THE MIS

THE MISSIONARY

by

Alex Cathcart

POLYGON
Edinburgh

First published in Great Britain 1988
by Polygon, 48 Pleasance, Edinburgh EH8 9TJ

The publisher acknowledges subsidy from the
Scottish Arts Council towards the publication of this volume

Typeset by EUSPB, 48 Pleasance, Edinburgh EH8 9TJ
Printed by Biddles Ltd, Guildford, Surrey

ISBN 0 948275 51 0
ISBN 0 948275 48 0 Pbk

This novel is dedicated to the
Linwood Philosophy Club and
the natives of Glasgow.

****

James Cameron Black tried to be a Christian; was ex-Cliftonpar Public School, and there was nothing he loved more than a decent game of cricket, but James Cameron Black had seen the bodies of the massacre. James Cameron Black had seen the corpses set to rot in the rain of a Rhodesian winter. Seen the prostrate bodies of the missionaries; counted three were women and five were men. Seen the bodies of the four younger persons, and counted them as four, including the three-week-old baby. Counted them, annotated them, for the Ministry of Information. James Cameron Black remained at the mission, where the bodies remained on the ground; remained for the reporters and the photographers, arranged for them to record it all in words and pictures for the newsbroadcasters of the world. Remained to see and hear and respond to the questing for answers to problems that had no answer in ownership of land or colour of flags or the proper spelling of acronyms or checks and balances. James Cameron Black had seen this, heard this.

And now James Cameron Black was seeing an American man in the made-up uniform of some holy man's army, dressed for battle with boots that were black and a beret that was green. Hearing this soldier talk of Christ and revenge, the gun and the Lord. Hearing a man say that many new volunteers were coming from America to Rhodesia to guard and remove the fear from the missionaries who would come to replace the dead. Hearing a man say that in the days of the Wild West all the people bringing the word of the Lord had a Bible and a gun. And James Cameron Black was listening as people applauded. And the man drank from a can as reporters prised the news from him. James Cameron Black left the room and found the lavatory and was sick as tears ran down and formed a mess on his face. There could be no more work for the Ministry of Information.

Outside, James Cameron Black wandered the streets of Salisbury as trucks passed with soldiers singing and tipping floppy hats to the ladies. In an avenue of English-style houses with English-style gardens James heard the sound of a church congregation lifting their voices in song. The sound was tracked, the gate gone through, and the church entered.

The congregation finished singing. A place at the first pew appearing was taken up. The vicar was lowering his head for prayer. James Cameron Black held on to the pew in front and prayed his own prayer for an end to the insanity which kept peoples apart and cried out as he remembered his part in the folly. Faces startled out of prayer were watching but there was no time left to care for appearances. James Cameron Black remembered.

Rising up, James removed himself from the main church and retreated to the entrance, staggered around, hunted around until he found the sacristy and entered through the side door. Inside in the midst of the blacks come there to hear and have worship, James Cameron Black, grown tired, weary of mind, collapsed on his knees and prayed again his own prayer.

Words tumbled out the mouth and tears ran constantly down the cheeks. Nothing in the mind but mental pictures of missionaries and young people murdered and missionaries and young people come to murder.

The church service may have finished here, time must have passed, the blacks are leaving this place, these knees are sore, the heart is sorer afflicted but this dark can be soothing and the cold is penitence penitence . . .

"Does anybody know this kaffir-lover?"

Someone was talking, talking behind, coming in front with black boots, a policeman.

"Doesn't anybody here know this man?"

Hands pulling now, under the armpits, James Cameron Black being hauled onto feet that were refusing to stay still, to stay, stay in one place, wandering. And these people, the place, blurring, becoming anywhere, any person, all around, everywhere, blurring and somebody has put the lights out.

***

In hospital James Cameron Black was injected into sleep and slept but wakened again and tossed. A white-coated doctor with an Irish accent patted a stethoscope on his chest, held his wrist and dropped it down again and murmured, winked at him and left. And James lay and watched the blades of the fan on the ceiling turn but he could not hear what they were saying. The blades came down nearer as he pulled at them with his eyes but they spun around, repeating circles, whispering, remaining neutral. A nurse came and helped him sit up, padded and patted pillows into his back. Two pills were next to put over with some water. She called him love but her voice came from a distance.

Sitting up, James found his head was too heavy for his neck and kept falling forward until he surrendered into head-hanging dozing. A flap opened up inside his head and James was looking through and seeing colours and people and there was Jesus and Jesus had no face but his outstretching hands were black and behind Jesus men worked and brought barrowloads of soil and pushed them into the river, the river flowed fast and the soil disappeared and father stood with his clipboard and looked, was shouting but no voice came, and he was shouting at Jesus and Jesus had a tennis racquet holding it out and the head of John the Baptist was on the racquet but Jesus had no face, and a donkey was chewing at the hem of his long white gown and on the donkey was a jockey with cap and whip and a shirt with a green band slashed through it and he was whipping the donkey but it refused to go, and men were pushing barrowloads of bodies and dumping them in the river, black bodies and white bodies and father senior Bwana Black threw away the clipboard and shoved a labourer away from a barrow and that barrow was full of little children and Jesus was strapped up for an innings and his face was black and he waved the bat and the bat was marked and chipped and father tipped the barrowload of bodies into the river that was brown and flowing swirling fast and the body on the top was James Cameron Black junior.

—Naah naah.

No one came running. A man in the next bed looked up at the shout, but never said anything.

And James rested for three days and three nights and on the fourth was asked to go. James thanked the nurses who had been tending him and left, returning to his empty flat and a full bottle of gin.

He could not go back to the Ministry of Information and help to create more extended versions of the truth, or compose more exciting, clichéd Press Releases for the bored Press of the world, who sent away deep analyses of situation Rhodesia until news of the latest massacre/atrocities set their pens and pencils and telexes into mad flights of fancy and fear for the future. In the hotel bars James would slide off his stool whenever one of the sons of the Press offered to buy him a drink, unless that person was one who could converse intelligently about cricket. But they were few and far between.

At the Cricket Club a few asked: how are you, old boy? but only for a while; for others were telling the tale that James Cameron Black was a kaffir-lover. The gentlemen of the committee were sorry to have to strip him of membership when he fell asleep on the grass beyond the far boundary with his fly open.

So James drank alone in his flat until afternoon, and would step out into the streets safe in the knowledge that in the haze of alcohol he would recognise no one, and no one would want to recognise him.

His favourite place was the corner of the street adjacent to the black Pentecostal Church of Christ, where he would stand under the trees and listen to the music and loud singing come through the open door. Some days he would just sit there, back against a tree, and pick up earth and allow it to flow through his fingers over and over again. And when the service had finished the black congregation would come out of their church and look and pull their children away from this strange white man who sat and dripped earth from his fingers.

One Sunday, sitting there, watching the dappled penumbra of the leaves flickering across the sunlight on the pavement, James began to drop the soil through the hole in his fist all around the shadow of a leaf. He looked at it, picked up some more soil, and surrounded another leaf, tracing its silhouette in dirt.

He did another one. He stretched forward, for this was one which wouldn't stay still, but moved about as the leaves moved in the breeze. James described the shadows of the leaves, and carried on up the branch, putting himself on all fours on the pavement and drawing around the edges in circles and ovals, and just plain squiggles of dirt. Behind him a black Mercedes car drew up.

A man got out of the car and stood behind a tree, but watched James as he crawled about on the pavement tracing out the patterns of the leaves. He watched for two or three handfuls, stepped forward and tapped James in the small of the back. James sat back on his heels but did not look up. He was admiring his handiwork. The man touched him again, on the shoulder, and spoke quietly.

"James."

James looked up, but had to squint into the sun. He lifted a hand over his eyes. Screwed up his face.

"James."

"Mmm?"

"James, c'mon."

James leaned further back. "The Lord called Samuel four times, you know."

"I am not the Lord."

"Ah. That it explains it then."

"That explains nothing, James."

"But you did call my name?"

"Yes." The man sighed. "James, don't you recognise me at all?"

"The voice. The voice. I know, I recognise the voice, but your face is in shadow. You have no face."

"If you would stand up you might have a better chance of seeing it. C'mon, James, up you get."

James tried to rise, but the man had to help him to his feet. James saw his face, and remembered. Remembered the claps on the back as he returned to the pavilion, remembered the man being there when the prizes were being given out, remembered his father had died working for this man.

"Mr Smith, sir."

"Yes, James, now let's get you home."

"Home? Home? I have no home. I saunter the world with my contemporaries; improvising, impervious to darts of criticism, hate or jealousy; held on an umbilical cord of superior innate righteousness to the womb of Mother England. Or is it Britain now? Not even great any more. Gypsy scholars men like me, you know; gypsy scholars, but gypsy scholars not foolish enough to stay with the gypsies. Ah no."

James stumbled on the pavement, but Mr Smith did not let him go.

"So where is my home? Where is this home you are taking me to? A promised land, or a land of promises?"

The black chauffeur had left the car and was holding a back door open. James was helped into the car. He huddled himself tight into the corner, his eyes looking beyond Mr Smith, out of the window, to the trees with their shaking leaves, to the church whose doors were opening. The first of the children were running down the steps from the church door. Laughing, happy the sermon was over, happy to be out, ready to go home, to dinner, the Sunday Dinner.

"Where is this home you are taking me to?"

"I don't know exactly yet, James. But my work here is finished for the time being. Rhodesia is no more, soon it will be Zimbabwe. I'm going home to Scotland for a while. I suggest you pull yourself together and come with me. There is little for you here now."

"Ah, Scotland. Land of the glens and kilted heavers of logs, ubiquitous engineers who perform miracles with pieces of string, and women in tartan sashes who sing folksongs written by the lady of the manor. And whisky of course. Mustn't forget the whisky. I don't suppose you have . . ."

"No."

"Ah, so be it."

The car pulled away. The minister was standing at the top of the steps, shaking hands with his departing congregation and James was going to Scotland.

James spoke into the window: "There are those who do say I was born in Scotland, you know. But I'm not so sure. I think I was born on the move."

James Cameron Black made himself relax; stretching his legs out in front, turning his head.

"Amen. Scotland then. It has as much claim to me as anywhere else. Drive on, Lochinvar. Do you happen to know the latest Test score, Mr Smith, sir?"

****

The man that was the voice of Scotland on the radio made a pun and a woman tittered and that was the news. The pun did not make Dave Parks laugh, nor titter, nor even smile. Maybe as middle age approached the sense of humour was hardening like the arteries. Slouched, bent over, sitting on the edge of the bed, waiting for the brain to function and call up the body for service. Morning service was on. The morning minute that set out the recipes for saving the world. Just an advertisement this morning. An American evangelist was coming on tour. Good God. Conversion to American know-how in the preaching of the Word. The preacher bade the listeners have a good day and be good and the world would be good. Goodbye. Eyes open. Seeing things that did not register on the brain. A voice from downstairs was competing with the voices on the radio and winning.

"Yup?"

YUP; that always got the automatic answer.

"MUP."

Then the disbelieving response. "GUP."

Now the final retaliation. "AMUP." And the brain had operated. It was time to move.

A look in the mirror and a reflection that the reflection should be denied credence. There was still some sign of reasonably hard stomach muscles. In the bathroom the bowl was missed, and wiped dry. The wash of the face was followed by the stand in the bath and the fiddle with the soap and the curses delivered at the shower that ebbed and flowed and was hot and was cold.

A white shirt was chosen. The old suit that was still the new suit was over the back of the chair after its press into service. The trousers were tight. That middle age starting right at the middle. Not really, this body slump was only natural after the winter. And the years at College. Summer would see if off. But it would be best not to bend down anyway.

Downstairs, Mary was sitting on the tiny tubular-legged breakfast chair that told the tale that she was spreading too. She was holding the paper up, its edge in line with her nose so that she could read the news that was history and watch the flat sausages fry in their own fat, all at one and the same time. There was no cereal in the cupboard or along any of the worktops.

"Any cereal?"

"Finished."

"Oh."

Sitting down re-emphasised the difficulties ahead with these trousers.

"Any chance of a bit of the paper?"

"No, I'm reading it."

"Any tea in the pot?"

"Help yourself."

The milk was already in the mug. The tea was black. Some margarine was spread over two slices of white bread; two sausages lifted over and placed on the bread to make an eminently resistible piece.

"Do you want one of these?"

"No thanks. They'll be like cardboard by now." Mary smiled and passed over the paper. "Nothing in it." She went to fuss somewhere over at the sink.

The paper was full of nothing in it and advertisements. Mary was speaking again but the ears were not picking it up.

"What's that you're saying?"

"I was asking, are you still going to that thing down the road this morning?"

"I'm still figuring on going, yes, why?"

"Nothing. I don't see why you think you've got to go, you've been away from the place long enough." Her head was down into the sink. The real message was coming. "I just don't want you missing the graduation."

"Miss it? How will I miss it? Get a grip. Anyway, some graduation. It's only the Diploma in Social Work, Mary. I don't even need to go and they'll still get it to me."

"If I wish to call it a graduation, I will call it a graduation. Just you make sure you don't get involved in anything this morning."

"Like what?"

"You know what I mean."

"More like who, you mean. Look, I'll meet you up there, all right. Quarter past. On the dot. OK?"

Her look over the shoulder was a glower; then the finger wagged. Best to change the subject.

"They're up early this morning."

The finger stopped. She was caught.

"Who?"

"Them out there. Them." Mary had to look out the window.

"Oh, them."

"Never quite sure whether I'm seeing the Mormons or insurance men."

"Or Social Workers."

"Ah now, Mary. You know it's denim suits for us mob."

"Used to be, you mean. Anyway, you're all in the same line, aren't you?"

"Nasty, Mary. Nasty."

It was getting on for ten. The demonstration was at half-past. It was time to be off.

"That's right, just leave the dishes." Mary was mind-reading again.

"I'll get them the night."

The shoes were given a final unnecessary dust, the jacket patted, picked at, put on. Dave Parks was ready. Maybe. "This tie OK?"

Mary's kiss was genuine. "You look good. Try and keep it that way for this afternoon."

"I won't be staying there long, Mary. But I've got to go. Show my face."

"I know."

The brown envelope and some money was being lifted from the sink-top. "Make sure you pay this, or it'll be us that'll be looking for a Social Worker."

The suit was definitely too tight and the trousers did not hang quite correctly over the eyelets of the shoes and a lace was broken.

A pull at the backside of the pants, a jerk at the sideside of them and a tug and a push at the frontside of them and they nearly made it. Nearly made it enough to do. Unless Dave Parks was for walking stiff-legged with the hands in the pockets permanently pushing down. The jacket was not too bad, but better left unbuttoned. More casual anyway. No chance of getting mistaken for a Mormon in this suit.

It was well seen it was spring. New growth was coming through in the gardens. New emphasising the dark rotten brown of the still winter-wet leaves whose time was past. Maybe it would be a good summer.

By the look of the numbers on the main road it didn't look as if this demonstration was going to be a runaway success. Or maybe that was what it did mean. There went the usual women, lugging the early shopping in the plastic bags and a few late men off to see if any papers were still to be had. This was Friday. Friday: the day for the jobs, though it used to be the payday. A few people waited at the bus terminus, waiting to get to the City; looking out, away down the road, but not able to make the bus come. This was the time of the long wait, when the drivers took their tea and respite from the early morning rush, and hash and bash.

"Hey, high-minded!"

Dave turned his head.

The three men were walking the same road. Together. They were walking slow and they were laughing. Maybe the trousers were really tight.

"Christ Jimmy, I never seen you there. How's it going, Pat? Tommy?"

Tommy was wearing his old Crombie. This coat didn't make his head look so broad. Tommy spoke from inside the greatcoat that had seen at least one great war and innumerable international incidents from Canada to Spain, and served as often as a blanket, as he slept on cold sobering doorsteps. "Not so bad. Yourself? You're looking a bit spruce this morning, me old son."

"Ach, I know. I've got this thing at the College this afternoon. Got to look the part."

"Don't give us that, you love it."

Four now were shuffling for space on the pavement; one walking half-inclined to the front, two shoulder to shoulder, and one half-inclined to the back. Four were smiling, all verging on laughter, but searching the collective memory for what it was that used to make them all laugh instantaneously. Three trying ha-ha hard to pull their old mate Davie Parks back in. Jimmy was looking well. A bit tanned. He always was kind of tanned right enough; but still, he was looking well. Jimmy spoke.

"Where you off to then?"

"Same place as you, I think, the Demo."

Pat chucked his chin out, raising his eyebrows, stretching his face. But he said nothing. Tommy took it up.

"I'm pleased to hear that, Davie. I'm sure that must show something."

Pat spoke.

"Aye. it shows he's nowhere else to go."

There was a quartet of disconcerted laughs. Lighthearted but serious defence was needed here.

"Give us a break Pat. I worked in the place for fourteen years. I still feel about the place, and what's happening is rotten. It stinks."

"Aye. We all knew a long time ago what was going to happen was rotten. But some of us decided to stay."

"And I didn't like? Is that the story? There wasn't a steward in there that fought harder for that place than me."

"Aye. Just some of us fought longer."

Jimmy intervened.

"Och Pat, give it a rest. If Dave wanted to leave, that's his business. There's nothing says he had to work in the press shop for the rest of his life. How did you get on at the College anyway? Is that you a Social Worker now?"

"After the day. I get the diploma the day."

Tommy's deep voice came up from the depths of his wrapped-up body.

"White-collar man now, Davie. Be buying your wee bungalow shortly. I think you're into an expanding business there."

Jimmy laughed. "Starvation Alley here you come, right into the Spam Belt you'll be going."

18

Pat spat. "And then you'll come down and tell us where we're going wrong. Ye'll be telling the women how to do the shopping to get the family fed on a pound and still get change back."

"Piss off Pat. I haven't even got a job yet."

"Aye, well, join the club."

That remark was a silencer. They walked on. More people were coming out now; from the side streets and the cul-de-sacs, converging, but it wasn't going to be a big turnout. Jimmy broke first.

"What do you make of these guys getting to auction the place then?"

"The whole thing's unbelievable, Jimmy."

Tommy rubbed his chin. "I've heard of a sale of work, but this is ridiculous."

Even Pat grinned. "Aye. I always usually tried to avoid sales of work myself. I always thought work was bad enough without having to pay for it."

Everybody laughed at Pat's crack, except himself. The face was back in the deadpan already. The walk continued, still shuffling for room, with Jimmy at the edge, sometimes on the pavement, most times off it. The silence was pressing in again. Dave Parks felt it better to talk. "Who's organising this demo then?"

Tommy answered. "Which one?"

"What do you mean? Which one, did you say?"

"There's two."

"How two?"

"The local Labour Party mob have organised one and the Scottish Nationalists have organised one. There's something for everybody."

Pat spat. "Aye. Workers to one side, Scotspeople to the other. Fuckin magic."

"You're jokin."

Tommy laughed a laugh that was big enough to lift the shoulders on the big coat. "No, no, it's true, Labour at the East Gate, Scot Nats at the West."

"Well fuck me."

Jimmy gave a final lick to a roll-up and handed it over. "Well Davie, what do you think your old Chairman Mao would have to say about this?"

A light was accepted. Tommy gave an answer. "If he'd read any Scottish history he would know it was par for the course."

"Aye. Where's MacLenin now? Just what is to be done? You see these people . . ."

He spat. He was finished. They walked on. Some old recognised workmates were on the streets. Some waved over. Not many. One man up ahead on the pavement opposite stopped; turned, walked back. Crying. Nobody commented. And there was the place.

The roofs of the different areas of the west side ran up, down, in a serrated zigzag that sawed at passing clouds in the sky. The east side was always more solid-looking, modern, a series of ranked buildings behind the administration block. Between the two sides a motorway ran south. Workmen were surveying the roundabout, in preparation for widening the access road. For no particular reason they went to the east side first. Behind the large glass door of the grand entrance a spiral staircase wound upward, impressing no one now, going nowhere now. A crowd was gathering. Inside his box the security man guarding the redundant factory sat, reading his paper, eating his sandwich, sipping at his tea. Two men in grey suits passed his box and he didn't challenge them. They did not look at him. They were reading their catalogues. Some men struggled with a banner, but a pole had broken. They rolled it up. A small Japanese lorry backed up to quite near the gate. The security man kept reading.

The ex-convener of the plant scrambled up onto the back tail of the lorry. He called it the sale of the century. But he was sure everybody hadn't come down to hear him. He introduced the Labour Party man.

A man in the sharp-cut twill coat was struggling to climb on the lorry. Two ex-stewards cupped hands across and gave him a leg up. His view was that this was another example of rampant capitalism and multi-national double dealing. Only a true Socialist programme could make sure that such obscenities did not happen in the future. It was essential for everyone to vote Labour. He cut his speech short because he had to catch a plane to London. He had to get back to the House.

A man from the Scottish Trades Union Congress was next. There was an oil stain on his sharp-cut twill coat.

Jimmy passed over another roll-up. "Anybody fancy seeing what's on at the other show?"

"Aye. C'mon away."

The crowd was small and easily passed through. They walked through the tunnel under the road. Two bidders passed holding yellow catalogues.

"Any bargains goin?" asked Tommy.

They ignored him, walked on, to wherever they were going next.

A voice was echoing along and round the tunnel. "Hey, big man, hey!" The face was in gloom, but the silhouette showed a man holding up a newspaper, waving it, and holding a bundle under his arm. Our Davie. Still selling his papers.

"Davie boy. Fuck sake. Davie. How you doing? Oh, man. Hey Jimmy, it's our Davie."

"I know, aye, you forget I see him every day. Or I used to. Hi Davie."

"How's it goin Jim? What do you make of the state of this man? What's the clobber for?"

"Ach, I've got to go and get my diploma the day. But how are you? How's the boys? Still fighting the good fight? Do you ever see The Tank?"

"The Tank's in jail, Dave. The steel works carry-on. Lifted him at teatime from his mother's place. Three fuckin hours after the do was finished. Thought we might have seen you there."

"Ach, well, there's a lot o studying, an exams an that. Got The Tank, eh?"

"Aye. No sign o you coming back to the meetings? I'm looking for somebody to give me a break with the papers. Wet nights and draughty railway platforms are disagreeing with my back."

"Know what you mean. Jimmy and I did it for years."

Jimmy was saying nothing but he offered Davie a roll-up. Davie handed the papers over to Dave in order to hunt in his pockets for a match. When the cigarette was lit he was handed them back. "Thanks Jimmy," he said.

"Have you anything on here the day?" asked Dave.

"Naa. The game was a-bogey when they shut the door on the place. This is just a side-show. Thought I'd come along and sell the lads a decent newspaper."

"Well, there certainly seems to be nothing doing at that side anyway. We're just going over here to see what the score is with this lot."

"Be bugger all likely. Anyway, nice talking to you Dave. I'll see you. See you Jimmy."

"Aye."

Davie went back out the way he came. Jimmy and Dave moved towards the end of the underpass where Pat and Tommy were waiting.

"HEY, DAVE!" It was that voice again. "You no for buyin a paper?"

Dave Parks laughed and walked back. "Much is it again?"

"Don't give us it. A pound to you."

"A pound? Oh wait a minute, man, I'm only a poor student. Here's fifty-p."

"You're a miserable bastard right enough. Here, give this one to Jimmy. Tell him it's for the roll-up."

"Right, I will. Be seeing you Davie. Tell The Tank I was asking for him. When you see him."

"Aye. We'll maybe see you around, Dave. Hope so anyway."

The lads had waited. Jimmy took his paper, laughed and stuck it into his jacket pocket.

There was a small buzz at this side. Something was happening. A woman had stripped herself naked and was pressing herself against the gate, calling on the buyers to rape her as well. Inside the gate some buyers had gathered, smiling, but most passed on into the plant. The security man on this side was standing up inside his box, goggling. A small group were stretching arms, trying to stop the police from reaching her. A television camera camel stood on the roof of a mini, focusing on the woman. Photographers' cameras were clicking and humming, as they knelt, stretched, held them up high and turned sideways, to capture the essence of the protest.

"Hope she's got big tits," said Pat.

"Eh?"

"Hope she's got big tits. Nothing like some bare tit to get you some coverage."

"She should fart in their faces," said Tommy.

An older woman with clothes on was shouting through a loud hailer. She was saying that this was another example of rampant capitalism and multi-national double dealing. Only an independent Scotland with its own Parliament could make sure such obscenities did not happen in the future. It was essential for everyone to vote Scottish Nationalist. She cut her speech short because she had to catch an aeroplane back to Brussels.

Out of the gates on the west side a low-loader lorry was moving. Slung on its back was a large machine. Its size made it easily recognised. Dave Parks knew it.

"Christ, look at that. It's the Two Hundred."

Some people raised shouts at the driver, most just watched as the lorry and its load eased a way out of the gate behind the police escort.

There was something moving in Dave Parks. Remembrances. Clear remembrances. Time when the machine was almost as real as himself. The two of them; moving in unison, synchronised, plate in, press down, plate in, press down, plate in press down, plate in press down, another one done, and another bob made, another one done, and another bob made. Stamping after stamping hitting the floor and shoving up the bonus. Easy stuff. Even doing the sleepy-time guy on the nightshift or drunk on the backshift. The Two Hundred moved at the same pace. Lift a plate and put it in, a pound note's really made of tin, lift a plate and put it in a pound note's really made of tin. Playing lightning chess with Jimmy. Stamp one move one stamp one move one. The sanity defence. And the big machine never disturbed any dreams. It just pounded on as background thumping until the mind came back and it was another one in and another one done and another bob made and Dave Parks had had enough. Or was it the writing on the wall for a single industry town?

23

Maybe. And there goes the Two Hundred. The other half of the team.

"I worked that bloody thing for years, you know."

Tommy laughed. "Christ. D'you think we don't know? No other fucker could get near it. Rumpelstiltskin. Tin plate into gold."

"Aye. Put a wee lot of wallpaper up on your walls that did."

Dave Parks was still concerned about the machine that was leaving. "That's as may be, but it was old when it was in there. It's bloody ancient that thing. Who'd be for buying that?"

Tommy was shaking his head. "You're out of touch right enough son. South Africa. That's where it's heading. It's off to the grand warehouse down south along with the gear from Birmingham, then it's off to bloody South Africa."

"You're joking."

"No joke, son. But I don't think it'll be pressing out panels for motor cars or washing-machines somehow."

"What d'you mean, Tommy?"

"Aeroplanes, my son. Aeroplanes. Aeroplane bodies."

"You're joking."

"Nope. For heaven's sake, they were in there giving interviews for the place before we had even shut down. Jimmy there was severely tempted you know."

Jimmy half-raised a fist. "That'll be right."

Tommy was for teasing. "C'mon now, don't give us it. You were the first right down there. You were the first right down the stores for the shorts and the old sjambok."

"Ah, piss off!"

The lorry and its outriders and its load had filtered on to the roadway and was moving slowly away. Away. Pat was staring after it too.

"Aye. I've fixed a lot of machines in my time, but that one was a beauty. She was a joy to work on. I used to love it when she had a breakdown."

"So did Dave," said Jimmy.

The woman had been wrapped in a blanket by two policewomen. The excitement was over. They bundled her into the back of a van. Tommy shrugged his shoulders then looked at his watch, which he managed to stretch out from under two heavy inches of scuffed Crombie coat. "It's past eleven lads. See any point in staying?"

Nobody saw any point in staying. It was past the eleventh hour and the pubs were open. Tommy asked Dave Parks if he was coming.

"No thanks, Tommy. I've got this thing this afternoon. I don't want to go up there with the smell of the bevy on me."

"It's your choice old son. Please yourself."

"Aye. We'll maybe see you again in another two years."

Jimmy took an arm. "C'mon, one'll no kill you. We haven't seen you for ages." Pat and Tommy waited.

"Right. OK, but it's just for the crack. I'll just have a blackcurrant and coke or something."

Tommy laughed. "That'll be the day."

"Aye. It'll depend on who's payin."

They moved back through and with the crowd until back on a clear pavement they formed their own loose line. The three asked questions about this course and this Social Work business. Most replies were met with disparaging jokes. Pat remembered a conversation when Dave Parks had declared that Social Workers were nothing but polis without uniforms.

"Aye. I mind it. But that was before we got wind the factory was shuttin." He spat.

The pub was empty. They went automatically to their corner. Jimmy was for getting them up. "You still want that coke an whatever?" Three pairs of eyes watched.

"Ah, bugger it, just make it a pint." Dave Parks' laugh was an embarrassed laugh. A beermat was twiddled through nervous fingers. Jimmy needed two runs for the pints.

The talk wandered over the morning's events: actions and inactions, rampant capitalism and multi-national double dealings, then passed backwards into industrial nostalgia; management wankers, the bampots, the comedians.

Tommy remembered Holy Joe that would get his tally in as quick as possible so he could put religious tracts in everybody's locker. "Never gave any to the supervisors but. Funny that."

Jimmy remembered the part-time song-and-dance man that came on the nightshift late straight from a show and was pulled up. "I had to plead his case. It was goin all right until he suddenly wipes everything off the manager's desk, jumps up on it and starts tap-dancin, and singin 'Follow the Yellow Brick Road'."

Pat remembered the time the steward had been taken up the spiral staircase to be introduced to the new American manager and he finished up chasing Dave Parks down the stairs and waving his fist and bawling, "I'll get you, you commie bastard, I'll get you." Everybody remembered that one.

Nostalgia left the workplace to return to tenement roots and the community, *gemeinschaft*, call-it-what-you-like, they loved it that much they all took the bammy job out here in the first place to get a house with a bath and a garden. From the tenements the next move was the fishing and into half-remembered pubs in weird places with weird country people. Literature took its turn on the third pint with Hemingway just losing the vote to Steinbeck, and somehow this merged into the World Cup. On the fourth pint there was philosophy. Marx led to Sartre led to Bergson, though right now Tommy's *élan vital* was being led by the heavy beer right into Laing.

Tommyisms were spewing forth: "Y'see, this system makes us do all sorts of things which aren't natural for living. Now. If we agree, and I think we agree, that to be natural is to be human, then what is not natural, is not human. So . . ."

Jimmy was rubbing his head. He was seeking refuge in the making of a roll-up.

". . . so, when we do these unnatural things, like standing on the line pressing buttons or whatever, for ten hours a night when every other bugger is sleeping, then we have to kid ourselves on that that is natural."

"Aye. I'm sure you're right."

Dave Parks was confused. "I'm not sure that I follow you."

"Simple. You know that feeling that you get when you've been on the line, churnin them out, first one, then another, then another, then another one an after that another one and the mind goes? Well, that's you dead."

"Aye. Dead. Carry on."

Jimmy had a finger up. He had something to contribute here. "Did somebody not say that was alienation?"

"Probably. But you're really dead. It's no natural you see. But this is the trick. You're not allowed to say you're dead. No even to yourself. If you had the cheek to say: 'I'm dead', they would say this guy is nuts, and bang you in the pokey. And no bugger wants that. So we just carry on and everything is perfectly natural. But it's still there. Laing says we end up with an I lookin for a me."

"Aye. Well that sounds like Scotland for a start. Though it's more like us being a me looking for an I."

Dave Parks was having a lot of trouble following this drunken philosophers' rambles. Dave Parks had been too long away from the Flosfy Klub. But something was brought to mind. "Antisyzygy. MacDiarmid. MacDiarmid said that."

Pat was smiling. Smiling. "I agree with you there, Dave. That's the shot."

Pat had agreed with Dave but the clock on the wall was showing ten minutes to two.

"Christ is that the time? Listen lads, I'll need to go."

"What are you worried about the time for?" asked Tommy. "It's only a measurement devised by us old human beings."

"And it's no real, eh?"

"Naturally."

"You try telling that to Mary."

Jimmy was disappointed. "What's so desperate about getting your hands on a wee piece of paper? I mean, if you don't get this bit of paper you'll still be a Social Worker, won't you? You'll still know what's wrong with us all, won't you?"

"I don't know what you mean about knowing what's wrong but I know what you mean."

"Well then. Why don't you stay and fuck them all?"

"I'd love to Jimmy, honest. I've not had such a good time for a long time."

Tommy brought in the practicalities for a change. "How you getting up there? The last City bus left five minutes ago."

27

"Aye." Everybody laughed. Dave Parks was nodding. Dave Parks was staying. Jimmy got the beer up.

Tommy gulped at his glass and prepared to continue with a drunk man's look at schizoids and schizophrenia. The air was warm; it was quite OK this. Even Pat staring that stare straight ahead had smiled. Dave's tobacco tin was pulled from the pocket. Jimmy was back in time to see.

"Christ, have you got some? The bugger's been smoking mine the whole day."

"Aye."

"Jimmy, I forgot I had it, honest. I'm that used to not havin it. Here."

Jimmy took the tin and shook it at his ear. "I don't think you've got all that much. You can give me one back when my redundancy money runs out."

"You might need to wait, I'm only an unemployed student, remember."

Pat had turned his head. He was looking at Dave Parks. "Aye. And tomorrow you'll be an unemployed Social Worker."

Tommy put his glass down hard. It was time to get on with this problem. " So, as I was saying . . ."

Dave Parks stood up. "I'm going lads. I think I can just about afford a taxi."

Jimmy's head went back. "A taxi? You must be holdin."

Pat spat. It was time to go. The chair fell over. Dave Parks was standing up. "Sorry, fellas."

The chair was replaced. "I'll see you guys, right?"

Tommy nodded. Jimmy nodded. Pat stared and said nothing.

At the door a voice called. "The next round is yours, by the way."

****

The roads were wet and overhanging hedgerows dripped drips of water onto the narrow pavement and onto shoes; and untrimmed thorny branches reached out, gripping at trouser-legs. Speeding passing cars splashed wet sheets from puddles that became flying oceans. All ahead people were strung out in spaced-out single-file, all heading to sign on. A young couple pushed a baby in a pram. The young father kept turning round, attempting to talk baby-talk to the child, until the pram wheels clicked his heels and he decided to give up. The pace was slow. Two miles was a long way to walk when there was no particular hurry.

Dave Parks had delayed his exit from home until the last minute had come and gone, just to have an excuse to walk fast to somewhere. A pat on the pocket reassured that the UB40 was there. Not that it mattered, particularly. The clerk would always supply another one if it got lost. There were plenty of cards.

Hedgerows gave way to the crumbling remains of the abandoned textile mills beside and under the railway track that carried no trains. One part of the old mill had been saved, and split up; divided up to provide the necessary space for the small units for the new small-business tycoon who some day might grow up to be Henry Ford and be the saviour of the nation. But most of the mill was boarded up.

The large solid stone houses built for mill managers by their grateful employers still loomed impressively. The shops at the edge of town did not. They were closed; some with boards clapped over the windows; others still showed inside traces of the past: broken counter-tops, odd shoes lying, cards of buttons scattered on a floor.

An old woman was hesitating at the pavement. Dave Parks put out a hand to take her bag and she clutched it tighter. She allowed this strange man to help her across the street. Dave Parks was going that way and had plenty of time. At the zebra two cars did not slow. But Dave Parks could wait.

The unemployment office was modern. It was light. The signing-on queues were not very long. This was Tuesday. Not that it mattered anyway. The card was pushed across. The girl pulled a little rectangular file held onto a piece of cardboard by a thick elastic band from a box holding many rectangular files.

"Sign here, please."

It was signed.

"Thank you." The card was pushed back into its place. Dave Parks had signed and confessed to being unemployed for another two weeks.

The route back was the same only in reverse. Most going back took the right-hand side. All strung out in a human loop. But the views from the right-hand side were much the same as the views from the left. More or less. All coming and going to make the moving finger write.

Mary was working today. It seemed a good idea to keep walking past the street; to keep walking, keep moving, walk on down to the library. On a piece of waste ground three men were watching two young lads swinging picks. A man in a boiler-suit was rushing over, tripping, carrying some kind of tree that dropped dirt from its roots in a trail as he ran. A bus went past but there was no one to be seen. At least on the bottom deck.

Somebody else had the paper. Two somebody elses had the papers. GEOGRAPHY HISTORY did not appeal, and Dave Parks had had enough of SOCIAL SCIENCES for a while. Across the road, the Community Centre was open, but in the lounge somebody else had the paper. There were only a few in; some women in from the shops for a quick coffee and a mind-saving blether, and an old man who smelled and hogged the paper. At the door two old men played chess, peering at the board through dull daylight. At least the new girl behind the counter was trying. She was smiling.

"Can I help you? Would you like a coffee, or something?"

"I don't, OK, a coffee'll be fine, thanks."

Steam took its revenge on the coffee for being rushed into service.

"Twenty-pence, please."

"Thanks."

A table was picked, the coffee put down and a chair drawn up. The table wobbled. Some coffee was spilled. Maybe somebody would come in. But it was doubtful. The old and the young used this place, the indeterminates preferred to ignore its existence. A police sergeant came in, spreading himself and his noisy nylon raincoat along a wall as he leaned an arm on the counter-top. He cracked loud jokes with the girl who was called Paula but he was watching Dave Parks. Dave Parks finished his coffee. The paper was in no danger of being surrendered. The cup and saucer were handed over. The policeman was smiling, maybe hoping for a hello, maybe not.

The girl smiled again: "Thank you."

"That's OK, I enjoyed the coffee."

Back in the library two other persons had the papers. It was time for home maybe.

Outside, that abstract bronze which represented the future as seen from the sixties pointed its curious circles and arrows across what looked like a sea and threw jagged edges this way and that. Every way but upward. It was definitely losing its inspirational magic. The man-made puddle that it rose out of was filled with crisp bags and toffee-papers and old windblown leaves.

A wind blew dust and papers across the shopping mall that had never had shops. Or not many for any time. The brightest shop was the shop that displayed the small white cards that advertised the jobs. A big clock inside showed it was still early. Dave Parks read the signs that exhorted him to work in tones that reminded of posters for the First World War. Dave Parks went in.

Inside it was warm. A man behind a desk did not look up. Above him the big hand of the big clock moved on, to a new minute. PART-TIME was nearest the door, next to the advertisements for the government schemes. These were under the blower that blew hot air down on Dave Parks, so these little white cards got the best of attention; a peer with the head forward as if to study the smaller print, a peer that opens up a space at the collar to catch the down-draught. Nothing much here and the hot air was making it heard to breathe.

Next section. Next lot. LABOURER. BOOK-KEEPER. BINGO-CALLER (Experienced only). Usual crap stuff. Usual crap wages. Nothing. Nothing here. Nothing here for Dave Parks. Not in this section; and not in JOBS IN OTHER AREAS. Nothing. For Dave Parks was not a bloody navvie that could work in the bloody Falklands. Neither was Dave Parks a DOMESTIC SERVANT or a PARTY SALES ORGANISER for lingerie or tupperware and Dave Parks was definitely too old for the YTS. COMMERCIAL sounded promising but really was for PART-TIME WOMEN.

The clock ticked off another minute, but outside it was raining again. Maybe another turn around the circuit would be interesting if nothing else. Or maybe a quick dash for the library and maybe the paper. The clerk had not looked up. Best to go. Never likely to be anything in here for Dave Parks. Nobody could make use of an ex-semi-skilled factory worker with a wee piece of cardboard that said this man is a SOCIAL WORKER, qualified to do Social Works. Help the misfits; once he had found a spot for himself to fit into. All that was wanted was the chance. At least in the plant they gave you a wee shot at the work before declaring you useless or surplus to requirements. Dave Parks. Surplus to requirements. And the clerk was not looking because he had seen it all before. Plenty times. Probably he had seen plenty Dave Parks hiding in here, amongst the dead-end job boards, and frames, for plenty empty ticked-off twenty minutes; seen plenty pretending to be sheltering from the rain, and/or huddling for a heat, pretending to be doing something positive with the time, that ticked away on the big clock, and couldn't care less. That clerk had probably sat there and watched as people made excuses to themselves for being here. Made excuses to stand under strip-lights that bounced bluish light off loud green and yellow decor and shiny dirty black creased orange plastic leather chairs. Bright like a painter and decorator's nightmare.

Maybe the screaming colours were to arouse the weary job-hunter from any stupor. Probably not. The place was just a bright dull nightmare. Everyone that came in here became part of it. Even the clerk there, just sitting, watching the shuffling round,

the studying of the cards, the looking for something that they had
been told was there for the early bird, or the late bird with the
hawk-eyes; him just sitting, was part of the nightmare; but his part
was part-time. He didn't have to shuffle and he didn't have to study
any card, but he had to sit out there, behind his desk, and look, and
the same clock ticked above him. But at least he was only killing
time until five o'clock. His nightmare was a broken one; relief was
bought with the wage-packet. Meantime, Dave Parks was still here.
Still not too sure why he was here. And the clerk had lifted his head
and was looking at Dave Parks. Looking from his comfortable spot.
Quite comfortable. Knows his slot. Few bob coming regular, all the
coffee he can drink, salad sandwiches on an inch of tuna, but likely
to buy the pub's lasagne on a Friday to get the weekend off to an
early start. Maybe this was all Dave Parks wanted. Maybe that's
what all this excursion into Social Work was all about. A secure
entry into a structure that would keep the family safe. A dash for
security before old age crept up. And old age was starting earlier
every day. Maybe.

The clerk's eyes were staring. Dave shrugged the shoulders
and stepped over and stood at the desk looking down. The man's
moustache was lopsided and there were inkstains on his breast
pocket.

"Can I help you?"

"Probably not. I just came in on the off-chance. The game I'm
in, I don't think they advertise in here."

"Oh." The man shrugged. He wasn't particularly interested in
finding out what game Dave Parks was in. The shrug told plenty.
The shrug was followed by a relaxed placing of the hands around
his head and an easy stretching forward of his legs. Dave carried
on.

"I'm really looking in the wrong place. I don't think you carry
what I'm after in here."

The man unclasped his hands, unstretched.

"Please yourself. I was only trying to be nice."

Probably that's all it was. It just never comes out that way.

"I'm sure, I'm sure, aye. Don't get me wrong."

"What are you after? Do you want to sit down and take a seat?"

33

Dave sat down. He leaned over and twiddled with the upturned corner of a sheet of A4 that lay on the desk. The sheet was littered with scribbles and doodles. The scribbles of a busy man. Important-looking scribbles. Telephone numbers. And grotesque naked women with beards and blue triangles of Biro fuzz.

"I'm not exactly too sure yet what I'm after. Could be one of a lot of things. Y'see, I've just qualified as a Social Worker."

"Is that right? Where did you go?"

"Up the Hill. I've had a couple of interviews, but, ach, I don't fancy my chances."

"You on the Region's list, as well as the District's?"

"Oh aye. Got to be. Must. Nothing doing with either of them just now, I don't think."

"Well, you've got to keep plodding away, haven't you? I'm sure something will bounce for you. At least you're looking. A lot of them that come in here, they're really only coming in here to pass the time, you know."

Dave Parks, newly qualified Social Worker, could be entrusted with these sentiments. Entrusted to agree. For Dave Parks it was time to be off.

"Aye. Very good. Well, I'll maybe see you again."

The clerk's call called him back from the door.

"Hold up, hold up. I blooming well have the very thing for you. Although I don't think it's permanent." An index finger was pointing out like a pistol. He kept repeating: the very thing, the very thing, and remarked that the thing was here somewhere. He had disappeared down and to the side of his desk. Long clean hands were rummaging in the brown wicker wastepaper basket. He kept insisting that the thing had been thrown in here first thing this morning, first thing this morning. "It was here, it was here." Little balls of crushed-up paper were being opened as he continued to lean downwards, and one by one had them scanned, recrushed, rejected. He leaned up again, lifting the bin with him. The rejects were being scattered along the top of the desk now. A polystyrene cup was accidentally decanted; the remains of thick vegetable soup made rivers around the islands of paper. "Bugger. But it's here. It's here. It came through from Central this morning."

He looked up and smiled that comradely smile before continuing. "I put it in the bin because I definitely could not see anyone round about here being suitable for the thing." He continued the hunt. "But you might fancy it. I mean, Social Worker, you've worked with people haven't you? Sure you have, at least in training."

"Sure I have, but what is this?"

"Just a — wait, there we are."

The bin was replaced on the floor. The rubbish was near enough swept back into the basket. The missing paper that was now found was held out in front and then laid down on the desk. The long fingers were rubbed along the creases on the important piece of paper; the clerk had become a pirate, spluttering and spreading saliva over this here Treasure for Davie Parks, ohar. The long index finger jabbed. Dave Parks looked. There was no big bold X. The mans head was up. He was grinning. Above that moustache an eye-patch would have been just the touch.

"Aha. There. 'Must have experience of dealing with people in a private and confidential manner'. I knew it was there."

"Can I read it?"

The clerk's head jerked up. He looked surprised. He picked it up and read it to Dave Parks.

The note asked for someone to provide assistance to a family in the rehabilitation of an older person into social life, with the usual mature outlook required and some knowledge of the welfare benefits system. Dave Parks couldn't help scratching his head.

"Rehabilitation? What does that mean exactly? If this is somebody just out of jail, they've got people that do that sort of thing."

"I don't think it's that somehow, although I don't really know much about it, I just took it on the old blower this morning. There's a phone number. Do you want me to ring it?" The head had to be screwed round to see the number.

"But what's it for? What are they after?"

The clerk pulled the phone over, lifted the receiver and held it up. "Will I ring?"

Dave shook his head, shrugged, nodded and said, "Suppose so, aye, on you go."

35

The white buttons were pressed. As it buzzed its first buzz the clerk asked for the name.

"Dave Parks."

"You local?"

"Just up the road there."

The telephone was being answered. A woman's voice was asking a hello. The clerk answered likewise.

"Hello? Hello. Job Centre here. My name is Mr Dicky, I'm ringing in connection with your request which was circulated this morning. I have someone here whom I think may be suitable for the post." The clerk was smiling and nodding at the same time. "Yes, it's a man, although you can't really discriminate, you know. However, yes, it is a man, and he's actually a qualified Social Worker." The smile was widening and the nods increasing. "Would you like to speak to him then? Good, good." The phone was handed over.

Dave asked the same question for beginners. "Hello?"

The voice at the other end was a woman's; high, but calm and very polite. The woman said that she did not wish to discuss the post too much since it was a highly personal matter. She asked if he could come out on Saturday afternoon.

"When? This Saturday?"

"Saturday afternoon, please. My brothers will be home then. You see, it really is up to them, all of this."

"All of what?"

"As I say, I'd rather not discuss it over the telephone. Can you manage?"

"Well, I suppose I can manage it, but where are you exactly?"

The place was the poshest area of the city. It matched the voice. The woman was asking if Dave Parks knew where it was. Dave Parks knew where it was; it was the place where apples grew for small boys to come and steal. Dave Parks knew it.

"And we're 24 MacNaughten. It isn't difficult to find, I don't think."

"No, no, that's all right, I know where you are. What time?"

"Shall we say half-past two?"

36

The time and place were repeated, and the goodbyes made. The clerk was leaning forward, taking his telephone, and replacing it even more neatly in its place.

"All right?"

"Oh. Sure. Just a bit weird, that's all. I still don't have a clue what it's all about, but there you are. I've to go out on Saturday." The clerk's face was sending out messages; he was waiting to be thanked. "Thanks very much, by the way. That was good of you to remember that."

"All part of the service. Can I just ask your name and address again, please?" The information was written down at the bottom of the creasy paper. "Champion."

"Right. I'll be off then."

The man opened his arms and hands wide, making an expansive gesture. Then he winked.

***

The bar was crowded even by the standards of a Saturday. The two domino tables were taken and the play had drawn a crowd around to watch, stand and sip, and look wiser than the players. Already there was a long list of initials on the slate, waiting to take on the winners as they appeared. A crowd was gathered under the television, watching the mid-day soccer special. Two experts were laying off the clichés and interviewing some manager that was looking for a result or his head would be on the chopping block, the thought of which did not make him perm any two from three, but any one from two. The Space Wars machine lay idle while the football was on, but silently the bright colours kept bursting ritually on the dark screen to advertise the thrills in store. Dave Parks hugged in close to the bar and waited for the pint to be poured. The place was mobbed and he had the daft suit on. The suit, the tie, the full gear. No denims; no casual jacket, no trainers, but a suit that didn't sit well over shoes that were plastic and shiny. The pint was lifted and the head stuck down into it. With one arm stretched holding the pint up, if he walked fast nobody would notice the suit didn't fit.

37

Men stood back to let Dave pass. They looked. They saw. Some feigned amazement. Some laughed. Some drew attention to the fact that Dave Parks was making a reappearance and inviting everyone to take a swatch at the cut of his jib. Cracks were made from mouths to ears and laughter was too loud as bar persons looked and let the beer froth up and over and down the glasses. Parks approached the Flosfy Klub table over in their faraway intellectual corner. Somebody shouted: did your cat die? Two fingers were raised up without looking back. The Flosfy Klub had convened, but they made space for Dave Parks.

Tommy had been holding forth on some book he had just read. Jimmy had his head down into his shag tin. Pat sat dead straight and deadpan. He was back on the pipe. Jimmy stopped licking and looked over the top of the cigarette paper. Tommy stopped himself in mid-sentence.

Pat's eyes moved. Then the mouth moved. "Aye, aye, look what the wind blew in."

"Mornin Dave," said Jimmy.

Tommy had a sip at his lager, settled the glass on the table, then spoke. "You're getting to be a regular again. But what's the good tin flute on for? You got another passing-out parade?"

Dave Parks had an answer: "Any passing out to be done it'll be done in here. Think half of them had never seen anybody in a suit before."

"Aye, but you're no just anybody, are you?"

Jimmy shoved over the shag tin. "How y'doin Dave? Don't worry about them. It's only unusual because you don't come here as often. And I'll be honest, I don't think I'd ever seen you in a suit before the other day." Dave Parks let go the shag tin. Jimmy might not have much left.

Tommy was curious. "So how you doin? What's all this sartorial panache in aid of?"

"Ach, it's a strange one Tommy."

Through sips of beer, and jokes that took off at a tangent, Dave Parks managed to get out the story of the strange woman at the end of the strange phone call.

Jimmy removed a piece of shag from the tip of his tongue. "What d'you reckon it's all about then?"

"I haven't a clue. That's what I came in here for. I want somebody to do me a favour."

"Might've known," said Jimmy.

Pat blew out a puff of smoke but signalled nothing. Tommy squared his shoulders. "Why? What's the problem?"

"I don't know. There's just something about this. It doesn't ring right. I just feel uneasy about it."

"Aye. Real tough area out there, and I don't think."

"It's not that. It was just something about that woman's voice."

Jimmy asked the question: "So what is this favour you want done?"

"Well, I wondered if one of you guys could give this number a bell at three o'clock and if I don't fancy the situation I'll use it as an excuse to get out."

Tommy looked. "Now wait a minute. Is that not putting the responsibility for getting you out on to us? I mean, suppose somebody here forgets and you get roped in, and it's useless, will you blame him later on? See what I mean?"

"Ah, don't give us that stuff. Look, I'm just asking, will somebody ring at three o'clock or no? That's all."

Jimmy leaned forward and took up a piece of paper from Dave Parks' hand. "I'll do your business. Leave it to us to bail you out."

"Will you do it, Jimmy?"

"Aye. If you give him the ten pence."

"Oh. Right, of course I will. Thanks, Jimmy."

The Flosfly Klub set its collective imagination upon what might happen to the worried man, but it did not sustain them for long. Tommy was back on the trail of a good argument. It was a left-over. The Scottish schizoid personality was still troubling him.

Jimmy said if they banged all the different nappers together it must come out right, because Hegel said so.

Pat blew smoke in the air. "Look, I told you lot, MacDiarmid's been there before you." Hegel and MacDiarmid needed more than one pint to be talked about correctly.

It was time for Dave Parks to be off. On his feet he addressed Jimmy: "You mind and phone then? Three o'clock. Just say what you like."

Jimmy was making mock. "Right, right, I'll tell them I'm the polis, and you're a raving loonie that should never have been allowed out. How's that?"

"Fair enough. I'm sure that'll do the trick."

They all nodded cheerio. By the door somebody made the crack: hey, Dave, did your cat die? Another voice was calling.

"Hey, aye, and you still forgot the ten pence."

****

The houses were big and solid and the avenues were wide and long and every alternate opening had red and white poles strung across, standing sentinel, barring the way for motorcars. Buses had been removed from this route long ago. There was no one walking on the broad empty pavements all shaded by trees that grew tall and straight a regular distance apart. Mock-Victorian Gothic castles, with meaningless gargoyles and mysterious ramparts to repel an as yet unknown foreign invader, competed with the serious straight edges of the Scottish architecture making its statement.

Plain white curtains in dark windows showed up those mansions now converted to take in the aged for those of sufficient income to grant the aged parent this eventide privacy and care. Grey gravel or red chips or flinty stones led from the road to the doorways of the houses. The gravel on the path of 24 MacNaughten was an indeterminate mixture of blacks and browns. The lawns had been cut in sharp edges to match the plain lines of the house. Only a small porch had been allowed to break the line of the house; as if a sentry-box had been considered a regrettable necessity. To the right a Victorian glasshouse threw silver-painted girders up, around and down, clutching and keeping the hothouse plants from escaping.

The tyres of Dave Parks' car and the gravel of the path grated together. The car was stopped. Locking up the car was like offering up an insult. To any thief as well. Rusty brown bits on the car seemed a brighter rust red than usual, and looking at it here there appeared to be more of it. The drive was crossed with actual scrunch underfoot, and a small piece of gravel made its way down the space between the ankle and the heel. The small box-like porch sheltered the front door. A square fibre doormat proclaimed WELCOME. Welcome. Psychiatric cases welcome. A large brass knocker on a brass plate hung over a brass letter-box. Somewhere inside a dog was barking its head off. Dave Parks' hand hesitated at the knocker. There was a buzzer tucked in at the side.

A class-conscious and wary-of-the-dog finger buzzed a small buzz on the buzzer. Inside a light went on. A silhouette of a small, probably woman person appeared on the frosted glass panel. Shadowy arms were stretching up there, down there, pulling and sliding bolts or some such and the door was opened. It was a woman. A dog was still barking somewhere, but the bark was muffled. Hopefully muzzled.

This small, improbable-looking woman had a slight hump on her back which forced her sideways enough to make her sideways looks be upward looks. She just stood or stooped, looking sideways or looking up, holding her bottom lip with two rectangular straight-edged teeth. Her eyebrows and cocked head asked the question.

"Dave Parks. I think we spoke on the phone."

"And here you are, Mr Parks. Good of you to come. Have you a coat?"

"No, no, it's not bad outside."

Inside a clock donged out some dongs.

"And so punctual. Do come in."

The hall was a long rectangle and had actual brown and deeper brown tiles alternating their way across the floor and the walls were hung with paintings of stern-faced people and sea scenes; and at the far end stood a long, tall, black grandfather clock, that ticked to the swing of a pendulum, right next to an umbrella stand at the foot of red-carpeted stairs. There were three walking sticks in the stand. Or two walking sticks and one umbrella.

"Have you a hat, Mr Parks?" The hand flew to cover the bald patch.

"No, no, I haven't. I've hardly any hair really, never mind anything else."

"Yes, of course. Come this way, please. My brothers are in the library."

The woman angled her way over the hallway to two dark double doors, knocked at them, pushed them open. Dave Parks followed; patting at the hair strands, pulling at the shirt cuffs. She stopped

42

in the centre of the book-encased room, held up her palm and fingers and indicated Dave Parks. "This is Mr Parks."

Dave Parks could not see anyone. The books could be seen. The padded wings of the padded leather armchairs could be seen. And there was somebody; tucked up, legs stuck up underneath, small and thin, engulfed by the wings of the chair, and pointing a brass looking-glass at Dave Parks. The narrow end. This little pixie was looking at Dave Parks through the wrong end of the telescope. Glasses chinked. Behind. Turning round brought a more normal man in a dark suit into view. He was pouring a drink. He was smiling at something. He spoke.

"Forgive my little brother, Mr Parks. He probably thinks that's a rare joke."

The red chair swivelled.

"It is not a joke. It's symbolic. Not that you'd know. You never read any of these." He was waving his hand around the lattice-barred bookshelving. "Accounts, that's what you do. Accounts. Where's the symbolism in that?"

"On the contrary, my dear Adam, that's precisely what accounting is all about: symbol recognition and reformulation or rearrangement to make new and different symbols, yet always the new different symbols contain the old within their parts."

"Fiddlesticks!"

The man in the suit came forward with a hand extended. "Smith, Mr Parks, Robin Smith. Glad you could make it, Mr Parks. This person, if one may call him that, is my brother, Adam. Ignore him when you can, and when you can't, thump him. Whisky? I took the trouble of pouring you one. I just somehow thought you would be a whisky man."

"No thanks, I'm driving."

"Oh dear. A cigar perhaps?"

"No thanks, honestly."

The pixie lowered the telescope. "And I don't suppose you like sex either."

The two brothers laughed out loud. The pixie fellow spun the chair, sticking his legs out at ninety degrees going round once, going round twice, three times, before jumping off and stepping over. Adam Smith was very small. His face only reached Dave Parks' shoulder.

"The joke is, Mr Parks, that just before you came in I bet Robin that you would be a paragon of virtue; no drinkee, no smokee and no bloodee anything else. That's all, that's the joke."

Parks stared down. The small fellow's eyes were big and bright; round shiny marbles set in a tight narrow face. The face looked up. Dave Parks looked down. The brows furrowing. Perhaps this was a test. Perhaps this Adam Goodfellow was due his first thump. Perhaps. But when in doubt, leave it out.

Robin was taking Dave's elbow. "Sit over here, Mr Parks. Forgive him, he's really quite harmless. As well as positively useless."

Dave Parks was guided to a chair opposite the bad pixie's padded leather Waltzer. The one called Robin pulled over a brass-studded straight-backed chair and sat down.

"Did you have any trouble finding us, Mr Parks?"

"Brother Robin, cut the cackle, just tell him what we want, just tell him, tell him."

Robin sipped his own whisky.

"Perhaps I should, Mr Parks." He took another slow sip.

"Mr Parks, you have come to us in answer to our request put out through these Manpower people, for which we thank you. You do have experience of working with people? And you do know about all these benefity things that people can claim and so on, yes?"

"I think so. We get all that sort of stuff in training, working with people giving them the benefits advice and so on, the usual type of stuff."

"Your usual type of stuff, Mr Parks, is very unusual indeed to us, but, to my point. Where should I begin? Are you sure you wouldn't like a whisky?"

"No thanks. Really."

Adam sang out. "Maybe you should tell it by numbers, tell it by numbers."

"Mr Parks. Our family have been involved in civil engineering for almost two hundred years. We have carried out work all over the world and in particular we helped to develop Africa. Our family built the railways and the roads that followed on the work of the

44

early explorers. Now we are not so important as we once were, but we still, how shall I say, make a living. My, our, father now heads the company, but he is getting on."

"You want me to help your father?"

"Oh, not at all, not at all. No, no, no. Let me carry on." The red leather chair was off on another spin. He obviously knew the story.

"My father worked very closely with one of the best civil engineers we've ever had, a man called James Cameron Black. There was not an engineering problem the man could not solve. My father felt very close to him, and when JCB had a son, father made sure he had the best education and, and so on and so on."

The pixie had stopped spinning. Now he was looking through the wrong end of the telescope again. It looked as if it was pointing up at Dave Parks' little bald spot.

Robin continued. "The son of JCB was very nearly one of the family."

The Adam Smith was beginning to bounce up and down in the chair, clacking the telescope, clashing the parts together, closing it up, opening it out. "Friend? Friend? What friend? The man's a fool. A fool. Only father wants to take anything to do with him."

Robin walked over and poured another whisky and returned and resumed. "Recently, Mr Parks, my, our, father was over in Africa trying hard to be useful, when he came across JCB junior in a rather distressed state. Out of some misguided loyalty to the man's father he brought him home and quite unceremoniously dumped him on us. We have, in short, been keeping this man ever since. And now we no longer care to do so."

There was the pause. They were waiting. Waiting for the sensible remark. The one that would indicate Dave Parks was the man for the job. Whatever that was.

"Mm. Couldn't you give him a job somewhere?"

Adam the elfin Smith cackled and slapped the arms of the chair.

"Rich. Rich. Oh, that is rich. The man's a drunk, a drunk."

"The problem, Mr Parks, is that over the years we have become, how shall I say, providers, rather than engineers. If a country wants roads or bridges, or wanted other countries to have them, we make

45

sure that the finance and some of the expertise is there. Our role is more that of a humanitarian expediter or, if you prefer, expediters of the civilities of life."

"I see, you mean the civilities that flowed along the canals and railways your father built."

"And that are still being built, Mr Parks, still being built. But not so much by us. To return to our problem, Mr Parks. Father has been well-meaning but misguided in attempting to look after the welfare of JCB junior."

"I'm no baby-sitter."

The red leather chair threatened to tip over. Fairy-head was clutching his sides.

Robin grinned. "JCB is fifty-four years of age, Mr Parks."

The legs were up again, but kicking up and down; he was smiling a smile that was set at forty-five degrees, walloping his head off the inside wing of the chair. His brother gestured to him to calm down.

"My father made sure his trusty servant was well looked after, Mr Parks, but it would appear JCB junior preferred to play the prodigal son. Unfortunately, his father was dead. And Adam and I do not exactly consider ourselves his blood-brothers." The Robin man's face became more serious. "I, we, have had enough of paying for JCB. It is time for the man to go."

"What does your father say?"

"My father is an old man, Mr Parks. We packed him off to the country. When he returns we shall present him with the *fait accompli.* Hopefully."

Dave Parks was the hopefully.

"Where is he going to?"

"We rather hoped whoever took on this job would help there. We don't particularly care, Mr Parks. It is time for JCB to be helped to help himself."

A cackling sound came from the red chair. "You mean, let the State help him help himself."

"My brother has put it rather crudely, Mr Parks. All I, we, want, is for JCB to be eased back into the real world and cease to be a financial burden upon all of us. I am sure, with his education, that

46

once he gets a taste of the real world, he won't be long working his way. We shall give you two hundred-and-fifty pounds to use to make the start, plus an hourly rate, plus expenses. Provided you do not take too long about it, of course."

Of course. Dave Parks stretched up and up. The shoulders were tight, tense. Stretching the arm allowed a sneaky look at the watch. Five past three.

"Well, Mr Parks, what do you say, as it strikes you so far?"

There was a knock at the door. The woman came in.

"There is a phone call for Mr Parks."

She waited, beaming, and showed where the phone was. It was Jimmy.

"Hi Jimmy. I'm OK. Thanks for phoning. They're quite pukka."

"Is it a real job then?"

"Aye, well, it's kind of complicated, I don't know whether to take it on board or not. I'll explain it to you later, OK? Thanks for phoning, but it's all right. I think I'll see you after."

"If you're sure. You sure?"

"Sure. Honest."

"OK then. I'll see you if you come back for a pint."

"Right. Cheers."

The library door was open, but Dave Parks knocked anyway. The woman stopped speaking, turned, smiled again and left, walking in that stooped way. Robin was sitting staring into the fire; the Adam was somewhere on his chair, moving it in half-circles. Robin looked up.

"Not bad news, I hope?"

"No, no, nothing at all. A friend was passing on a message for my wife. She was leaving instructions, in case I don't have the key to get back in."

"Ah, good. Always be prepared, eh?" His eyes were looking over the whisky glass. He was waiting. Dave hesitated, then sat down in the chair. It was low and leaning forward. Robin was higher. There was a puzzle here.

"Can I say something? Why don't you just pick up a phone and phone the DHSS or one of the Council's Welfare Rights officers?"

47

The elfin one had moved the chair round to face the dulling fire. A leg was stretching out, stretching out, stretching, stretching, aiming a pointed toe-cap at a fading lump of black, grey red coal. The foot connected. Grey ash fell from the lump, bright sparks went up the chimney and after the action the lump remained the same dull red. Three men watched the fire. Three men were silent, until Robin spoke.

"Reasons. Apart from our own ineptitude in these matters, we feel that we would not like it to be known that we were having dealings with the agencies of the State, as it were. We prefer to act privately." He stood up and went to the drinks tray. The man was showing signs of impatience.

Dave spoke towards him. "That's OK for you to say, but what about the client? He might be missing out on his entitlements, depending on his circumstances or his stamps or whatever. He might be missing out."

"I can assure you, Mr Parks, JCB has been getting more than his fair share. Much more. That is why it has to stop. We do, however, recognise that his background to date has not exactly kitted him out for dealing with whatever it is he may have to deal with. That is why we are prepared to pay you to guide him, counsel him, ease his path, until he can stand again as a free agent."

Free, the man said.

The poking foot crashed into the grate and threw up a cloud of ash and sparks. The shoe with its toe of ash was being pointed at Dave Parks. It spoke.

"Or become the prisoner of the State. What do you say to that, Mr Parks, could be, eh? Could be, could be, could be . . ." He swung in time to the mouthings.

"All I can see is that this JCB man needs help. Can I talk to him?"

The pixie went off on a spin. Robin stood up and looked down. He spoke. "JCB does not live here. We have him placed in a guest-house on the coast. And his time is up. We wish him to be independent, and the owners wish the room for the summer season, in order to make more profit from it."

Dave Parks gave in. "Can I have a whisky, please? As I understand it, I've to take this lad and find him a place and get him on the supplementary, is that it?"

Robin had been over and returned with a whisky. He smiled. "If that's what you call it." He handed the whisky down. "I'm sure you will find him most agreeable material to work with. He has a First from Oxford, you know. Philosophy."

Adam jumped out of his chair and began marching up and down the room, the telescope tucked under his left arm, right arm swinging, trebly voice singing. "First, first, first, first, first, first, first, first." They could only pretend to ignore him.

Dave spoke up. "I'm not exactly a dummy myself."

"No offence, Mr Parks, I was merely trying to give you a pen-picture. Will you take the post?"

"If I do, my rate is five pounds per hour, plus these expenses."

"Excellent. Good man."

Adam jumped. Now he was standing, balancing, on the straight-backed chair, looking again through the wrong end of the telescope.

From his inside pocket Robin produced a document. He looked through it. He hummed, took it over to a desk, picked up a pen, and made some adjustment to it. The document was given over to Dave Parks. It looked very official and full of official-looking phrases.

"Can't we just shake on it?"

Adam cackled. Robin held out a pen. "That is such an upper-class myth, Mr Parks." He jabbed his fingers at some dotted lines. Dave Parks signed. Something was rubbing at the shoulder. Adam Smith was standing looking down the correct end of the telescope, focusing on the signature, almost touching it with the body of the telescope. Dave Parks wanted to be out.

"I won't be able to do much this weekend, but I'll go and see the fellow, probably Monday."

"Handle it whatever way you will, Mr Parks. Whatever way you will. Here is the address of the guest-house. It's quite a charming place, quite charming."

Adam the elf was back in his chair and was humming tunelessly and spinning backwards and forwards aimlessly. Robin had the Parks elbow again and was leading out into the hall. The woman was buttoning up a green raincoat above green wellies. She smiled, but said nothing. At her feet an alsatian watched, but remained quiet.

"Mr Parks is just leaving, Florence. And don't stay too long out with the dog, there's a good girl. It's still rather cold yet."

Brother and sister smiled at each other with their lips. The woman and the dog went first, Dave followed Robin out on to the driveway. Robin gestured Dave to follow him. He led around the side of the house to a garage. After fumbling for the keys he opened the door. He stood back and pointed in. "This is yours for the duration. We do not want any transport problems, do we?"

Dave Parks did not. The car was a family saloon. By its registration it was only two years old. Brand new to Dave Parks.

Robin spoke. "It was one of our reps' cars. If you leave the keys for your own, I mean, after you take anything there is to be taken, it'll be garaged here. If you like. Just if you like."

Dave Parks liked. There was nothing in the banger that anybody could want. Unless they wanted cheap jump-leads and a foot-pump that only worked if you held the nozzle on yourself. A few days with this would be a pleasant change.

The keys were exchanged. Robin closed the door with a quiet click behind. It started first time. Robin leaned in the window. "A pleasure doing business with you, Mr Parks."

Dave Parks insisted on a mythical handshake and was off.

****

There were plenty of spaces in a car park provided by a benevolent supermarket; an abundance of choice of empty space that created confusion in the ranks. When there was so much to choose from it was hard to come to the ideal conclusion. A piece of tarmacadam between two white lines was chosen for no particular reason and there the car was parked. Sea smells came in on a cold wind that Dave Parks drew in in gulps as he locked up and pulled at the door handles just to be sure. He gulped, hoping, but not entirely convinced, that it was a wind that was blowing some good.

The streets of this town were narrow; tight tenements shutting out the light. Two cinemas faced each other: one closed up and the other proclaiming the Bingo. An assistant in a newspaper shop provided a morning paper that was the only one just left, and a smile, and told the whereabouts of the guest-house with another smile. The place was right on the front.

The streets grew narrower. These did not run straight to the front. These ran off one another in curves, obtuse angles and oblique angles and sometimes straight across right angles, a Pavlovian maze that might have built up excitement in a young Dave Parks but for now produced only annoyance.

Inside a video games palace a man knelt and poked at a machine with a screwdriver in preparation for the some kind of summer that was to come again. A pub stank. Its door was open for deliveries and last night's smell was let out; a narcotic nicotine mixture, swilled in sweat, urine and damp poverty. Inside, a radio was playing a somebody-done-somebody-wrong song. A tubby woman with wisps of grey hair that dropped out below her turban pulled her pinny down and proceeded to scrub the terrazzo steps of a discotheque bar that called itself 'CHUCKLES'. She talked to herself.

People passed by but kept their heads down against the seeking wind and nattered and nodded nose to nose to one another, or singularly shuffled and studied the ground that passed under between each step.

Dave Parks passed on by and round and up another street and there was the front, and the sea. A grey stone wall ran above the beach with little pointed turrets at the points of access, and it ran, and ran along past the green that would be for putting and the empty pool that would be for paddling, and the spare piece of ground where the showpeople would put up their tents and set up their stalls for hoopla and the palm-reading, where everybody wins a prize.

In memory Dave Parks knew this place, or the place that it was then, as he was then. Remembered the big steam engine; the early rise to get a good place on the beach; the fun that destroying sandcastles could bring; and the torn faces of teenage girls who didn't know what they wanted but knew it wasn't here. If it wasn't here then, it wasn't here now. Passing summers brought back some of these girls as mothers with their own happy families, but probably some of these would be women who knew they had no chance now of ever finding that place they had hoped to be. The 'sixties and 'seventies had failed to penetrate any further than the bingo and the disco and the video parlour. The battered, uncomprehending, refuge-seeking spirit of the 'forties possessed this place; this out-of-season place that was painted in the forty shades of Scottish grey.

A solitary, boarded-up, white caravan that was Joe's Diner, whenever, sat like a washed-up sea-slug. Lost, hugging the stones of the promenade in cold hibernation. At the bandstand a piece of plastic repair on a window pane. Ripped free; flapping; cracking at the wind. No one else walked the pavement beside the sea wall. The tide was out, far out, as if contemplating staying out. Even from the Sea-Views a visitor would need a pair of binoculars. Green slimy weed stuck on rocks beneath the harbour wall and stuck on row-boat hulls that were imbedded in muck-brown sand. Dave Parks hauled himself away from the sea wall and crossed the wide promenade to the pavement beside the houses.

The paint on the villas peeled in flaky bursts of curling paint that revealed further flaky bursts and depressions of crumbling plaster underneath. Gold-lettering on glass panels above the doors was faded and peeling, only etching out the titled fantasies, HAMELDAEME or DUNROAMIN. The church with its expansive driveway was now a store for electrical goods. The board proclaiming the name of the last preacher was bent backward at several different angles, more likely to have been hit by a truck than have been bent by the wrath of a storm. The brightest colours were being provided by the FOR SALE notices in the windows of some houses that were being given up. On a hill the solitary ruin of a castle tower half-stood with its masonry tumbling down and out in train behind it. A dog leapt at something in its imagination across the knoll that the rest of the one-time stronghold had stood upon. No one appeared to be walking the dog. This was a holiday place of the past where traditions were slowly being surrendered up to newer flights of fancy in warmer climes, and happy times on cheap crossings and cheaper booze. This was a holiday place of the last resort. And from a house here James Cameron Black was being asked to leave. Because someone else had to have the room. Perhaps this landlord threw free whisky in with the night-time Bovril or perhaps his rates were cut-price if the boarders brought their own coal. And here was the number where James Cameron Black was to be found; a square villa of orange sandstone and faded red and yellow curtains. No name. Weeds were growing through the cracks in the flagstones of the path which was set between two rectangles of wet overgrown grass and purple weeds.

Before a knock was possible the door opened and was held open by a small, thin man with spectacles and a military moustache, who shivered at the cold blast. He looked at this caller standing there with arm upraised, then looked backwards over his shoulder. Behind him, on the stairs directly facing the door, a man was being pushed downwards, and was resisting, but failing. The door-opener again looked at this man on the doorstep and again he looked back. He said nothing. His face declared indecision. A woman was beating upon the shoulders of the man on the stairs. She screamed. The man apparently was a fool. The foolish man fell. He tripped from the top, and hit every stair as he tumbled. The standing man looked again at Dave Parks. His face asked for help. The woman clumped on high heels to the bottom of the stairs, stepped over the still body, settled herself, and began to boot him with the curling toe of her right foot. The receptor got the message and covered up his head. At least he was alive and not that foolish. She was kicking and shouting: Get out, get out.

The doorman turned. "You'd better come in," he said. "There's a draught."

Dave Parks entered the hall. The door was shut. The thin man smiled. Dave Parks smiled back. The woman kept kicking the recumbent body. The floored man was trying to speak, but covered up again.

Dave spoke. "What's up?"

The little man checked over his shoulder that the question had been directed to him.

"I'm not quite sure. I think he said something to her, you know, kind of personal like."

"Oh."

The woman stopped. "Now get out, bloody get out."

An eye appeared from behind a protective forearm. "But madam . . ."

"Don't you say another word, just get out, as quick as you're able."

"But my baggage, madam."

"When your rent's paid you'll get your baggage."

The little man turned to Dave Parks, pursing his lips, stroking his moustache. "Can I help you at all? Is it a room you're wanting?"

"Actually, I've called to see this man here. I think. I take it that's Mr Black?"

"Oh." The man pointed. "Him? Yes, that's him."

At the sound of the name, Mr Black's assailant turned towards Dave Parks. Her face was long and unsmiling, a lengthy turned-up chin accentuating the smallness of her eyes.

"And who are you? Are you a relation? You his brother or something?"

Dave Parks was glad to be on terra firma on the ground floor. "No. I'm a sort of Social Worker. His family, or friends, or whatever, have asked me to look after him."

54

"Aye, and he needs it. His rent's overdue. I don't suppose you know anything about that?"

"It's OK. I've got the money here to pay that. You'll get it."

"I bloody know I will."

The man on the floor moved; just a little at a time; a stretch here; a stretch there; and cautious looks everywhere. He came up on to one knee. He was broad. Not fat. Broad. Black hair with still plenty of it with silver streaks on the sideburns. His face was tanned. The usual healthy-looking colonial that made Scots look sick. A handsome man, for his age. He stood up. Slowly. A hand was put to the small of his back. A final stretch brought him up to his full height. He was a tall man. His eyes were grey. His forehead was cut, and bruised patches were forming.

The little man picked up a yellow duster from a hall table and began dusting a full-length mirror on the wall.

Dave Parks stepped forward towards the JCB junior, and lifted his fingers towards the man's temples. "You all right?"

The man smiled. Teeth were perfect, annoyingly white against the tan.

"Fear not, sir. As I fell, I remembered the words of the Lord. 'As an adamant harder than flint have I made thy forehead; fear them not, neither be dismayed at their looks, though they be a rebellious house'."

"Aye, well, if you say so. Might be better with an aspirin though."

"And who are you, sir?"

Dave Parks extended a hand. "I'm Dave Parks." And could not resist it. "Cameron Black, I presume?"

"Yes." The man's eyes were grey. The new-found James Cameron Black extended his hand and his grip was strong.

The woman pulled the shaking hands apart. "Well, listen you, whoever you are, he has got to go. And I mean go. Right now, if not sooner."

A duster finished flicking dust off the mirror. "Excuse me," said the man, "would anybody like a cup of tea?"

"There'll be no cups of tea made in here today. And that's final. This one is just going. Clear?" They were all looking at Dave Parks — stranger.

"Can he go and get his gear first, Mrs?"

"Fine. But tell him to make it snappy."

The woman turned and went through an open doorway into what appeared to be a living-room. Dave looked at this James Cameron Black. This JCB was holding up a palm. "I have heard and I obey, Mr Parks; although I am not quite sure who you are."

"I'm just the man that's come to take you to the promised land. I'll explain it to you outside."

"Say no more. So be it for now, my friend." James Cameron Black turned and went up the stairs muttering to himself.

A voice came from the other room. "Hector." Hector dropped his duster, picked it up, red in the face. He beckoned to the caller who had been left standing in the hall. "HECTOR!" Hector stretched over and held the living-room door further open for the visitor. This Hector was looking for an ally. Dave went through.

The woman was sitting on a chair holding an accordion erect on her lap and peering over it at music on a music-stand. She was peering and frowning. Hector crossed over and turned the page.

"Thank you," she said. "You can sit down and wait."

Dave sat down on an old deep armchair. She began to play. It was a tune that had been in the hit parade about thirty years ago. Dave Parks remembered his mother putting her knife and potato down in the sink and dancing to it as it played on the radio. Some kind of Nordic-Slavic polka.

"Do you know him?" she asked, and never stopped pulling and hauling and squeezing at the box.

"Not really. No; no, I don't. Some people that know him have asked me to see he's all right, that's all."

There was a pause while a big strain of music was pushed out.

"He's not you know. Not all right in the head."

"Is that so?"

"Yes. By the way, do you have the rent he's due?"

"Yes, I'll pay it, don't worry."

Her foot moved from tapping with her toes to tapping with her heel. Dave Parks could not play a mouth organ but there was a certainty creeping in that this was not exactly virtuoso stuff.

"He was full board."

"How much is that then?"

"Seventy."

"Seventy?"

"I said he was full board. You can ask him." The music played on.

"No, that's OK, it's nothing to me. I never said a word."

Her left hand got out of co-ordination with the right. She noticed the difference and peered forward. Dave Parks pretended not to hear. The wallet was extracted from inside the jacket, eighty pounds taken out and eighty pounds held out. The cash was going down. The accordion was placed down beside the fireplace.

"Thank you. Need a receipt?"

"I think so; the paymaster is an accountant."

"Oh. One of them."

She crossed to a writing-desk set under a window. Hector came through bearing a tray. He had made tea. The tray had three cups on and a plate full of digestive biscuits which looked ready to fall over the edge. A biscuit fell. Hector stopped. He looked up the room to the window. He continued on. The tray was manoeuvred on to a glass-topped coffee table. The Hector stepped back quickly, taking his handkerchief from his pocket as he did so. The biscuit was picked up, blown, flicked at.

"You can have that one," she said, without looking up.

Hector bit it. She finished at the desk, walked over, and a receipt was given and taken. She sat down and Hector picked up and passed her tea over to her. A biscuit was declined. Hector sat on the arm of her chair. They sipped tea. Hector smiled. They sipped tea. Dave Parks smiled. The woman did not. She sipped tea. Dave Parks sipped tea.

Hector broke first. "Have a biscuit." He held over the plate.

"No thanks."

Another biscuit nearly fell off but the man moved his arm and his body and it balanced. The tension was too much for Dave Parks.

"I see you play the accordion."

"Yes."

They sipped tea. Noises could be heard from the floor above. The tea was supposed to be calming. Talk would make the time pass faster than this steady sipping in silence.

"Played the accordion long?"

"Yes."

Dave Parks decided to plunge ahead and try to make the words here flow into at least the semblance of a conversation.

"I always fancied the accordion when I was young. The man up the stairs used to play one. I think he used to play that tune you were playing there. What was it called again?"

"The Swedish Polka."

"That's right, that's right. The Swedish Polka. I've never heard that for years. That was a big hit, wasn't it?"

"I think so, yes."

Three extra words there. From now those TV interviewers would be looked at in a new light. Still, three extra words. Promising. Maybe Hector fancied a chat.

"What about you, Hector. Do you play?"

Hector shook his head. But no words. And the tea was finished.

"How long has Mr Black been here?" Her mouth was opening. She was going to say something. Success.

"Five months. An older man brought him one night. Said him up there needed rest and contemplation. I liked that man. He was very distinguished. I liked him."

Dave Parks was not for exploring the inference that she did not like her lodger, or Dave Parks perhaps, or even Hector maybe. The head was put down into another sip of the tea. But she continued.

"He's a fool, you know. Talks nonsense all the time and drinks and mutters to himself, and he's not above a bit of the dirty talk for all he tries to talk like a minister." She put her cup in her saucer and sat up straight. "Thought I was his skivvy, you know. Soon put a stop to that. Anyway, I've had enough of him. We need the room. The season will be right on us before we know it."

"Oh, I seen signs of that this morning."

Hector nearly slid off the arm of the chair, but caught himself. There were questions to be asked, but Dave Parks did not like to ask the lady. Footsteps sounded on the stairs, then stopped. Her cup and saucer were lifted on to the mantelpiece.

"You can just stay out there."

Dave Parks put his tea things on the floor. Hector put his on the tray, smiled, and lifted the visitor's cup and saucer on to the tray and lifted her ladyship's from the mantelpiece to the tray. She stood up. Dave Parks stood up. She held out a hand.

"Well, Mr Parks, I wish you joy. That's all I can say."

She remained, but Dave followed the tray-bearer out into the hall. Hector squeezed past JCB who stood beside a long canvas sports bag and one large suitcase. The buttons on his black blazer gleamed, and on the breast pocket was a badge showing two crossed cricket bats above a wicket, with a ball between the handles. Hector came back, squeezed through, again with a smile, and opened the door. The wind chilled. JCB bent to grip his luggage and aimed his voice at the living-room door.

"I'll be gone then, woman."

There was no reply.

"Thanks for the tea," shouted Dave Parks.

There was no reply.

Hector came down the path with them, shivering and remarking that it wasn't summer yet by a long chalk. At the gate he was reluctant to let them go, chittering and chattering on about how Scots never dress properly for the weather. An upstairs window in the house scraped its way up. It was her. The landlady's head came through.

"Hey you, you, you forgot this."

She withdrew from the window. A full-size cricket bat came hurtling through space. It landed on the wet grass. JCB ran forward and picked it up. His face was red. He shook the bat high and shouted at the figure sheltering behind the curtain.

"Desecration. Desecration. This is a desecration, woman. You're vile, vile. A vile, vile woman. I shall be glad to be gone from here. Do you hear? 'It is better to dwell in a corner of the housetop than with a brawling woman in a wide house.' Do you hear?"

Her head came through the window again.

"Hector, you come in here."

"Hector, if you have any sense you will construct yourself an attic. An attic, do you hear?"

She probably heard. Hector said his goodbyes and walked up the path, opened the door, and closed it. JCB rejoined Dave Parks at the end of the path. Carefully Dave Parks made sure the bolt on the gate was home. Then he freed it again, and swung the gate open. That was the way Dave Parks had found it.

They walked slowly along the promenade. No one else was taking the sea-breezes. James stopped. He touched Dave on the arm.

"Wait. I must go back. I should not have shouted at the poor woman."

He turned and marched back towards the house, turned into the path and stopped halfway up. The bags were laid down. He lifted his arms and hands above his body and began to speak in a loud voice.

"O Lord, who hearest everything and knoweth all things, hear me, a perfect sinner, and forgive me this day for the sins I have committed, by thought, word and deed. Forgive me the manner in which I have treated your other creatures this day and shine your light upon them and recompense them for my sinful ways. See me, O Lord, hear me, O Lord, and forgive me, O Lord."

The arms and hands were dropped and crossed in front of him. He began to sing in a louder voice:

> "The Lord's my shepherd, I'll not want.
> He makes me down to lie
> In pastures green: he leadeth me
> the quiet waters by."

Dave Parks stood at the end of the path.

The 23rd Psalm   Tune: Crimond

Somehow it felt wrong to even step past the gate. The man's voice was strong. No one came to the door or the windows of the house. There was no one on the promenade to hear. The man was singing solo and Dave Parks was listening solo. There was a white van coming along the road. It was slowing down, but it flashed left and turned up the driveway of the electrical store. The words were singing in Dave Parks' head. In his own voice. Word perfect. James Cameron Black was giving it everything he had, lifting his chin up and belting it out. Dave Parks was finding it hard not to join in. Those words were floating down from the mind to the mouth and almost sneaking out in whispers. Dave Parks gave the head a shake and snorted through the nose. JCB's cup was overflowing and there was only one verse left. Dave Parks knew that.

> "Goodness and mercy all my life,
> Shall surely follow me;
> And in God's house, for evermore,
> My dwelling place shall be."

Scotland's Psalm   Dave Parks knew that.

Dave Parks began a clap and stopped. James looked over his shoulder, smiled, and turned his face one more towards the house. His arms were raised high, fingers extended.

"May the Lord make his countenance to shine upon you and bestow all blessings of his house upon you, that you may know the grace and the peace of his son, Jesus."

It was wrong for Dave Parks to think a few music lessons wouldn't go wrong either.

James was standing, staring. "I forgive you, woman," he shouted, "I forgive you."

Nothing and nobody moved at the house. He waved, lifted up his bags and walked down the path, and down, out. With a skip he fell into step with Dave Parks.

"Is that you OK now?"

"That, Mr Parks, is me OK now."

They walked to the car. Dave tried to explain his mission. JCB understood. Or so he said. At the car he paused before getting in.

"I'm to become a ward of the State, is that what you are saying?"

Dave leaned over the roof of the car. "Well, I suppose that's one way of putting it. Unless you get a job or something, and I don't know where you're going to get one of them."

They got into the car. James had a difficult job with the safety belt. Dave the driver leaned across and fixed him in. Before he started the car Dave Parks had to scratch his chin and scratch his head at the back and then scratch his forehead.

"Is something troubling you, David?"

"No. I'm just wondering whereabouts in this place to go next, to find you a place like."

"Do I have to stay in this place? It is such a depressing little town."

"No, not really, we can go almost anywhere, but it's finding a place that'll take people that are on the supp ben."

"Sup ben?"

"Supplementary benefit. Look, JC, James, there is no cash going to come in for you except from the supplementary benefit. Most places don't like their punters to be on the supp ben, that's all."

"I see. But within those constraints I can go anywhere."

"Well, within you know what I mean."

"Can I say this? When I was driven down here by old Mr Smith, may God bless him, I'm sure we came through a little fishing port, not far from here. That's where I really would like to go. It really looked quite charming."

"There? You'll never get a place there. That's full of the yachting and gin and tonic brigade, behave yourself."

"That is where I wish to stay."

"I've no doubt you do, but there'll be no chance."

"Shall we try? Perhaps the Lord will guide us."

Dave started the car. Maybe they would get lucky. The roads were clear and inside the car it was warm and out of town a weak sunshine tried its best to shine on everything. And somebody was paying Dave Parks for this. Driving up country roads in a reasonable car on a reasonable day. As long as the passenger stayed reasonable.

"What was the old dear beating you up for?"

"Absolutely nothing, nothing at all. I came upon her dusting the dresser and just happened to say: how amiable are thy tabernacles, O lady of hosts. She was not amused. I'm afraid she's a woman of limited education, and even lesser humour."

Dave Parks could not stop a laugh. "You don't get away with that sort of thing nowadays you know."

"So I have observed, my dear David."

Dave Parks laughed. JCB laughed. His head was back and his laugh was loud.

The road became more reasonable as the town was left behind with the empty harbour and the jettisoned, rusting oil depot, and passed the caravan park for the city dwellers, who still came in search of the weekend peace next to the sea and the farms where the cows watched the cars go by and up into the places where ribbons of bungalows had place-names to themselves until they merged in again with the anonymous fields. The passenger was staying reasonable, rubbernecking the views on either side and occasionally peering forward. Sometimes the man put his head down and stared at the floor mumbling, until he jerked himself up and looked at the countryside around for another space of time. And sometimes he spoke and asked questions about the Smith family, benefactors. In particular he wanted to know if the old man Smith had decreed his fate. This question had been asked more than once.

"Do you think these instructions are from the old Mr Adam?"

"Don't think so, James. I've a feeling he's on the road out. No, I think it's definitely the young Mr Smith that's giving the orders."

That made the James Cameron Black look again at the floor. And mumble mumble some more.

The whitewashed cottages, with their red-tiled roofs and lopsided chimneys, hove into view; running down from a high hill to the very edge of the sea. This place no longer had a fishing fleet, but the world knew of it because its small breakwater harbour was photographed and shown on pictorial calendars by photographers keen to show the world that Scotland was like what the world thought it was like. A cobbled square acted as municipal car park. Men were digging some kind of fertiliser into troughs of soil to make ready for the summer display. The town hall looked closed. A café had red chairs stacked on white formica tables. A hotel that had an ivy-covered porch displayed a yellow sign that had black stars and black knives and forks picked out on it.

"Don't think there's much use in trying there, James."

"A touch austere for my taste, Mr Parks, just a touch."

Down by the harbour, along streets the width of a motorcar, in blocks of houses that used to be the fishers' rows, four-square windows had signs in them that said full board, or bed and breakfast, or b.&b., was available. Some gave a full English breakfast. Small sets of stairs separated the doors from the pavement. At the bottom of each set of stairs, one each side, polished, varnished, iron-hooped half-barrels stood, all in line, cleared of the growth of the previous year, now ready, waiting to receive the geraniums and blue and purple lobelia with the white alyssum that would bloom so bright for the summer.

"How's this suit you mister?"

"Admirably. Admirably."

"Well, don't count on it. OK, let's have a bash."

The first door was tried. A curtain moved, but no one answered. The next brought out a woman who rubbed her hands on her apron and said it was too early in the season. And she didn't want permanent boarders. Another woman smiled, then frowned when she heard the words "supplementary benefit". For others it was the letters DHSS that brought the shake of the head. A clean sweep was made of a long row. Dave Parks gave it up.

"I'm afraid this is going to be it, James. Everywhere you go in this place. They need the money OK, but they don't want to know about the DHSS. We're at the wrong end of the market, old son."

James was looking disappointed.

"No room at the inn, my friend. It seems singularly bereft of other human beings, this place. I'm beginning to have second thoughts about it."

"Well, as long as you're not pregnant we'll find you some place. There's bags of room, but I'm afraid it's horses for courses, old son, and you just might be heading for the stable. Anyway, let's go for a coffee."

A café made out of the back of a baker's shop was found. It was clean. And empty. The baking smelled good. Two teas, two scones, and jam were ordered. Dave Parks went to the lavatory.

In the mirror the face did not look at all red, never mind suntanned. A little boy came in, filled his hands with water, wet his hair, and stood under the hot-air drier combing it. He dried his hands on his jacket and made for the door again.

"Blow-dry mister," he said.

James was chatting to the waitress as she put the order on the table. He got a big smile for his small-talk when she left.

"Looks good, James."

"It does indeed, David."

The scones were hot. The butter was melting on them.

"So how come you came to be in Zimbabwe, James?"

"My father preferred it there, and it was an ideal starting-off point for the other states. Geographically speaking. He wanted to retire there. The climate, you know."

"Is he still living anywhere? Or what, is he dead?"

"He died at the beginning of seventy-eight, David. He was getting on. I think he missed mother. She had died in sixty-four. In Bournemouth."

James was being very deliberate in spreading the butter. And the information. This was getting to be a sad tale.

"So why did you stay on after that? I mean, apart from your Ma and Da dying, it was just about time to get out, was it no?"

"It was either a time to go, or a time to stay."

"Oh aye, if you look at it like that."

"David, I was not one of those who believed, still believe, Rhodesians never die." James bit into his scone and a piece of jam fell on the white tablecloth. "England, or Scotland, meant relatively little to me. If anything, I felt more at home in Rhodesia/Zimbabwe. And I suppose, well, I suppose I had some notion, duty, of being the last of the great scholar-administrators. Wise old head and all that. I worked for, for the government."

"Important guy then?"

"Not quite important enough. I tried not to think too much about the war, just carry out my duties, wait for the foregone conclusion to come. I hoped that I might be of service to the new rulers." James wiped the sticky spot of jam with his open palm. "It was not to be."

"Well, at least you're here to talk about it."

"Is there more tea?"

"Sure, plenty. I'll be mother."

"Anyway, the cricketing is poor in Zimbabwe now."

"You're never for telling me you let the Mr Smith bring you back because the cricket was rubbish?"

"Not exactly. When he found me I was, I suppose, in a sorry state. But it's true. Cricket is in danger over there." James was smiling, but half-serious. "I remember sitting in a bar in Harare. The girl was fawning over Mugabe on the television set. Nothing unusual in that, but then I heard the word cricket and my ears pricked up. I just caught him saying: cricket had never really been popular with Africans, words to that effect, and he was considering allowing the game to die. The game to die. Even consider it. That, my dear David, was the tin hat. And here I am. I even tried to stop drinking. I resolved to come back to England where people knew the value of cricket." James leaned back in his seat. "Unfortunately, I never made it under my own steam, or any other way."

"You mean you ended up on your arse in Harare."

"You have a simple way of putting things, David."

"If you say so, James. Anyway, I was getting a bit personal there. Sorry."

"No damage done, my friend. None whatsoever. But these revelations are depressing me. Let us be off, or from, or whatever."

"Sure. But I honestly think you're best bet is the City. It's all the City folk that play cricket in Scotland anyway."

"Then the city it shall be. Tell me, David, is there an hotel called the Imperial still there? My father always stopped there when he came home to visit the Smiths. I seem to have it in mind it was rather a charming place."

"Everything's charming to you, James. But I don't think charming is the right word for the Imperial. No way you can stay there. No way."

James stood up. "If it's all right for my father it's all right for me."

"Aye, well, we'll see about that."

The bill was paid, the legs stretched, the last lungfuls of air drawn in. James fastened in. Choke out. No bother, the car was away like a wee train.

B roads became A roads and entered the motorway. Up from the coast the roads came into the City on the south-side, past the docks with their petrified giraffes, and the warehouses and the industrial estates. BLOCKS TO LET, the housing estates, but here traffic slowed down, behind each other, one at a time, as others waited to turn in to city centre streets, before, and after, Dave Parks. Lights were at red.

"James, I'm going to drive down here past the Imperial."

"Yes?"

"See when we get there, I won't even have to stop. It'll be on your right-hand side."

Traffic lights turned green. It was time to go, move over, get into the right-hand lane. From the lights the street ran down in a slope. High-rise blocks on the left. A propped-up wall with only spare ground behind on the right. Further down on the left a brewery had claimed the surrounding streets as its own. Right down on the right a grimy red sign with half of its letters missing hung slanted on the side of a building. It was time to slow the car down.

"Can you see it?" It would be hard to miss it.

"Yes." The tone of the voice told he had seen and understood.

Scraps of curtains hung in windows in a continuing grey wall. Men sat stooped forward, sleeping, on the marble stairs, heads resting on arms, resting on knees. Some man with a long beard and wearing two dirty greatcoats was begging from a woman who rushed to the edge of the pavement. She had probably meant to cross the road earlier. A drunk man and a drunken woman were arguing with one another, and spittle was flying between them.

"You still for the Imperial, James?"

"You have made your point, David."

"I thought I might, but that still does not solve our wee problem."

This street was a long one. There were no turn-offs. Not here anyway. The car could only be pointed in front until at the far end a right turn made itself available. This was unfamiliar territory. The same as the rest, but unfamiliar. Streets looked the same, but this was an area the young Dave Parks had never come near. Different religions. But now Dave Parks was a man. But the area was still unfamiliar. But probably all right. But.

"I'll head over the river, James. I'm more familiar with that side of the City."

"Whatever you say, David."

Another right turn and this was a cul-de-sac. The gear stick was struggling, struggling, and screeching, and refusing to go into reverse. Dave Parks had to swear.

"David."

"Sorry, James, it's just I don't know what's happened here."

"Eh? No, no, I wasn't meaning that, no, not at all, look there, in the window of that house."

At the end of the cul-de-sac stood a square house, on its own, detached, out of place in this district of tenements ancient and modern. A house painted green, with dark blue rectangles around the white painted windows. The house stood. A dull light barely lit up a curtain in a downstairs window. In an upper window a faded yellow piece of board with big black lettering carried the message: VACANCY.

"That place? You fancy that place?"

Why not fancy that place? Not fancy that place because the young Davie Parks was inside the big Dave Parks and still being not too sure. Why not that place?

"D'you fancy it? In there? I don't really see why not, I don't suppose."

"Perhaps the Lord has been our guide."

"Aye, maybe, maybe no. Personally my money is on Dave Parks and his ignorance of this area. Still, might be worth a try."

Forward gears were no bother. The car slid in next to the pavement. Some kind of grassy park set a margin down one side of the rectangle. On the other, spare ground left by fallen tenements had been planted with shrubs and trees and a couple of benches sat waiting to be sat upon. A litter bin was overflowing with beer cans.

"Ah well, James. Here we go, here we go, here we go."

The street was clean enough, right up to the path going up to the door. A hedgerow ran in ill-defined waves around narrow strips of garden in front. Perhaps the hedge-cutter had got seasick. Somebody inside was singing. High and loud.

"Lohengrin," said JCB."

"I'll take your word for it."

JCB stopped with his head cocked to one side, listening, but Dave Parks thumped the door. The singing stopped. Sounds came from inside that were not musical. The door was opened. A woman dressed in some kind of red silky dressing-gown stood, one arm holding the door open, the other wiping across her forehead. The face was flushed. A dragon wound its way round the material with a forked tongue finishing up around her chest.

"Yes?"

"My name is Dave Parks. Sorry to bother you but the . . . I'm a social worker. I'm trying to find a place to stay for this man here. His name's Black."

"Is he working?"

"Well, he, no. He's not long back in the country, actually. But I'm sure he'll get a job no bother."

"D'you think so? What does he do that makes him different?"

Dave Parks was stuck for an answer. And her eyes had the beating of Dave Parks' eyes. Her eyes went for a look at Mr Black, taking in the face then moving right down to the shoes.

"Shiny shoes. I like shiny shoes. Shoes are always a dead giveaway, you know."

Dave Parks was frowning but she was the woman with the room.

"That's funny that. You're the second person I've heard say that the day. Imagine that."

"Yes. Imagine. Is he quiet?"

"Very quiet. Just likes to mind his own business and maybe listen to some opera or stuff. This is a professional man we are talking about."

"Opera? Do you like opera?"

"Yes, although it's a long time since, well, since I was in a position to indulge myself. I was enjoying listening to you singing."

"Oh, you were. What was I singing?"

"*Elsa's Dream*. Wagner."

"Mmm. Come in then and we'll talk. It's bloody cold out here."

She turned and led the way down a hall. She was in her bare feet. "Make sure you close the door," she shouted back.

The hall was dark. Doors indicated rooms along both sides. The stairway split the bottom hall in two. The woman was standing in front of an open door. "This way."

This way was into a large room; square; with a high ceiling. From the high ceiling a lit glass chandelier dangled. Light only made it halfway down the walls. A grey-headed woman sat in a wheelchair, looking up. A small accordion case was stacked in a corner behind her, next to a door in the end wall.

"My sister, Laura Kipple. I'm Theresa Kipple. Who are you?"

Dave Parks gave the name. Mr Black remained quiet; he was grinning at the woman in the wheelchair. Theresa Kipple sat down, making sure her gown covered her legs. Some of her toes were painted. Some not.

"Is he drawing the social?" she asked.

"I've just taken charge of him. But you must know if I've to get him any money I've got to get him fixed up somewhere."

"I don't know how I must, but I do. I've only got one lodger on the social here, though. And he's been here a long time. I prefer them to be working. Sometimes I have to leave my sister alone here, know what I mean?"

There was no question. There was no answer. The sister spoke up.

"I like him." She was looking up from her wheelchair at Dave Parks.

The one called Theresa corrected her. "It's not him that would be staying, Laura, it's the other one."

"Oh."

The bottom lip on the mouth of Theresa Kipple was being chewed. Her face was making it known she was considering it. Dave Parks tried to clinch it.

"I can pay rent in advance."

"You'll need to. If he gets in, it'll probably take a couple of weeks before his cash comes through. He's a pathetic-looking soul, isn't he?"

"Don't think so."

"Mmm."

"If I may be permitted. I have not exactly said I wish to remain here."

"I like the way he talks," said Laura.

"I think that's fair enough," said Parks, worried about losing out. "Could we see the room?"

"You'll see the room when I decide if I'll take him."

That was fair enough to bring a silence. Now the landlady decided her toes needed close scrutiny. She leaned forward and over and studied the toes of her right foot as she waggled it. Without looking up she asked a question.

"What is it you do for a living, Mr Black?"

"I have been many things in my lifetime, madam, but I suppose one can say I was a civil servant for most of them."

"No call for civility around here. You might have a chance as a servant. Do you get a pension then?"

"Alas, no. I'm afraid the circumstances of my departure from my last post rendered that condition invalid."

"You mean you don't get one?"

"Precisely."

"Hmm."

"I really do like the way he talks."

The Theresa Kipple looked at Dave Parks. "Where do you fit in? You work for the Social Work, or what?"

"No, not really. I was just asked by a friend to get James settled, that's all."

"You won't be coming about, poking your nose in?"

"Once he's settled, that's it."

She turned to James.

"Situation is this. There's five lodgers here, and only one of them is on the social. I prefer my men to be working. I don't want any snoopers hanging around here. The place is bad enough as it is. We only want a nice quiet household. Is that understood?"

"Roger."

"My men come and go as they please here and they all mix well. The kitchen is shared, the men use the bathroom upstairs. Always. You'll get breakfast, supper and sandwiches for your work. Forty-eight pounds. That all right?"

"Admirable, I'm sure. But I am rather at the mercies of David here."

David Parks had been mesmerised, lost somewhere.

"Oh right, right. Sounds ideal. But we still haven't seen the room."

"Can you pay the ninety-six?"

"No problem."

71

Laura was clapping her hands. "I'm sure he'll like it. I'm sure he'll like it."

"That's as maybe," said Theresa, rising and leading the way out.

The stairs led up and became a landing. Three doors left, three doors right, and one straight in front.

"That's the bathroom."

She opened the door, and turned a face that defied anyone to step past and actually look. As she led around the landing she nodded to a set of stairs in the corner that ran steeply up to a small door.

"There's a Mr Gordon lives in that room. He's the other man on the social. But you'll get to meet them all when you move in. OK, if you move in."

Two men were standing on the landing, looking in the right direction and trying to nod in the right places at this information and waiting to see the room.

She stopped at door number three. Lucky for some. A key was brought out from a pocket in her gown, put in the lock and turned. Room number three awaited inspection. Room three was clean and tidy. More than large enough for one. Usual dresser. Usual wardrobe that had survived the Blitz. A card-table, folded up, lay against the wall. The window looked out on the cul-de-sac. A man and two youths were working at the grassy margin. The bed had a light above it. The carpet looked new.

James tried the mattress with a push, then another push, harder. "Excellent. I like a hard bed."

There was no change in the woman's face. James was looking at Dave.

"What is your considered opinion, David?"

"It's you that's got to live here, James. It looks OK to me."

"Then, that is that."

Theresa Kipple's face did not change. She waited. Dave Parks decided to back out. James followed, beaming at Theresa. Her face did not change. The door was locked behind them.

Making their way along the landing, they had to stop as a man came out of a room, locked the door, and turned to go, adjusting a soft hat as he went. He was wearing a raincoat that dropped shapeless down to his ankles. A green scarf was tied around his neck, muffling his head in between the hat and the collar. He pulled at the hat brim to acknowledge the landlady.

"That you off, Mr O'Brien? Well, keep a good eye on things then, and remember, if there's anything suspicious, go for the police right away."

The man tugged the brim again, moved along the landing and down the stairs and out. The landlady stopped the two at the hall. Theresa Kipple was spelling out the demarcation zone. Dave Parks paid up and James could move in right away if he liked. James Cameron Black was already at the door. He opened it, stepped outside and there he was waiting on Dave Parks to come and tell him what to do.

"C'mon, James. We'll just get your gear out the car and that's you. You quite happy with the place now?"

"Quite, quite, David. Don't worry, I'm sure it shall be fine."

The handle of the cricket bat had got stuck in the corner of the boot. James worked it free. The gear was out and on its way in. The landlady stood in the hall behind the wheelchair. The wheelchair was pulled back to let the men and the luggage pass through. From her hand a cigarette stuck out from her fingers. Laura sat smiling, sometimes screwing her head round and up to smile wider at her sister. A new arrival was being watched. As James passed Laura she tugged at the sleeve of his blazer, stopping him.

"What does your badge say?"

"*Nil Desperandum,* my dear lady."

"Oh. Nice. I like you coming to stay."

"And I too."

Dave Parks held back, waited. The Theresa looked around and blew some smoke above her head. James bent his head down to Laura.

"Do you believe?"

"Pardon."

"Do you believe upon the Lord?"

73

"Oh, yes, yes. Yes, I do."

"Then you and I shall read our Bibles together every day."

A puff of smoke was blown Dave Parks' way and a head was shaking and brows were knitting.

"James, c'mon. I'll have to be getting home, my son."

James straightened up and brought along himself and the sports bag with the cricket bat on top, following on, up. Theresa closed the front door.

Inside the room Dave bounced on the bed. "Aye, not bad, James, not bad, right enough. Not bad at all."

"It will be sufficient for my needs, I am sure."

"Right, tomorrow, James, you sign on. I'll be here as early as I can."

"Sign on?"

"Sign on. The dole, the unemployment."

"You make it sound as if I were going to enlist."

"Well, so you are; in the grand national reserve army. First battalion the shite brigade, if you'll excuse my language."

"Tch tch tch tch. Dear, dear, David."

"Well, anyway, dole first, then the social. When we find out where it is."

James snapped to attention, slapped his heels together and saluted. "Yes, sir."

"That's the ticket, old bean." Dave placed a tenner on the dresser. James acknowledged it.

"Before you go, David, may I say a prayer for your safe deliverance home?"

"You can say as many as you like James, but I've got to be off. Oh, and by the way, see until you're in here a bit, go easy on the Bible readings and that. I don't think the Theresa person is too sure about that."

"My dear David, when I needed someone in Harare, the Lord sent me Mr Smith, and when the time came it was you the Lord sent to guide me. I am meant to be here."

74

"Aye, well, I'm just saying. Anyway, I hope that Lord of yours is at the social tomorrow, and fixes that reverse gear."

"Nil desperandum, David. Nil desperandum. And I shall pray for you."

The man went on his knees beside the bed, clasping his hands. Dave Parks shut the door.

****

A waitress was coming through from the dining-room and hungry Dave Parks was willing her to be looking for Mr Parks to tell him everything was ready and waiting to be served up.

"I think this is us, Mary."

Right over to the bar the waitress came and she was asking if sir was ready to eat now. Sir. Mister Sir. Sir Mister. Sir Dave. Sir Dave Parks. Sir David Parks. Yes sir. Sir David Parks, former UB40, about to be employed, was ready; just as soon as the last of this little dry white wine could be got rid of. Up and over. It should have been taken slower; that kind of gulping might be good enough for rough whisky but for dry wine it only clapped the cheeks in. Mary was sipping hers. And she was taking the last drop through. Anyway, it was follow the leader time through to a table by the window looking out on to the hotel gardens, and these looked kind of mysterious with shiny leaves in the shrubbery reflecting the light from the building, and dark earth that did not.

Mary was enjoying this. And why not? It had been a long time since the last time. A long time. Mary worried too much. Converted abstract time into worry lines.

"You comfortable, sir? Table all right?"

"Yes, fine. OK Mary?"

"Oh, what do you think? We're fine, thank you."

A smile without teeth came across, and the waitress was off.

Starters came; served by a younger woman with an emotionless face. At least no smile was sincere. Time for Dave, Sir Dave, to spread the napkin on the knees, using the pause to check the layout and function of the cutlery. This was just a habit. In case the people had made a mistake or forgotten one of the tools. Or you never know, they might sneak an extra one in there and that could cause problems by the time you got to the pudding. But it was simple. From out to in. And a separate knife for the butter.

76

Never changed. Rules were good that way. Once you knew them, it was simple. Must've been hard in the early days but, when they were making them up. Few faux pas's then. But now it was simple.

Simple. Smoked mackerel, paté with oatcakes; no problems here. Although oatcakes could be crumbly. So's a pound note. Just break a piece, spread a piece. It tasted peppery.

"How do you find it, Mary?"

"Nice. Lovely. Maybe a wee bit peppery, but nice just the same."

"Mine as well."

There was the glass, and there was the jug. And there was the glass for Mary.

"Would you care for a glass of Adam's ale, dear?"

"No thanks, honeybunch, I've still got some wine left."

"Nineteen eighty-three was a bad year anyway."

The wine was on its way. The older waitress was bringing it over. She held it up, by the neck, resting the bottle on her palm. The label was supposed to mean something. A nod would do. There was food in the mouth. At least it said Chianti on the label. That was right enough. The cork was being attacked as if it had no right to be there.

"Nineteen eighty-three was a very good year, sir."

"Yes. I mean, is that right? I don't really know too much about these things, but I think I read that in one of the papers or something. I thought it would go with our order." That was as much a question as a statement.

"Sir had made an excellent choice. This wine is excellent with both of your meals. But particularly yours, sir."

"Thank you." Now for the token taste. For those with discernment in mouthwashes. It was all right. "That's fine, thanks." Two glasses were poured and the bottle left.

The waitress left. "Enjoy your meal, sir. Madam."

The younger girl brought the main course followed by a young man in a maroon dust-jacket that had stains on. He was bending almost double, balancing two trays of vegetables between his body and his elbow. Vegetables were placed on the plates with a flourish and a silent pause that asked if enough was enough. When enough was enough the glasses were raised. Mary was going to say a toast.

"Here's tae us, wha's like us?"

"Gey few, an they're aw deid."

That toast went down just as well with the Chianti as it did with the whisky. The steak was perfect. Perfect for Sir Dave Parks anyhow. Blood left in the centre.

"How's your spaghetti, Mary?"

"Beautiful, it really is beautiful."

"What did you call that again?"

"Spaghetti Marinara."

"I'm none the wiser."

"Just a fish dish in a sauce with the spaghetti. That's all."

"Sounds good."

Whether it was a good year or whether it was a bad year, the wine was OK. Maybe two bottles would've been better. No. Too much. Maybe they could have liqueurs with the coffee or something. Supposed to be sipped anyway.

"Dave?"

"Yep?"

"Are you sure this is all right? I mean, that money, is it yours to spend?"

The worry lines were into a frown there. Couple of years deep.

"It's mine OK, Mary. They owe me money. Look, we're here to celebrate, not to worry. As of Monday I'll be your actual Social worker. D'you want to read the letter again? I mean, maybe ten times wasn't enough for you."

"No, don't be daft. But what will they mean by temporary?"

"It's just temporary; but Mary, now I'm in I can apply for any vacant post that crops up. Don't worry. Sir Dave Parks won't be temporary long. Anyway it's a start."

"Where is that place anyway? Is it far enough that you might get that car allowance?"

"No, no; it's quite near the centre of the city. It's quite near where I put that guy James at teatime. Just down from the market."

Salome the head waitress was back and asking if sir was satisfied and this time asking madam too, without appearing as if she had to have a think about it. It was satisfying.

78

"What you going to do about that man? And the car and everything?"

"Well, I've got to the end of the week. I'll get him to the Social tomorrow, and that's really it. I'll maybe take a run up and see him. Maybe on the way home from work. D'you hear that, Mary: the way home from work. How does that grab you?"

"I'm sure it'll grab the electric people as much as me. Will that be you done with him then? Will you take the car back and tell them you've got to start work?"

"That's about the size of it, Mary. And present them with a bill."

"Make sure it's enough to cover the electric."

A sweet was refused, but coffee with liqueurs was the order of the day. The cigar could come out now.

"Where did you get that?"

The matches had been put somewhere. "It's the last of the duty-frees your George brought me. I've not got a bloomin match."

"That waiter will give you a light. Ask him."

"That'll be right. Ach. I'll just smoke it when we get down the road."

"You're daft."

"I don't like. Ach. Maybe I will."

A tentative finger went up and an attentive waiter came over. "I seem to, forgotten my matches. Can you give me a light, please?"

"Surely." A lighter was produced, the flame adjusted and the light taken.

"Thanks."

Coffee and Glayva and the Tia Maria were here. Magic. Mary was really enjoying this. She enjoyed a night out and a dinner. Dave Parks was quite partial to the odd dinner here and there, also also, also also also.

"Well, Dave, I wonder what the poor are doing? It must be great to be able to do this whenever it comes up your humph."

"Wouldn't it just? I'll make you a promise, once I start getting a wage, or should I say, salary, we'll have a meal out like this every week. Or some kind of night out any-way."

"I'd rather save up for the house."

"Well, if you keep getting a wee turn from the agencies we might manage that as well."

"I'll believe it when I see it."

The cigar was out. There was no way a waiter could be asked to light this. Last one. And it was out. A bit big to leave. Back inside the box. Back inside the pocket.

"Dave, what are you doing?"

"Well."

"Couldn't take you anywhere."

"Not unless I had plenty cigars."

Mary looked like Mary when she laughed. Laughing or not laughing was Dave Parks like Dave Parks? The laugh was only a smile now over a coffee cup.

"You never told me what the lads thought about this thing that you're doing."

"I never seen them. I was supposed to go back and see Jimmy, but by the time I got back and everything. I'll maybe see them on Saturday."

"Oh. You figurin on goin to the pub on Saturday, are you? Is this you starting again?"

"No, not particularly. I'm not all that bothered. I suppose it's changed a bit, it's never the same is it, if you've been away for a while, but I just thought . . . I'll see, I'll see."

"Just thought you'd go in and bum you've got a job. I can read you like a book."

"I hope it's a dirty one."

And there comes Mary leaning over the table, looking a good drink and a good meal younger, and laughing.

"I don't need the porno."

When she looked that look and laughed that laugh and spoke that message it always brought the nervous tickle and made the skin move. It was time for the bill. Time to pay. Notes were left lying on the little saucer with the odds and ends of silver that were lying around the pockets.

"You leaving a tip? Thought you didn't believe in it? That's not like you."

"Ach, let's just say it's the Robin Smith man that's paying the service charge."

"I hope you've done the right thing."

"Eh?"

"See the wee waitress woman? She works during the day in the butcher's. Sometimes they get a bit shirty if you know them and you tip them. That's right."

"Ach. C'mon. They might act annoyed, but they never give you it back."

Mary was not for returning to the bar. A return taxi was called from the foyer. An arm went round Dave Parks' waist and pulled him in. The taxi came, and inside the taxi as well she cuddled in, and pulled and leaned, and laughed that laugh.

It was tickly.

The baby-sitter was agreed with, and nodded to, and after the report was dismissed and ushered out the door and it was upstairs for a quick check on the kids, and so to bed.

"Enjoy yourself?"

"I'm not finished yet," she laughed.

****

The number of people waiting to get in and sign and be away was a surprise to Dave Parks. Nine of the a.m. and now even individuals, groups, couples, threes and fours were hanging about waiting. Waiting to get in, to sign the name, and get on with the day. A young man came to the inside of the door. He bent down and loosened off the bolts, opened the door, fastened it back. He came out and ran up the short flight of stairs that led to the street. He fiddled with a bunch of keys and unlocked the padlock which was holding the little barred gate closed. JCB stepped in front of the man as if to ask something.

"JCB. This way." Dave Parks was taking him by the arm.

Those in front had formed up in single files at their particular allotted section of the counter: that part with their own shared signing box number hanging above: 1 2 3 4 5 6. No one had gone to the section marked ENQUIRIES. What was there to know? It's a simple system. A young, yawning woman came forward and asked if she could help.

"Can this man sign on today? It's his first time."

There was a pause. Her look was going from Dave Parks to JCB. She was shaking her head.

"I'm sorry. When you sign on for the first time you have to make an appointment. I think maybe you'll have to come back in the afternoon."

She began to look at some kind of register which lay on the counter. Dave Parks put a stop to that.

"Excuse me. I know that. What you said. Maybe I should've explained. I'm a Social Worker. I'm trying to get my client here signed on so we can get to the Social. You know what like it is down there if you don't get in early."

The girl was looking up. Again the pause. "Wait till I see Mr Johnson."

82

She went away. Somewhere. Dave turned to speak to James but James was looking round, taking it in: the clerks sitting emotionless, clerks sitting busily, clerks walking busily, clerks speaking; emotionless; people silent in queues, people waiting, people staring, people emotionless looking. The girl returned.

"Mr Johnson says if you take a seat he'll see to you himself. What's the name?"

"Parks. Sorry, that's his name. I mean, that's my name. His name is Black. Mr James Cameron Black. Sorry. Thanks. Thanks very much."

The place was more crowded now. People made gaps in the queues to let them pass through to the end of the hall where three rows of the plastic-covered benches sat in front of a segment of the counter which had been transformed into private cubicles of separated space by the strategic placing of orange hessian-backed barriers set at coy angles. They sat.

"First time you've ever been in one of these places, James?"

"I think so, yes. Yes it is. Interesting in their boredom I must say."

"Think so? Wait till we get to the Social."

A voice called. "Mr Black? Mr James Cameron Black?"

Mr James Cameron Black stood up. Dave Parks stood up. A man was beckoning, indicating one of the angled enclosures of counter space. The man sat down on his side of it. James sat down on the other. Dave Parks stood by his side. The man slipped the elastic band from the rectangle of grey cardboard and pushed it up his wrist until the band refused to go any further. A form was pushed over with a pen.

"If you just fill this up, Mr Black." The man studied other forms.

James picked up the form which had been shoved over. James was looking at Dave. Dave gave him the slip of paper they had filled in before leaving Madam Kipple's. James copied, then set down the pen. Mr Johnson or whoever took it back, read it.

"Looks fine, Mr Black." Another form was produced. "Would you sign here please?" It was duly signed. The signature was studied. Emotionless. A printed card was slid over.

"This is your UB40, Mr Black. This is your signing day. Monday. You are a B, so you're a Monday signing. This is your signing-on time. You're a B, so you're nine o'clock. Not a very popular time, I'm afraid. You sign again this Monday, and then it's every two weeks thereafter. Until you get a job of course."

"I see. I attend here every two weeks, at nine o'clock."

"That's it. Now when you come on Monday, go to signing box number one, but thereafter you go to signing-box number two. All right?"

"Yes. Signing-box one on Monday and then I attend at box number two."

"That's it. Now Mr Black, we do ask you to take care of your UB40. They're worth money you know. A UB40 will get you into the theatre half-price you know. Even the Royal makes concessions now. If you do lose it, however, just tell us and we'll give you a new one. All right? Good."

Very good. It was not half-past nine yet.

"Now do you wish to claim Social Security?"

"Yes." Dave Parks almost answered out loud.

"Then you'll need a B1." Another form, pink, B1, was written on, and put in a brown envelope, which was licked, and stuck shut. "Take this to the DHSS offices in Almond Street. Just give this to them there. I think that's you. Any problems?"

James was looking at Dave. Dave was shaking his head.

"Fine. Good-day Mr Black."

On the way out James stopped and started reading a poster advertising courses for redundant managers and/or executives. Dave took an arm. "C'mon James. This place always gets mobbed. You've got to get there early or you're there for the day."

James nodded, followed. Dave Parks led on. "I think the place we're looking for is on the other side. It's about two or three streets away, I think. Look out for an old coal yard."

James was striding out. Dave Parks was fit, but this man took some keeping up with.

"James, for goodness sake give us a break. D'you always walk as fast as this?"

"I suppose I do, yes. I've never actually thought much about it. Is that your coal yard over there?"

Green and rusty brown corrugated iron separated some kind of yard off from the street. A sign could just be made out. It said something about coal merchants on it. They crossed over. Round the corner they were in Almond Street. People were moving up a set of stairs through glass-plate doors into a featureless brick building.

"Looks like us, James."

The place was warm inside. Warm like the wards of a lunatic asylum. Warm to keep the people inside warm. Not hot. Warm. Sleepy warm. The place was warm with bodies. People hid behind papers, a woman was knitting, some slumped forward putting their weight onto their thighs, and stared at the floor. Children were running around, their laughs and yelps echoing off the low nicotine emulsioned ceiling.

"Take a ticket, James."

"Pardon?"

"Take a ticket. See that thing there? Just pull on that thing there, the paper, the paper. That's your number. When your number's up you get called."

James tore a strip of paper out. It came easily.

"How many's in front of you?"

"I'm sure I don't know. This paper says number sixty-nine."

"Sixty-nine. Could've been better. But I've seen it worse. Where do you want to sit?"

James studied the sixty-eight plus others spread throughout the waiting-hall on the grey plastic upholstered benches. James was looking. A frown was gathering on that brow.

"Where do you fancy, James?"

"Does it matter?"

"Oh, it matters. It matters, OK. Y'see, we don't sit at the edge. That means we avoid the weans. Don't sit in the middle. It gets a bit too warm in there. If there's ever any danger of anybody losing the wool, you can bet it's in the middle. As well as that, it means there's twice as much chance of people wanting to get by you. The middle is definitely out. Now don't sit in the front, because everybody passes that way to get to the counter and sometimes you can't help but hear some of the sad tales. And they might not want you to hear. Know what I mean? So, we sit at the back. One side or the other, but not at the edge, if possible. But there's a problem here as well James. Do we sit at the side nearest the lavatory or the side furthest away? Nearest it's a shorter hop, but also nearer the smell when people go to use it. In and out remember that door's open. So there you are. But you've got to work it all out quick, cos failing any of what you're after, you just sit where you can get a seat."

A space existed on a bench next to two women who sat, head inclined to head, mouth inclined to mouth, to gossip. They stopped talking. James and Dave sat down. The women shuffled in their seats without creating new space. James ended up on the edge. The women continued.

"So I said to her there was no way I was going to suffer a darkie doctor coming out to me at night-time. She was my doctor and it was her I wanted."

"Aye, you're blooming quite right."

"Anyway, she says if I felt like that I should leave her Panel, but I know she was only bluffing. I've got a big family and my family every one person in it uses her, and it's no as if we use her that often, y'know what I mean?"

"Oh aye. Aye. Sure, I was the same when it was yon Jewish character. I had to threaten him as well. Geordie never liked him. Never. That's why we changed. No that that was much good. They seem to be the same wherever you go."

"Think you're right. Cigarette?"

"No thanks."

Dave sat. James sat. James was looking around. Dave Parks was overhearing. Dave Parks had forgotten something.

"We should've bought a paper."

"Pardon?"

"A paper. A newspaper. We should've bought a newspaper. Although sometimes it's *War and Peace* you need in these places."

"Oh, I see, yes."

"So there it was, lying there on the table, a blooming great side of a cow, half a one. He was that drunk he just walked in and lifted it straight off the butcher's hook. Not one soul noticed. Cos it was a Christmas Saturday I think."

"That Geordie's an awful man."

"He'll never see us starve anyway."

A child came and knelt and crawled and was hiding behind James's legs. Dave leaned over. "Don't look down, you'll give the game away. He's playing Cowboys and Indians."

"I know David, I know."

The Cowboy or Indian crept forward, very slowly, then scuttled back. No goodies or baddies could be seen. But they must have been there. BANG! BANG! The shots came from behind. Two desperados had crawled round behind. The Lone Ranger was dead. But he was refusing to die. He punched one of the other two. The one that was not a girl. His arm was back to punch again. James clamped his fingers around a wrist. "Mesopotamia," he said.

The child stood stock still; eyes wide, looking at James, looking to Dave, looking back to the man who had said Mesopotamia. His free thumb went to his mouth. Teeth nibbled at the nail. The wrist was let go. The boy ran down rows and sheltered in at the side of a woman. From here he looked back. Wide-eyed. The two others had run away laughing. Dave Parks was laughing too.

"What did you say to him there?"

"Mesopotamia. My father used to say it to me when I was being mischievous. I could never quite affix the proper emotion to the word. Even when he shouted it with a red face. It invariably left me totally confused, by which time I had forgotten whatever nonsense I was involved in."

"That right? Must be a use for a word like that somewhere. Maybe the big goodies and the big baddies should use it as some kind of Mantra. What d'you think?"

"I prefer the Ten Commandments myself."

These two women had been listening, watching, trying to know. There were children involved. Now they resumed where they had left off.

"So that's me stuck and no cooker."

"Well, you should qualify."

"Bloody better. This primus stove lark is no bloody joke."

James had his hands clasped. Now he had joined those who study the floor. Now and again a frown would plough up the flesh

87

on his forehead. Dave Parks would leave him to his silence.

Smoke was drifting up now, gathering in little blue-grey clouds below the low ceiling. Two polystyrene tiles were missing. Smoke was being sucked towards the gap. Number nineteen was called. She shuffled out of her place in the crowd, fixing her headscarf under her chin to be tidy. Clock said ten twenty-two. James's shoes were shiny. Dave Parks' were not. Someone had carved BONGO LOVES NO CUNT on the back of the bench in front. A tall woman passed slowly, head up, looking straight ahead, in front, looking towards the lavatory door. A child in harness toddled beside, smiling, but concentrating, balancing, looking up for applause with each stuttering, successful step. Dave Parks saw. Dave Parks smiled. But the toddler didn't see. Mother stepped backwards, she bent and clipped the reins onto the child's harness.

A young man in blue denims and a black leather jacket got up and walked to the back of the waiting-room. He stood with his back to the benches. He was looking up and out of the window. The man turned, held his head in his hands, pulling the hair back from his forehead. He shook his head hard, let out air, put his back on the wall and rolled a cigarette. Clock said ten thirty-six.

"I'm going for a paper, James. You hold the fort."

"I don't think I have any pressing engagements, my dear David."

"Right."

It was good to get outside. Air was fresher. There were some shops on the other side of the street. A half-decent walk away. A half-decent slow walk. Two papers bought: one the five-minute special that wasn't bad for sport or page three buffs and the other had a better crossword. Reading one on the way back helped the walk last longer. A lorry beeped its horn. It was coming up on the pavement backwards. Around the side of the DHSS it tipped a load of topsoil. It drove away and the driver waved. At the top of the stairs a man was coughing and spitting over the side. Dave Parks rolled a roll-up and smoked it leaning on a handrail. There was nothing to be thought about. He was just here at the Social with a man that had never

88

been here before. Cigarette was finished. Time to go back in.

Clock said eleven thirteen.

JCB was on the floor. JCB was on the floor and the Lone Ranger was on his back, gripping the horse's lapel and punching its back and yelling. The two others were running around, watchful, laughing, maybe envious, sometimes touching James, sometimes not. James began to buck like a bronco. Cowboy squealed and held one arm high in the air. A woman came up and pulled the boy from the man's back, whirling the boy round and skelping his arse as he landed. James was frowning. Two other cowboys stepped back, and back, and went away. James rubbed his hands together, wiping one off the other, and tried to dust grime off the knees of his trousers. Dave sat down and passed a paper over.

"You're a stranger in a strange land, sunshine. Kids aren't allowed to talk to strange men, even in Red Indian language."

"But why did she punish the child? He was playing."

"Well, she couldn't very well skelp your arse, could she? Just stick yourself behind the paper."

James got up. He was moving down towards the woman and her child.

"James. James. What you doing? What's the matter with you?" Dave Parks moved after.

James was standing over the woman. His palms were stretched out.

"Suffer the little children to come unto me, and forbid them not: for such is the kingdom of God."

The woman looked up at James; up at Dave Parks. "Is this your pal? You better take him out of my sight."

"James." Dave Parks was tugging at the sleeve of the blazer. "James."

James shook his head and turned away. Dave Parks spoke to the woman behind his back. "Don't worry about him, Mrs, he's a minister. Honest. He's a minister."

"A creeping bloody Jesus, you mean."

"No. A minister. A minister."

A child was pulled in tighter.

89

The two women on the bench moved along as fast as they could go. They watched. Silent. Checking the situation. James had his head down and his hands clasped between his legs. His lips were moving. For Dave Parks it was time to do the better crossword.

ACROSS
1. Prehistoric monster replaced by definite object (9)
5. Home is the hero, a bit late (8)
9. Did Aristotle's have glory in it? (6)
10. Serves you right (2, 2, 2)
11. Quintessentially, I don't think (3)

DOWN
1. Wrong way round soldier (4, 2, 5)
2. Father to the cold winter world? (5)
3. It's all over (9)

Where's the anagrams?

Thirteen across. Linked to a dirty soil. Ten letters. Oh, what else? There's another one. Arena. Case it for the Emperor. Nine letters. Easy. Warm in here . . .

So I told him wherever he goes I'll be there he wouldn't be able just to walk away like that you were always able for him Jessie I wish I was a bit like you like that but I suppose it would never do if we were everybody just the same and help me Father of all number twenty-four please did you hear Mrs McGhie passed away did she last week it was never heard fly me to the moon six four across must be wrong should have seen the weans roundabout way of saying no that right guide me tell me where you wish me to be right rammy it was used I used to know her daddy as well nice wee buddy he was christ the things we do for money oh man the smell from that lav is diabolical forgive them Lord for they know not number twenty-five hope this job doesn't have too much of this carry-on suppose it will what number are you extinct bird not that again surely I'm after you then wish they'd hurry up for heaven's sake listen to that James the guy's no right sooner roll on Monday Bellesmyre it's not the same place number thirty fairly getting through them last time I was here it was murder murder do you think that man's OK aye he's OK Mrs just leave him be he's talking to somebody used to fight a lot in Bellesmyre how many s's in that green and the blue the usual crap don't you worry I know exactly what to say to her if she's who I get wisdom that passeth all understanding thought that was surpasseth suppose he knows what he's saying quieter now at least the professors have stopped going about there in mufti number thirty-three two fat ladies nearly had a full house the other night waitin on two just that right solidarity that's it hope it's not as bad as people say it is probably just labelling what are you for doing if you don't get the special needs that boy's leaving his mother again Father in the art world what the fuck do I know about art hope he keeps away from James did you see Diana on the telly last night her needs a good feed oh but they're really good watched the picture but it was talk talk hardly any action Amen Amen did you hear that Amen there's something up there sooner we start in Bellesmyre the better eleven down as ten across two two two too rich for my taste but I know a lot of people like it the boy's back the women aren't talking they're watching and it's only twelve fuckin o'clock oh oh.

James was up on his feet. He was lifting the boy off the ground, up, on to a wide ledge at the window. The boy was sitting with a face that was half-scared, laughing scared. The two others were running, coming to see what they were missing. James lifted them up too.

"Right? Are you ready? I want you to listen to me. Do you like singing?"

Something like nods came over.

"Would you like me to teach you a song? Listen carefully now."

The little girl gave a big nod.

"Now, can you do this?"

James rolled one arm over another. The children copied.

"Good. That's it, that's it. Now listen to the song:

> Running over, running over,
> my cup's full and running over.
> Since the Lord saved me
> I'm as happy as can be;
> my cup's full and running over.

Can you sing that? Can you? Right, let's try."

Two boys giggled, but the little girl was serious. Her voice joined with the leader's. Towards the end the boys tried.

"Wonderful. Wonderful. Let's try it again and don't forget to move your arms like me."

> Running over, running over,
> my cup's full and running over.

They sang their best. The mother came up. Then another. And another. They stopped behind James. Between James and the children was the Lord. They were smiling at the children. James was silently clapping his choir.

"Now a new bit. Can you do this? Point to the sky, where Jesus lives, and then yourself." He jabbed his chest with his finger.

They sang the new bit. And they pointed to the sky and they pointed to themselves. The children sang and tried to roll their arms and point to the Lord and tell the world who me is and in between they giggled and laughed.

"That was really good. Now can we join it all up? And sing loud so Jesus will hear you. Ready? Go.

> Running over, running over,
> my cup's full and running over.
> Since the Lord saved me
> I'm as happy as can be;
> my cup's full and running over.

Again, louder, louder."

The children sang out loud and people turned heads and lifted up heads and smiled at one another and another number was called. Number forty-seven. The boy's mother stepped forward and lifted the boy down. "That's me," she said. Other mothers took their children down and away, smiling and nodding at James. James came back to his place on the bench.

"Kept them amused James."

"Perhaps. This is a joyless place. Children. In here." He shook his head.

The nearest woman on the bench leaned over. "That was nice. My mammy used to say the Lord likes to hear the voice of the singer. You've got a good voice." James looked surprised. The woman carried on. "I haven't heard that for years. I was near for joining in myself. It's funny how you don't forget them, isn't it?"

"Did you want to sing?"

"Well, actually, I was a wee bit. It's a good tune that. It was my favourite. I used to give it laldy."

Her companion was eager to speak to this man. "No. My favourite was 'What a Friend We Have in Jesus'."

"Oh aye, yes, that was good too."

James stood up. "Then shall we sing it?"

"Och, away ye go."

"Don't be daft. In here?"

"We can sing to the Lord anywhere, madam."

James began to sing, quietly, facing the women, and conducting himself with his hands out, palms upwards. He sang just a little bit louder. The woman called Jessie put her bag on the floor and began to clap in time. She sang. Her voice trembled, but she sang. She pulled at her friend. Her friend began to sing.

James began to clap. Dave Parks folded and unfolded the paper. James was keeping the beat with each clap. James was looking at Dave Parks. Dave Parks began to clap. Roll on the right number. But Dave Parks was laughing. All of a sudden a laugh. People were looking round. Kids were running up. A coughing man stopped coughing. Women on the bench in front picked up their hands and clapped Some joined in. The founder members sang louder. The children were clapping. Clap clap clapping and laugh laugh laughing. James sang louder. Clerks looked up. Number fifty-one was called and nobody moved. People now were looking at the clerks, signalling, encouraging them to join in. The more the clerks looked up and looked down the more the people clapped and sang and sang and clapped and sang louder. Even Dave Parks sang the remembered song. It came out without any effort:

> What a friend we have in Jesus,
> All our sins and griefs to bear!
> What a privilege to carry
> Everything to him in prayer!

What a privilege to carry
All our hopes to him in prayer,
Are you weary or downhearted?
Take it to the Lord in prayer.

A door opened at the side. A man in a grey suit was signalling behind him. A policeman came out. The man pointed to James. Over came the policeman. James received a police tap on the shoulder.

"Sorry, sir. I've got to ask you to be quiet. That's not allowed in here."

James stopped. Here and there the others stopped. The singing wound down until there was no one singing. Not even a preparatory cough was being made. James waited till all was quiet. He addressed the policeman.

"What is not allowed?"

"Singing, sir. With your voice, sir."

"With my voice? How else should I sing?"

"What I meant, sir, is that sometimes singing can be allowed. If it's a radio, sir. But even then it's got to be quiet, sir, like on these headphone things for preference, sir. People do have work to do in here, sir."

"I see. Well, if singing to the Lord interferes with the work of the departments of government, then by all means let us be silent."

"Yes, sir. Can I ask you to be seated?"

"Number fifty-nine."

"He's with me officer. I'll see to him. He just got carried away a wee bit."

"Who are you?"

"Just a friend."

"Well, just-a-friend, keep him sat down, will you?"

No sir for Dave Parks.

"Yes sir, I will sir."

A number was called. One of the ladies' section of the choir went forward. Another number came. The other founder member excused herself past and away. James sat down as the policeman and the man in the grey suit moved away and back through the side door.

"Think you roused them up a bit James."

"I enjoyed it."

"I'll bet you did."

Number sixty-nine was called. Dave followed James into the cubicle. The girl looked tired. She took the envelope and extracted the B1.

"James Cameron Black?"

"That's him." She looked up.,

"Can he speak for himself? If you don't mind. Who are you anyway?"

"Just a friend. Just a friend."

She was looking, eyes half-shut, lips tight.

James spoke for himself. "I am James Cameron Black."

"Is that the Reverend Black?"

"No, not at all. Goodness me, no."

"Oh. It's just that somebody said you were a minister."

"I minister to the Lord always, but I don't think that makes me a minister."

"Oh. Right. Shall we get on, Mr Black? Let's see what we can do for you."

James Cameron Black was taken through the check-list slowly, patiently. Not once did she turn to Dave Parks for clarification. Her body was inclined between Dave Parks and the forms as she ran through it with the point of her pen. James answered and nodded affirmation on the second run. His answers were the truth. James would be on the bare minimum. The girl wrote on the bottom of a couple of forms, passed the pen to James and James signed. She studied the signature.

"I think that's about all there is Mr Black. You will probably receive a Giro once your claim is processed by Newcastle. It may take a couple of weeks. If it's any longer, please don't hesitate to contact us."

Dave fiddled with the corner of her blotter. There were no naked men with Biro fuzz on this one.

"Is there any chance of a special needs payment for him?"

"What for? Does he keep bad health? Does he need a special diet? Hmm?"

95

"Well, he's on his own and a couple of weeks . . ."

"Mr Black does not qualify. Thank you, Mr Black. If you have any problems please contact us." She took the forms of James Cameron Black away to be processed. James got up.

A child waved to James as they left the building. Air was warm outside. A team of men were spreading out the topsoil where it had been tipped. Two were stripped to the waist.

"Do you know your way from here, James? Where you live is just three streets down on the left, then first left again. I'd like to get away, and the car's parked away the other way."

"Three to the left, one to the left. I shall quite enjoy walking, David. Give me a chance to explore my new surroundings. When shall I see you again?"

"I'll give you a couple of days to find your feet, then I'll come, say, about the end of the week? How's that? Don't worry. I won't be losing touch."

"I am not quite completely helpless, my dear David, but just as you said yourself, I do feel a stranger in a strange land."

"Look, don't worry, James. Actually, where I am going to work isn't too far away. Bellesmyre is just over that way."

Bellesmyre. Pointing. Mistakes.

"James, I will come and see how you're getting on. From what you said this morning that place seems OK. Is that right?"

"I have no complaints."

James was holding out a hand. Dave Parks took it, shook it. James spoke.

"Give my regards to the misters Smith when you see them. Tell them I understand."

"Sure. I will. I will. I'll be off now James. I promised Mary I'd try and be back for the kids coming out of school."

"Of course."

James turned away, looked back, waved. When James was away Dave Parks kicked a sapling that was growing from a man-made hole in the pavement. It was a hopeful, flowering cherry tree. Unspent petals fell on the pavement. Passers-by tramped on some. Dave Parks tramped on some.

****

Jimmy and Tommy had their heads down into a chess game. Pat was missing. Dave sat down beside Tommy. The broad head never lifted. He continued to contemplate the next move. A young woman practised throwing the darts by herself. Jimmy looked up, across, and smiled. Dave Parks nodded back. Tommy made a move. It looked as if he was playing a Sicilian defence. It was Jimmy's turn for the head down. Tommy lifted his pint.

"How you doin, my man?"

"Ah, not so bad, big man. Yourself?"

"Ah, so-so. Usual."

"Pat not in tonight? I thought he liked his chess on a Tuesday?"

"Haven't seen him. Maybe he'll be in later. You lookin for him like?"

"No. Just askin."

A man came over; stood; looked down at the board; looked at the three; looked at the board; looked at the three; walked away. Jimmy was pursing his lips and pulling at them, then moved a pawn, opening up his king's bishop. Standard move. Tommy leaned forward. Jimmy spoke.

"Did you get on all right with that job? What was it all about?"

"Ach, just what I thought. I'll tell you when you're finished."

Tommy moved his queen out. Putting the bolt in place. Tommy settled his back into the upholstery. He was smiling. Maybe he was three moves ahead. At least. The big man took a sip at his lager and left Jimmy to the problem. The smile was turning on Dave Parks.

"That right what I hear? You're initiating some old bloke into the mysteries of working-class existence?"

"Eh? Who was telling you that?"

"Betty met Mary at the shops. She was telling her."

"I'm sure she never said what you just said."

"Maybe no exactly, but that seemed to be the gist of it. But even what you were saying yourself about the phone call, that doesn't sound too far away."

Jimmy made the expected move and looked up. "Aye. By the way you never came back last Saturday, what happened to you? We were all hanging on here waitin to hear what it was all about."

"It was nothing really."

"Nothing really? You went to a lot of trouble beforehand surely, for nothing really."

It was time for Dave Parks to study the board. Tommy took the pawn on offer. Jimmy took his. But he was not finished.

"So what was it all about then?"

Tommy's eyes were on the board, but it was a fair bet his ears were on Dave Parks' mouth. The players played. Making moves on the board, but listening at the same time. If the story was stopped to politely allow them quiet to concentrate, heads would lift, shake or nod but always egg on to the finish. They laughed at the picture of this bloke leading a revivalist meeting at the Social. Then there came a quiet. A silence. Either because the game was at a crucial stage, or because every word was being listened to and being joined up with words of the past. Tommy knocked his king over as the story reached an end.

"It's yours in another six moves."

"I know. I think you lost it two moves ago. Did you forget about the bishop?"

"I did actually."

Dave Parks had stopped in mid-sentence. They had heard enough to be going on with. They had been listening. Listening to every word. They had paid attention to the words. Now they had heard enough they were ignoring the speaker. Jimmy stood up.

"Pint, Tommy?"

Tommy nodded. Jimmy turned towards the bar. The girl at the dartboard had been joined by another woman. Dave Parks' pint was nearly empty. Jimmy was turning back.

"You for one, Dave?"

"Sure, but look, hey, let me get them."

98

Jimmy stopped, sat down, handing up the empty glasses. "I think we'll let you."

There was only a few at the bar, nursing their pints the way they nursed their redundancy money. The old song-and-dance man of the Yellow Brick Road was shaking his head at Dave Parks in some kind of watery-eyed acknowledgement. Perhaps he might appreciate it if Dave Parks bought him a wee half. Maybe better not to. The man got a nod back.

The chess had been put away. Dave put the pints down. Jimmy said: cheers. Tommy took a drink from his and put the glass down in that definite way. A debate was somewhere about.

"So, you're a self-employed Social worker? That's the game, eh? Resettlement of cast-offs a speciality."

"Give us a break Thomas. What was I supposed to do? They were going to get rid of the guy anyhow. Surely it's as well I do it as anybody else? Maybe some nutter might've got a grip of the guy. Surely it's better that he's my client?"

"Your client? He's your client? Whose client are you?"

Jimmy laughed. "What are these people paying you? Five pounds an hour? And a company car? Aye, maybe it's just as well he's got you right enough."

Tommy was looking at Jimmy. Now he was looking at Dave Parks. An argument was coming.

"Surely there must be more to it than five pounds an hour? Can I say this to you Dave: I always thought you educated types were supposed to lead people out of the cave, not lead them down into it, or teach them how to survive by chewing candles. Know what I mean? As you tell it, this guy James is no longer required by his class, and not having an inkling of the ways of the underworld, they send for a guide. And you jump at it for five pounds an hour."

"Don't forget expenses," said Jimmy.

"Oh, and don't forget the car either, eh?"

It was time for a defence. A Dave Parks defence. "I think you're reading too much into it, Tommy. I'm just trying to get the guy settled, away from a situation where he's not wanted. The fact that he's not wanted is scarcely my fault, is it? And don't give me that 'no man is an island' crap."

"Hardly. But listen to yourself, man. Settled. Settled where? Settled in to the ways of the unemployed class. Is that what you mean?"

Jimmy has something to say. "Can I just say something here? Dave, see when you were in that house, did you ever try and persuade them to keep this bloke James, look after him? I mean, according to you, their old boy picked him up in Harare, does that not make him their responsibility? I mean, I never asked him to bring the fella back, but it's my taxes, or taxes that I used to pay, that are goin to keep him."

There was an opening.

"Come off it Jimmy. If you follow that logic, the fact that the boy is a British citizen means nothing, his only existence is under their roof. All they did was bring him here to his own country."

"But what does that mean? Does that mean now they're fed up wi him they can pass him on to the rest of us? Using you to lead him away?"

"Ach, bullshit!"

Bullshit. An abstract concept encompassing a certain inability to argue the point.

"No bullshit at all."

Jimmy was miffed. Not beaten but miffed. Tommy took it up.

"Maybe we should be a little more optimistic about this. Maybe this lot can be given the benefit of the doubt here. For surely if they didn't have some sense of responsibility for this man James, they might not have sent for the likes of Dave here."

Jimmy laughed. "You don't believe that, do you? They just did not want to be involved in sending the bloke down. What they were lookin for was somebody to make it all go smoothly for them."

"You guys are no real. Would you rather they just tossed the guy to the wolves?"

"At least scavengers are independent," said Tommy.

Jimmy liked that one. "Nice one, Tommy. By the way, Dave, it's no us that's no real, it's you that's living the fantasy. You're helping this guy down that way." He pointed to the floor. "Middle class, working class, aye, unemployed class, all together stompin at the Social. Ah, here's Pat."

Pat had come in and was making his way to the corner. Jimmy leaned over, whispering. "Tell me this, Dave. You were in the factory, right? A shop steward, right? Always goin on about Socialism, right? Tell me this: would you have taken this job on if you hadn't needed the money?"

"Aye, aye. When did you start gettin out during the week?"

Pat pulled a chair over and sat down, smiling a smile that was too big.

"I had a meal the other night and there was a file in the cheesecake. You want a pint?"

"If you're buying, certainly."

The bar was a pleasant change. Three women were at the darts now. One was marking the score as the other two played. Lightning the bartender was mercifully slow. The pint was a bit short. Pat accepted the pint with thanks.

"I was ready for that. Thanks Dave. Tell me, how did you get on about that job?"

"Oh, don't you start."

"Eh?"

"These two have been slagging me to death about it. I don't need you to join in."

"I wish I had come down earlier."

"I believe you. Anyhow, I've something else to tell you."

"Pray tell, pray tell," said Tommy.

"I've got a job in Bellesmyre. With the Social Work. Community Worker."

The three drank their pints. There was no visible reaction. Dave Parks had a new job and his mates could find nothing to say. Jimmy put his pint down and pulled his shag out.

"Bellesmyre. Bit of a place that, is it no?"

"Aye," said Pat, "I think that's where Custer had his last stand and the natives have still got the swords to prove it."

"Piss off, Pat. That was years ago. It's quietened down a lot now."

Jimmy passed over a roll-up "Is that the place where yon university dame went to live and clocked everybody?"

"That's the place."

"Aye. That's the place, That's the place where the top end o the street knocks fuck out of the bottom end and vicey-versey. Don't fancy working in there."

"Well, I don't mind it. I'm telling you it's nowhere near as bad as some other places."

Tommy slapped Dave Parks on the back. "Well, we'll take your word for it, old son. Congratulations, if you think they're in order. Now you can move up from having one misfit to look after to having a couple of tribes o them."

Pat was shaking his head. "Pure animals in there, man. You'll never be a Social Worker in there, you'll be a zookeeper."

Tommy nodded agreement. "Not only that, he'll be a spectator as well."

"Aye. And no bars between them."

Jimmy was blowing smoke to make room for a laugh.

"He is not his brother's keeper, you know."

"That's exactly what he's become," said Tommy.

"Christ, give it a bye you lot. I'm surprised at you. There's a lot of positive stuff can be done."

"Aye. Oh aye. Positive, says who?"

"Pass out the candles to them, eh?"

"What? You know, you lot make it very difficult to come in here with a bit of good news and go out the same way."

Tommy pointed a finger. "Ah. You know you always go out the same way."

"Aye, in a box."

Jimmy got up, gathering in the empty glasses. He must've seen the face getting red. "Well, the best of luck to you anyway. I wouldn't have your job. Except for five pounds an hour, of course."

Pat went with Jimmy towards the bar, but stopped and began talking to a well-dressed man. Pat's hand went up and his fingers made signals to the barman. A glass of whisky was brought to the man beside him. The man lifted it, nodded, drank it. Pat returned to the table.

"Who's that you were talking to Pat? His face is familiar."

"Frank Stone. Used to be gaffer in the maintenance, remember? He does the contract work now. Gets me a wee turn now and again."

"Oh."

Jimmy came back and the conversation was kept light. Dave passed over a roll-up and everybody laughed as Jimmy held it up to the light. Pat wanted to play chess. The board was set up. Conversation was killed, but at least the game would hamper the argument as well. Pat was playing Jimmy. Tommy sat on the other side of the players. Dave Parks gulped the drink. It was time to be leaving.

"I'll see you blokes, OK?"

"Aye. Oh, by the way, did you give this man his ten pence back?"

"Forgot all about it. Sorry, Jim."

Ten pence was dug out of the trouser-pocket. Jimmy took the coin, kissed it, and dropped it into his shirt-pocket without saying thanks.

On the road home a decision was made against buying chips or whatever. It wasn't the weekend and the kids had school in the morning.

Mary was surprised, to the extent she even made a cup of tea and some sort of tuna salady sandwich, and brought it through to the living-room. Another two cars were bouncing their way down the hills of San Francisco and threatening to leave tread marks on the carpet.

"You're just in time for the film."

She handed over the tea, settled herself on the settee, stretched her legs over her husband's legs and smiled up.

"What did the lads say about your new job?"

"Ah, nothing much."

"Nothing much?"

Somebody was advertising a thirty-thousand pound washing-machine with a free house thrown in.

"What did they say?"

"I told you, nothing much. What did you expect them to say? I think they were pleased for me all right. OK? What's this film about?"

"Oh, nothing much."

****

JCB's landlady was in voice this fine day. The voice was high and happy-sounding as if this was the day the rents fell due. It was a shame to knock on the door and disturb her in full flight. The voice was getting louder as she came to answer the door. The singing stopped just before some really high note and she opened the door. She had the same gown on. Except this one was coloured green and in the sun it turned silver in places. But the forked tongue of the serpent ended up at the same place. When Dave Parks lifted his eyes she spoke.

"Oh, it's you. I just sent away a Jehovah's Witness. If you'd been him again I was for buying the bloody *Watchtower* just to be shot of you. Him."

"You don't get rid of me that easy."

"So I see."

"Hope I'm not disturbing you. I thought I'd pop over and see how James is getting on."

"Getting on? He's hardly been here."

"That's one of the problems."

Her shoulders and chest rose up, and fell down to an exasperated sigh. "You know where his room is. I think he's in."

Something was making Dave Parks take the stairs two at a time. Looking down from the landing he could only see the landlady and the green gown with the serpent and its forked tongue head to the main room. She looked up. Dave Parks gave an embarrassed wave. She shut the door. Voices were coming from inside number three. Dave knocked. JCB answered.

"David. I didn't expect to see you today. How are you? Do come in."

James stood aside. A bald-headed man in a shiny jacket of dull brown material was kneeling on the floor, bum in the air. Somebody smelled. The man did not look round. He was concentrating on something on the floor. Around the man books sat, tent-like, or piled in threes and fours. Various accoutrements and two pillows lay at the edge of the carpet. A small fire was burning in the grate. On the hearth a dirty holdall sat, covered in coal dust. James began to make the introductions.

"David, this is Mr Bandy Jardine. He lives here too. Bandy was kind enough to bring me in some coal and start a fire for me. Bandy. Bandy."

The man look round and up from the carpet.

"Bandy, this is David Parks, the gentleman I've been telling you about."

The man's eyelids were narrowing and his lips tightening. He frowned and turned back to whatever he was doing on the floor. James scratched his head and smiled at David.

"So what brings you up here today?"

"Ach, I just thought I left you in a bit of a hurry yesterday. Thought I'd better come up and see how you're doin. Struck me I never enquired as to how you might be for gear."

"Well, I slept well enough thank you, David, eh, but, um, gear? Do you mean cutlery and so forth?"

"Aye, well, maybe, but I was actually thinking of clothes and stuff. But now that you mention it, I suppose if you're staying here we'll have to get you some tools."

The Bandy was muttering away to himself. James was smiling and nodding quickly. Stretching across, he removed some clothing from the back of a chair and placed the bundle on top of the chest of drawers.

"Do sit down, David." David sat down.

"Right, thanks. So what do you reckon you'll need? I take it you've got soap and stuff?"

"Oh, yes."

"How are you fixed for messages?"

"Messages? Messages? Telephone, you mean?"

"No I don't. Tea, sugar, eats, that kind of messages."

"Ah, well, we share the kitchen as you know. I'll probably have to lay in a stock of such things, tea, biscuits, whatever. We do all have a little piece of cupboard to call our own."

The Bandy let out a sound that was a cross between a bronchial cough and a wordless curse. He lifted his head, but spoke into the fire.

"Keep your gear in your own place."

"There you are, James. Sound advice from the man that knows. Do you want to go to the shops then?"

The man Bandy was turning his head around, frowning again. The face was round, red, but the eyes were the giveaway. Tiny pupils set in red eyeballs. A frown was pulling the forehead down and one half of the top lip was being drawn up. This was a face picked up from an eave of some mediaeval church. This man would have made a fortune as a stonemason's model. He was angry about something.

"Perhaps later, David," said James.

"OK." There was a silence.

The room looked bigger than it had on Monday, and much lighter. Sunshine was coming through the window right on to the bed, alighting on a multi-coloured panelled quilt.

"See you get the sun."

"Yes, very pleasant. I dare say it will pass away quickly today, but in the summer, yes, should be quite, quite pleasant."

The silence took over.

It was getting that Dave Parks was none too sure why he had come. The JCB seemed confident enough. Not in the least down in the dumps. Drinking. The bastard had been drinking. It was in the eyes. Just too sparkly. That's what it was. That explained the silence. Dave Parks had walked in on a bevy session.

"How do you get on with her nibs down there?"

"Perfectly well, I think. I've only passed her once or twice. Seems a pleasant enough type."

"She's a bitch."

The Bandy had been listening. Dave was looking at James looking at David. A bitch. Interesting.

"What makes you say that?"

"Nothing. She's just a bitch. Steer clear of her, Jimmy."

That could have been addressed to either Jimmy Parks or Jimmy Black, or, see her, Jimmy (plural), she's a bitch.

Dave Parks wanted to know more. "What makes you say that? I mean, you must have some reason for saying it."

Bandy was back at the muttering. He muttered as he moved a salt-cellar on the rug; moving it, muttering; muttering, moving it again. James was merely sitting, sparkly-eyed, smiling, shrugging his shoulders. There was no information being volunteered. Dave Parks was going for a look out the window. The man and the boy were still fiddling about in the grassy margin. From up here one could see over them, over the shrubbery, over a bowling club to the river, to the small skyscraper buildings of the city. A man was pulling a heavy roller over the greens of the bowling club, head down, pulling it behind him.

"Not a bad view here, James."

James came over. "Yes, it is, isn't it?"

On the river floating cranes were grabbing buckets of earth from the quays, swinging out, and dumping the earth into the river. James pointed.

"What are they doing there, David?"

"Not quite sure. I think it's supposed to be some kind of desert island when they're finished. There used to be a dry dock there. Somewhere."

"For fuck sake, James, offer him a drink so I can get one."

Bandy bounced the plastic salt-cellar off the floor. "Never mind, I'll get it."

James's face was reddening. Bandy was spraggling under the bed. Two bottles of wine were brought out. It was the cheap stuff. The undertaker's friend.

"Would you care for a glass of wine, David? For thy stomach's sake?"

"Not for me, James. But you and your pal wire in."

Bandy was back under the bed again. This time he brought out two mugs. The insides of the mugs were stained red.

"You sure you don't want a snifter, mister?"

"No thanks, you two go ahead."

"Right. We will."

Bandy poured wine into a mug for James, some into a mug for himself, pouring until the last drop dripped from the bottle and shaking it could yield no more.

"Ah well, here's your health," said Bandy.

"Cheerio," said James.

"Cheers."

Bandy's face was cheerier now that the wine had resurfaced. Dave could only try to make amends for breaking up the early morning session.

"You lived here long, Bandy?"

"About a year. Year too long. Ach, actually it's not too bad." He whispered: "You've got to watch her. She can be a right bad bastard at times."

"How?"

"Mmm. Just sometimes you never know where you are with her, and when she's in a wee mood she thinks she's Lady Muck and treats you like shite."

James seemed a little shocked. "Oh, I'm sure she's not as bad as that. Certainly never gave me that impression."

"Ah well, you'll find out."

Bandy scratched at one of the two coils of tousled hair that ran down each side of the bald space. Underneath his jacket he was wearing a tartan shirt, with the tail hanging free outside oil-stained grey greasy trousers. But the boots were new. Or nearly new. Riggers' boots.

"What is it you do, Bandy?"

"Nothing. Nothing. I've been on the disability for years."

"Bandy's a driver," said James. "He drives big trucks with the trailer things."

Bandy was shooting daggers, and the bald head was turning a pink that matched the eyes. He was making a gargoyle face again. At James. The man looked a bit unstable, and vicious. He turned to look at Dave Parks.

"Who do you work for?" the man asked.

"Me? Nobody. Yet. Ah, wait a minute. I'm not interested if you're doin a wee bit on the side. It's none of my business. Honest. I know the score."

"Like fuck you do." Bandy gulped some wine from his tin mug and opened the other bottle. "You want some of this?" He was looking for some credibility.

"OK. OK. Just a drop."

James got up. "I'll fetch a glass." He left the room.

Bandy refilled the mugs. "What are you to him?"

"Nothing. Nothing really. Some friends just asked me to get him settled somewhere. That's all. James hasn't a clue about the system. I think he's used to better things."

"Aren't we all? He'll be all right here. One or two a bit dolly dimple but he'll be OK."

James returned with a tumbler that was as grey and opaque as if it had been washed around on a beach for years. "Best I could do, I'm afraid."

Bandy poured up to and just beyond Dave Parks saying: that's enough. Glass and mugs were lifted. And the wine was vile. This was the wine that was imported in bulk: barrels of boke poured into bottles in the licenseed grocer's basement. Most people had to be drunk to drink it.

A Dave Parks smile tried to disguise a grue. "Some stuff. So what were you then Bandy, an artic driver?"

"Aye. I did a bit of shunting for a contractor after the boys brought them up from the south. Even yet, if he's short of local drivers, he might give me a shout. But it's getting harder. There's so many going about nowadays."

"That's true. Even the old moonlighting is under threat from your chinas these days."

James sat on the edge of the bed, smiling, listening, sipping and smiling.

"Bandy was showing me how he came by his disability just as you came in, David. He was in the army, you know."

"Was he? That's the game. What were you in?"

"Argyll and Sutherlands."

"That right? What was it they did again? Thin Red Line, was that them? An old Scottish Soldier, eh?"

"If you say so."

"Were you in that thing with Mad Mitch? That was the Argylls, wasn't it?"

"That's just what I was showing James here before you came."

"Is that right? Well, carry on then. Don't let me stop you."

Bandy took another slug of his wine, wiped his mouth on the back of his sleeve and placed the wine mug down.

"Right, well, I was just saying, people had been leaving Aden for some time. Our lot were trying to ensure a safe route back to the port."

The man shoved a book to the end of the carpet, maybe to indicate docks. Maybe to indicate it was in the road. Dave drew back his chair to make more room for the Director of Operations. The pillows were being flounced up and one placed at each side of the carpet. At the foot of one of the pillows three books were set up like tents.

"That's us," said Bandy. On top of the pillow opposite, the salt-cellar was placed. "This is one of them, but we can't see him right now."

"Was this before or after the Entry?" asked James.

"Before, before. Just about the same time. Will you listen?"

"Sorry, old chap."

"So there was us more or less dug in. Gettin popped at every now and then. Come the night-time our platoon gets gathered up for a night recce. It made a wee change for us." Bandy let himself fall forward onto his elbows. He picked up three lumps of coal. "This is us."

The eyes were staring. He was speaking to his front, to himself as much as anybody. Bandy was away. Dave Parks and James could hear what he was saying, but it looked as if Bandy could feel what he was saying. The eyes were widening to see more of what was in the memory. And as he saw it, felt it, he told it. Different feelings maybe, but somehow it was a familiar tale. The burly sergeant — not a bad lad; the relief of getting out to do something; the eagerness; the cold of the night sand; the dark night; the quiet night; the stomach tight; the nervous crawl; the sudden moon and they knew they had made a bloomer.

"What was wrong?" asked James, on cue.

"We had wandered right into a wadi called Metra tel Kebir. This was us." Bandy indicated that the space between the two pillows was the wadi Metra tel Kebir. The lumps of coal were set in the middle between the two pillows. This was us. Books were widened to ensure they really looked like tents. This was them. The salt-cellar, an HP sauce bottle and a fort-like castellated ashtray were placed forward and behind the coal patrol.

"What did you do?" asked Dave. "Go back?"

"Bloody hell, no. We were there anyway so the Sarge wanted to know how many there were."

"Maybe he should've asked for a roll-call or something."

Bandy's face turned up. Up towards Dave Parks and up at the edges. The round face had become an elongated one.

"You being funny? Are you? You being funny? We're talking about fighting men here. Men that went on to die here. I hope you're no being funny."

"Sorry, OK, sorry, carry on."

James had stood up. Now he sat down again. From outside there came the voices of two people shouting something to each other. In here the sunshine beat down on Metra tel Kebir.

Bandy got back down to it, moving the lumps of coal up the pillow; up, up, and up, moving them slowly, leaving a black dusty trail, turning his head now and then and watching the lookouts. On top of this soft dune pillow Bandy stopped moving forward. The platoon was turned to the left, making for the back end of the tents. He made a guard move; but not far. The tall sauce bottle wobbled. The platoon moved on, with the commentary, slowly, in whispers.

"Right at the back of the tents. We were trying to get a check on what hardware they had. We were just about to skirt round, have a quick looksee, but then the bastards came at us."

His face was shapeless in its anger and pain. Dave and James looked at each other. Bandy was not looking at anyone. His eyes were shut tight, but that pain was getting through. He let out a cry.

"Aaah. I'll never forget it. Those bloody great camels charging at us."

"Camels?" asked Dave. "Camels? In the night? A camel cavalry you mean?"

"Naw. Naw. No cavalry, just camels. We had crawled right into their camel herd."

"Camels?" asked James.

"Aye. Fuckin camels. Great smelly bastards came at us, snortin and coughin an us too scared to move, lying there flat an those big hooves just kept comin an comin."

James stopped biting his lower lip. He scratched an ear. "So what happened, Bandy?"

"The sergeant, he rolls away from one." Bandy tried to roll over on the rug and failed. "But all he does is roll right under another one. A hoof copped him, right behind the ear. He was out. I got up and ran for him. Somebody was firing at me, or firing at somebody, but I gets beside Sarge, but just as I was pulling him out from under this beast, the bastard leans forwards and tears a great bite out my arm." Bandy was tapping his left shoulder.

Dave Parks' forehead fell into his hand. The head was shaking. A laugh could not be stopped. Bandy was spitting.

"Suppose you think it's funny? You ever been bit by a camel?"

"Oh dear, oh dear, oh mammy. No. Not that I know about. Come off it. Camels? In the Crater? Give us a break. The Crater was a housing scheme like Bellesmyre or some of them."

The Bandy was on his feet. That face came over to be face to face with the laughing listener.

"Why the fuck do you think they call me Bandy?"

Dave Parks' face was already straight. The shake of the head was given.

Bandy raised his left arm. It hung out in a curve. "See it?"

Dave Parks was looking, but not seeing too much. The arm was being held up and out to the side. Curved. It curved in a radius from shoulder to fingers.

"It can never be straight again."

"Oh. I see. You've got a bandy arm, is that it?"

This Bandy man's face was finding an undiscovered shade of red.

"You laughing at me, son?"

"No, no. Not really. Honest. I've just never met a man with a bandy arm before."

Bandy turned away, kicking lumps of coal to the side. The platoon was being dispersed throughout the wadi. There was no doubt. The man was angry. He turned back. Standing, he could look down on a Dave Parks that was sitting. It was best not to move. Bandy was there, stood in front, the hairs in his nostrils were ginger. Probably singed by the heat off his face.

"You think this is funny?"

He was reaching across, pulling his jacket free of his left shoulder. Clumsily, he unbuttoned his shirt, yanked at it until the shoulder stuck out, exposed. A ring of purple-white indentations lay around the joint. What could be seen of the upper arm was white. Bandy poked a finger on it. "In there, son, plastic; in there."

There was something wrong here. Dave Parks had felt low this morning. Fed up. Something eating away at the head. A visit to James was only something to be done. Something to ease out the low feeling. And here Dave Parks was in a room, a furnished flat, wall to wall failure stamped on it. Dave Parks was in here listening to this. Outside birds were singing, somewhere out there a man and a boy were pruning shrubs and smelling woodsmoke and an ox of a man tended his regulation grass; City men were making deals, men and women were working and striving and starving, and inside here Dave Parks was looking at a wild man with a bandy arm and tooth-marked memories of an Arabian night. This grin was self-sympathy, was some kind of exasperation, was nerves. And that started the Bandy man screaming.

"You still think it's funny? Funny? Funny? Do you? Funny? You young bastards are all the same. You know nothing. Nothing."

The jacket and shirt were pulled back over the shoulder. He was staring; staring at an irreverent listener that found it hard to be sorry and probably didn't know anything anyway. The staring Bandy gave up the stare first, turning away, stepping towards the door. He stopped. He turned back. He lifted the bottle. He looked at it. It had some wine left in it. The Bandy man stomped away again, screaming, shouting: you know nothing, you know nothing, nothing. He left the door open behind him.

James was looking down into his tin mug. He placed the cup between his feet and straightened up. "Well," he said.

A shrug of the shoulders was all the answer he was getting. James moved across and closed the door. Dave decided to speak.

"Forget about him, James. Steer clear of him. The man's a ponce."

"A what? A ponce? In what sense?"

"The only sense I know. A ponce is a ponce. The bag of coal, the wee bottle that you couldn't resist, that's just the sprat to catch the mackerel."

"And I'm the mackerel?"

"Let's be honest, James. Round about here you're definitely a fish out of water. And I think you're nearer to being a mackerel than a shark; James, the coal, the wine, then he clocks you're the officer class and he's away on the old war wound routine. Come on. Before you know it you would've been supplying him with the wine. And I don't mean the communion stuff."

"I think this assessment of yours may be rather quick, David. The man has committed no wrong against me. Personally I found him quite an interesting chap."

"OK. Please yourself. Maybe you'll have to find out the hard way. Experience is the best learning. Anyway. What about you? You're definitely going to need some gear. Have you any cash?"

James pointed an imperious finger. The blazer was hanging on the back of the chair. It was passed over, and he rummled inside a pocket and withdrew a thin wallet. From inside the wallet James took out a five pound note. "That's all I have."

"Oh. Is that it? A fiver. That won't get us much."

Inside the head the Dave Parks computer was showing that most of the advance from the Smiths was away.

"I think there's only one thing for it, James. I'll have to ask the Smiths for more cash."

"You don't believe they will give you any, do you?"

"Won't know till we try, will we? I wonder if her nibs has a phone down there? Suppose she has."

Dave rose from the chair and crossed to the door. He opened it. Bandy.

Bandy's face. Nose touching nose. Wide eyes above this purple-speckled nose, above a mouth that showed white secretions of saliva set in the corners and spat. The hand was coming up. Medals. A palmful of medals tied on coloured ribbon up into the face of Dave Parks who only wanted to get to a phone.

"Y'see these? They're no nothing, pal. These are no nothing. Y'see them? Y'see them?"

The breath was vile. Wine and inner decay reeking past black stumps. Medals of honour and evil breath right under Dave Parks' nose. A defensive hand eased the clutch of medals away.

"Look, look, for pete sake give us a break. What do you want me to say? I've said it. I'm sorry if I've upset you. Right? I appreciate everything you guys are doing. OK? Now let it go, eh?"

Moving past him wasn't easy, but it was done. Behind, the man kept shouting.

"Let it go? Let it go? If we had let it go at the Thin Red Line where would you be, son? Where would you be if we had let it go? Communists, that's where we'd be. Communists, ya toerag."

The stairs looked like an escape route. The face kept looking down over the banisters shouting: Corunna Cambrai Lucknow Alamein. And the Crater. And the crater. French names, places. Battle honours probably, sounding as good as curses.

The landlady's door was reached. The curses stopped even before a knock was placed on it. Somewhere above, a door slammed. It was Theresa who opened the door. If she had heard the row it could not be seen in the face. A small face. High cheekbones. And overdone with make-up. She was still in her gown.

"Sorry to bother you, but have you got a phone I could use?"

She was letting the answer take its time, standing, studying the man that was doing the asking. She was looking in Dave Parks' eyes for something and Dave Parks wished he knew what it was. She was speaking.

"We've got a phone. But it's in here. If it's, em, personal, well, em, put it this way: there is no way Laura and I are leaving the room, although we'll do our best not to listen. Best we can do."

"That's OK, that's OK, that's fine, thanks very much."

"Charmed, I'm sure."

She stood aside, pulling the door wide. Dave passed her, head up, willing not to look where the serpent was feeding. A couple of different heavy perfumey smells stirred the stink of Bandy's breath from the nostrils. This Theresa Kipple was strong stuff. In the corner of the room Laura Kipple was stretching from her wheelchair, arm extended, trying to reach the accordion case set against the wall. She was failing. Her face was strained. Dave Galahad crossed over to her quickly.

"Want me to get it?"

Laura Kipple fell back into her wheelchair, looking up. Her face looked a weary woman's face. A grin nearly made it.

"Oh, it's you. No thanks. I've gone off the idea. Thank you."

The wheelchair was wheeled around, and driven into a patch of sunlight made by the sun coming through a large window. Sister Theresa was coming from the door.

"He wants to use the phone."

"Oh. I hope it's not bother or an emergency or anything." She was looking up at Dave Parks as she spoke. The look on her face put the question mark on to her statement of hope. Dave felt obliged to answer.

"Not at all, not at all. It's for James. I only want to ring some friends of his."

Theresa had sat down. She was selecting from a range of small round and triangular bottles clustered on a table at her chair.

"Carry on," she said.

The piece of paper with the number was brought out from the breast pocket. The telephone was picked up, and Dave was dialling; dialling and sneaking looks across as Theresa the landlady was bending over and putting the paint on her toenails. There was some thigh there, but Dave Parks drew his looks away elsewhere. She was only a woman. Every woman had thighs. Men had thighs. Somebody was taking their time answering. The gown was slipping more. Somebody should hurry up. The call was answered. It was the woman, the sister.

"Hello, can I speak to Robin, please? This is Dave Parks here."

"Who?"

116

"Dave Parks. Dave Parks. Your brothers asked me to take care of James for them."

"Oh. Yes, Mr Parks. Hold on please, I may catch him before he leaves for the city." She had put the phone down.

Theresa Kipple was admiring her big toe, staring at it as if contemplating the brushstrokes. Laura had her head tilted back, face up, eyes closed. The spread of sunlight spotlit her face. Her lips were moving. Her fingers were moving as if playing the tune the lips were humming. Laura's lullaby.

"Hello." It was Robin Smith.

"Hello? Mr Smith? Dave Parks here."

Relating the request was going to be a waste of breath. Dave Parks knew that. But there should be some sympathy here. Surely. Too well hidden. Dave Parks knew that. Even as the tale was being told and accounted, and the needs of the man upstairs laid out, Dave Parks knew, and felt an idiot. There would be no more cash here. James was on his own. But it had to be asked for. And the denial came wrapped in the usual bullshit.

"I do appreciate what you're trying to do for James, Mr Parks, but I'm afraid we cannot go beyond our original agreement or add to the original monies paid to you. We had hoped, actually, that your expertise would help James over these early difficulties."

"Look, the man needs gear; pots, pans, whatever. It won't take much."

"Mr Parks, limited as my knowledge is, I do believe there are charitable agencies which can help. When we took you on, it was because we believed you could do this much better than we, and the price was agreed. Why, if we give you any more monies, well, it might have been cheaper to do it ourselves. I'm sorry. Please keep in touch."

"Sure. I'll be bringing the car back anyway."

"No hurry."

The telephone was put down. The whole thing was a putdown. That was it. But something had to be done. James had to be settled before Monday. James. Oh fuck. Maybe this would do it. Get him over this hump and that would be it. With a bit of luck once the job in Bellesmyre was started that would be Dave Parks finished with the James man. Dave Parks was beginning to sound to Dave Parks like Robin Smith and his weird family. Something had to be done. The guy needed some kit to survive with. And this Smith cash was way down.

"I think you can put the phone down now."

This woman in the gown was sitting, holding up a nail varnish brush and laughing.

"Sorry. I was dreaming."

"Some dream. By the look on your face it was more like a nightmare."

"Could be."

"What's the matter about our Mr James?"

"Ach. He needs some stuff and his relations won't cough up the cash to buy anything."

Laura's eyes opened. "Always the way of it." The eyes were closed again.

Theresa Kipple was looking down at that big toe again. She was moving it back and forth, up and down, finally settling it up on its own above the others.

"Can you apply for special needs?" she asked.

"Ach, I tried that the other day. Not that I tried very hard right enough, but it's such a bloody hassle now. Might as well throw the Yellow Book away and hand the people over to the moneylenders."

"What is it he needs?"

"Usual stuff: stuff to cook in, eat off, usual tools. He's got nothing and even less of a clue."

"That's not normally a problem if you've got money."

The singing landlady was sitting back in her chair now; crossing her legs, pulling the gown over them. Her mouth opened and closed a few times. This woman was thinking. The lips were being pursed like a preparatory kiss.

"Tell you what," she said, "give me a minute to get ready and I'll take you where you can get some stuff cheap. I feel like going out anyway. It's been a wee while."

"Thanks. But he's only got a fiver and I've only got a few quid."

Laura laughed, disturbing dust speckles that were floating in the sunlight above her face. The sun was picking out individual hairs above her top lip. Theresa was smiling at something too. Something was funny to the two sisters.

"Don't worry. Have you got your car?"

A couple of nods answered.

"Good. Right. Meet me back down here in half an hour." She rose, holding the gown around herself. "Half an hour," she said. The door was opened and closed behind Dave Parks.

At the top of the stairs the Mr O'Brien was coming out of his room. He was wearing the long raincoat. But the sun was shining. Room was made for the man to pass.

"That you off to your work then?"

"Aye." The man passed on.

James was putting clothes into the set of drawers. Straightening up he let a shirt hang down in front of his chest.

"I'll have to find someone to do my shirts for me, David. These are becoming terribly creased with all this packing and unpacking."

"Do your shirts for you? Do for you? You daft or something?" The man had been hurt.

"Oh, come on James. Look, you're on the Social now. D'you know what that means? You'll be on about sixty to seventy quid at the most. You'll have to pay her nibs down there, you'll have to eat, you'll have to put clothes on your back, and you want somebody to do for you. I'll do you if I hear you come away with this patter again. Give us a break. Christ man, you're done already."

"Please don't take the Lord's name in vain, David."

"Right, sorry, but screw your nut. Listen, her nibs is taking us somewhere to get you some things to get you by. In half an hour. Right? Can you be ready for that? You look a bit rough. You'd have been better shaving instead of playing at wee soldiers."

James rubbed his chin. "Goodness. I do need a shave. But I was sure I shaved this morning."

"That's that wine, James me boy. That's not your communion stuff you know. So, reassure yourself with another shave. On you go."

James lifted a neat array of toiletries which he had placed on a towel at the foot of his bed. The towel was slung over a shoulder. Dave Parks received a salute.

"I go. Cleanliness is next to Godliness."

"That right? Well, I think I know plenty of people that might think God must be a right dirty old rascal."

"David. How can you say such things?"

"Easy. With my mouth. Now on you go. Never mind any sermons. I'm not in the mood."

James left. The door stayed open. Across the landing another door closed. Then the voice came. The voice that sang for its supper in the Social. James was belting out a hymn. Dave Parks knew that one as well.

> "O God of Bethel! by whose hand
> Thy people still are fed;
> Who through this weary pilgrimage
> Hast all our fathers led."

Dave Parks closed the door on it.

****

It was right on the half-hour and she was ready and waiting at the door. There was no move from her as Dave and James came down the stair. She waited; waited until they came, waited until Dave leaned forward and opened the door, then she stepped out and waited at the edge of the pavement while Dave Parks took three attempts to close the door. James stood beside her, waving to Laura who was waving from the window. She had dressed in red, a simple, straight-cut two-piece that fitted perfectly. She tucked her arm into James's as they walked to the car. The man and the boy in the shrubbery were sitting under a tree, the paper wrapper of the sandwiches spread out. The man was pouring the boy some tea from a flask. A look at the watch confirmed dinner-time. One o'clock. In Edinburgh somebody would be shooting off a gun. Maybe all the clocks were bammy in Edinburgh.

"This yours?" she was asking, as Dave stopped.

The head came back from Edinburgh and nodded.

"Nice."

"Well, it's not actually mine. I've just got a loan of it."

Once away, she directed them to the centre of the old city, giving instructions through the streets and finally indicating a lane that Dave Parks had never known existed, though he had passed it lots of times for sure. The passenger was pleased to be informed of her driver's ignorance. Off this wynd there was spare rubbled ground behind a hotel. A tramp sat on some kind of ventilator and steam was passing up all around him. There was room to park. The car was parked. The tramp shouted something.

"Where to now?" asked Dave.

"Along towards the Tollgate."

The streets were busy with people, most of them probably going back to work after dinner or some squeezed-in shopping.

"Up here," she said.

121

"Right Mrs."

"My name's Theresa."

Theresa. Why had Dave Parks been afraid to call Theresa Theresa?

"Sorry."

The way she led was through a cobbled pend that gave way to a rectangle of depressively pitted cobblestones, surrounded by grey tenement buildings with long iron-barred railings at the windows. Some of the bars had been painted. Rust protective reds and easily maintained blacks. Theresa was heading for a small doorway in a building to the right. James was looking flushed. He was grinning and not grinning and looking round all ways, as if to confirm that he had not been left alone with the pathfinder general in front.

The doorway led into a narrow, dark close, from which stairs ran up, lit only by what light scraped in a window at the bend in the stairs. Theresa led up the stairs. She knew where she was going. At a door she paused. James paused. The leader-off nodded towards the handle. James opened the door. It opened into a tight hallway. An upright piano, with some kind of Grecian vase overflowing with grapes embossed upon its front, took up half the space. Beyond the piano a heavy mahogany sideboard of plain shiny wood and rounded edges imposed itself and had to be squeezed past. It would have served as a high altar. At the end of the hallway was some kind of square room. Here where the hallway joined the room, where people milled around, Theresa stopped. The Theresa was waiting. But there was no door to be opened.

The room was square. Odd chairs and sofas and coatstands were stacked around the edges of the room. Prints, paintings, embossed and plain mirrors, hung haphazardly on the walls with little oval, coloured stickers or square, white-numbered tickets stuck haphazardly on the frames. The place smelled like James's room. Theresa was standing still. A standing crowd at the back here made it hard for anyone to see. What could be seen was that Theresa wanted to be seen. And she could wait.

At the back here, two office doors led off into some kind of showrooms. Through the glass doors it was noticeable the jewellery display units were covered over with the green felt. A man pushed past to get in. Still Theresa waited. At the front of the room two rows of people sat on benches set high off the ground, a benchful on either side, facing each other. Three people in the middle of one of the benches looked young. They were laughing, but the eyes were sad. Most of the rest looked old. With white faces. Tight white faces. Tight white faces with lines that ran deep. Especially the women. And they were mostly women. Below the people on the high benches other people sat on other benches set on the floor, a table separating them. The table ran down the centre of the room to a black, highly varnished partition. At the far end of one of the high benches a woman with tugs of hair like strands of steel wool sat with her arms folded across her chest and looked over gold glasses at Theresa. This woman wasn't sure. She turned to another woman at her side and whispered in her ear. Now they both looked at Theresa. Others were looking at Theresa. Her wait was over. She had captured the audience. A touch was asking James to let the arm go. James kissed the back of her hand and let her go. She showed no surprise, or pleasure. Some conversations were ceasing. The woman in the corner was sure now. The name was called out: Tessie. She waved. The standing crowd parted a little to let the women on the bench have a clearer view. Theresa blew the woman a kiss. The woman waved harder. Others waved.

In the front row a man unclasped his hands, turned around seeking, smiled a wide smile, and doffed his brown trilby to Tessie. A young man in a woolly pullover was making some kind of clearway to Tessie Theresa. The crowd was clearing. Behind the young man, placed at the top of the table, a man dressed all in black sat in a wide cane chair. His neck was turned so his face could smile at Tessie. He had three gaps in his teeth. He stretched an arm out as he spoke: Tessie.

"McPhillan." Tessie was indicating the chair. "Steal my grave as quick?"

"Oh, Tessie. It's my back. You know I've always had a bad back."

"Aye. It's our Da's back," said the young head above the pullover.

McPhillan senior took a grip of his boy's arm. "Right, son, right. Anyway, you've not been turning to, Tessie. You've never been here for a while."

"That's true, I suppose. But how come the chair's black? Did the red not suit you?"

McPhillan went red in the face. "Ach well, it was needing a new coat. And Tommy the auctioneer always did think it was a bit distracting."

"Oh, I know. It'll still be distracting now that you're sat there, but for different reasons."

"Well, I must say he's been able to get on a bit without your legs dangling in front of his face."

"McPhillan, you talk rubbish."

People close enough to hear were laughing, those further away smiled anyway. Those talking stopped talking. Some strained to hear if there was going to be any more backchat and probably wished they had heard the first bit.

A crowd was building up in this standing area at the back. A thin man in black leather jacket and faded blue denims pushed past out of the crowd into the narrow hallway.

"Lot of rubbish, that," he said. He pointed with a nod of his head. Around the walls, notices, crudely drawn in black and red crayon, proclaimed: This Is A No Smoking Aria.

Dave edged into the hallway beside the man, took out his tin, rolled one, lit it, and leaned on the sideboard that could have been a high altar.

"You come to these things a lot?"

The man shrugged. "Just sometimes, if I'm needing some stuff for the stall."

From the showrooms at the rear four people emerged, led by a lanky man carrying a thin sheaf of white papers. Behind him came a young man or woman with short-cropped hair, followed by an older man and woman. The four moved around the outer edge of the crowd. They moved to the end of the room and passed through a door set in the partition. The young person took up a seat at some kind of desk. The desk must have been set on a platform. The clerk was high, looking down over the partition, biting a fingernail and spitting it out to land somewhere. Halfway across the room, in the centre of the partition, one panel had been cut out. Here, on the high platform, a bosun's chair with a thick heavy cushion sat. The lanky man was jumping up on to the platform. On the platform he looked giant. He picked up the cushion, patted it, arranged it on the chair and sat on it, stretching his legs out in front so as to rest them on the table in front, in front of the noses of the bidders. Auctioneer presiding.

"Right. Good afternoon to you." He waved the papers, conducting.

"Good afternoon," the bidders chorused.

"What we have for you today is a clearance sale. Some rubbish, some good stuff. If you get any antiques there's been a mistake and we want it back. Failing that, we don't want to see the stuff again."

"Why don't you get some good stuff in?" somebody shouted.

"If you lot would take away this stuff we might have some room for some."

People laughed; somebody blew a raspberry.

"What we have for you today is a clearance sale. Three estates. Just the odds and bobs. So, I'm in a bit of hurry today, so let's keep it moving."

Theresa was beckoning. The cigarette was crushed on the floor.

"What kind of money have you two actually got?"

James pulled out his five.

"I've got about the same."

"Is that all?"

"Well, maybe six or seven."

"You're not too bloody sure, are you? Never mind. Should be enough. You pay and collect. I'll do the bidding."

The auctioneer had a cardboard box in front of him. Little objects were being extracted from the box. "What have we here? A toast rack, some table mats, oh, here we are, hey, look at this." A small statuette of the little boy pissing in Brussels was held up. "Few of you never seen one of these for a long time. Right, pound the box."

Nobody moved.

"Oh, come on. Is this to be one of these days? Fifty pence."

A woman standing near poked her head above the shoulders in front. On tiptoes she nodded a bid.

"Right. Mrs Scullion. Put it away Dick."

The helper stowed the box away into a numbered box on the wall behind. Floor to ceiling, the space had been divided up into numbered boxes. The oval enamel number plates were chipped, rusting. The clerk made a note. The woman working with him passed up some more stuff. Brass.

"Usual brassware here, nice pouring pot, two plaques. OK. A pound."

A finger went up on the left.

"Pound I'm bid, Pound fifty. Two. Two fifty. It's with the bidder at two-fifty. Right two-fifty. Mr McPhillan. And that's an orange sticker on that one. Orange estate." The clerk made a note.

Next lot was three kettles. The laid-back auctioneer picked one up and handed it back down to the woman helper.

"Take that back, Mary. That's electric. That'll go itself."

Somebody booed.

"That's enough of that. D'ye think it's outside you're in?"

Two kettles were put up, held up to show their nice clean bottoms.

"Fifty pence the two." The auctioneer pointed in Theresa's direction. "Fifty pence. Is that our Tessie I see there?" No one else bid. "Fifty pence. Blue sticker. Is that cash, Tessie?" Tessie nodded.

Another cardboard box was up. As he delved the man was shouting to Tessie Theresa. "By jings we've never seen you for a while. You got through your man's money already? Good to see you. Time we had a bit of class around here."

Theresa laughed with the crowd. Dave Parks was pulled into her side. She was pointing to the partition. Dave Parks was to go down there somewhere. After pushing through, the door in the partition was reached.

The clerk was looking down from his high-desk height. "They for you?"

"I think so. Aye. Fifty pence."

A pound note was handed up, kettles lifted from a shelf. Change was given out of two wooden bowls set in the desk. Trying not to hit anybody with the kettles, the place in the crowd was regained.

"Put them against the wall," said Theresa.

Lots were being put through quickly. Three paintings with their frames hanging off that might have been Rembrandts missing for years went for a pound. Golf shoes, somebody's record collection all in a case, a typewriter that nobody had any more use for. Things were going in a series of nods, upright fingers and shakes of the head. Another cardboard box was put up.

"Box here, pots, pans, even a wee teapot here. Frying pan to batter the old boy. Right, a pound."

Dave Parks' hand nearly went up. It moved. Dave Parks was feeling excited.

Theresa put her hand on his arm. "Not that stuff."

"Eh?"

"See the box? See the 'W'?"

"Aye. Aye. I see it."

"Warrant sale. We don't touch it. Some of these younger ones do but . . ." She made a spitting noise.

A finger went up from the bunch of three young people on the bench. In their judgment or ignorance the sign did not matter. There was no other bid.

"They're yours," said the auctioneer.

The bidder leaned up from his seat to take the box, but the auctioneer had already handed it down to his helpers and started extolling the virtues of the next lot: a cobbler's last. The young bidder was stuck half-in, half-out, of his place. The auctioneer stopped describing the last and turned to the customer.

"You cash, son? I'm sorry. They're put away now. You can pick them up at the end of the auction. Who's for the last? Fifty pence."

Next up was another typewriter. Food mixers, bathroom scales, artists' paints, golf clubs with and without bags, photographs of a Pope, of unknown soldiers, chipped plaster horses' heads, tools, barometers, thermometers, pedometers, and another set of pots and pans and odds and sods. Theresa signalled and the pots and pans were hers for a pound. Dave Parks fetched them and piled them with the kettles. James was standing with both hands clasped behind his back, leaving Theresa both hands free. After another typewriter and six pairs of engineer's callipers had been sold, Theresa bought a bundle of knives and forks tied together with string. Again they were paid for, brought back, and piled with the rest. And already Theresa was bidding for something else. Something in a green tartan holdall. She got that. And Dave Parks was away once more to fetch and carry.

Inside the bag were two shoe-boxes. Inside the boxes were two pairs of women's shoes. A shiny maroon, all-plastic patent with plastic gold-leaf spreading across the instep.

"These for you?"

"Kidding? No, I wanted the bag to carry the stuff in. You don't think I would go through the town with you two lugging all sorts of stuff at my back? I have a wee bit reputation, you know."

"So I see, Tessie. Will I chip these shoes?"

"Lesson number one, Mr Parks. You never throw stuff away. Never ever."

Theresa moved forward to speak to some people. Other people made way for her. She moved over to stand at the side of, but in front of, McPhillan in the chair. Leaning forward, she was pushing her backside into McPhillan's face, forcing him to lean down to one side in order to see the auctioneer and keep his face free from the backside of Theresa's skirt. He was trying to look unconcerned. Dave knelt to pack the grip.

The goods were proving a hard fit in the holdall. Pot handles stuck out this way and that way. Pans took up bellies of space, rectangular boxes did not fit. Out the pots came. Out the pans came. In went the boxes. In went some pots. In went some pans. Out stayed some pots. Out stayed some pans. Dave Parks looked up for inspiration. James had a finger up. James was bidding. Pots clattered to the floor. Dave stood up. Even standing he could not see what was on offer. Theresa was engrossed in her gossip or whatever. The auctioneer was pointing. It was with another bidder at a pound fifty. James was sticking his finger up again. But James did not have any money. This guy had no money bar what Dave Parks had for him. Dave Parks tried to attract his attention. And it was there for two-fifty. And whatever it was, was his. James came over.

"Was that you, David? Do you want these for yourself?"

"I don't even know what they bloody well are. Never mind. What were you up to? What is it anyway?"

"Will you go and get them for me, David, please."

"Oh, I suppose so."

Get them. Get what? Two tea-maids and a butler probably. The assistant Dick was holding the door open. There they were. On the shelf.

"Is that what I'm down for?"

"You for cash?" asked the clerk. "Well, that's them. Two pounds fifty."

Dave Parks lifted the pair of cricketer's pads from the shelf. They were covered in dust.

Theresa was waving cheerio to her friends on the benches. The auctioneer stopped a spiel. "You bidding or fanning yourself, Tessie? We don't see you for years, then you come in here and disrupt everything. Any more of this, I'll set McPhillan's boy onto you."

"It would take a man."

McPhillan's face turned red. And so did his boy's. The crowd laughed. Theresa turned, moved through the crowd, returning to her two companions of the day. Maybe she had noticed. She must've. Maybe not. Didn't matter. Where could a pair of cricket pads be hidden? They wouldn't even fit in the holdall. Dave Parks was getting angry.

"James, what is this all about?"

"David. The pair I have are almost gone. I gave my best pairs away to my boys in Zimbabwe."

"Flogged them for drink more likely. James. James. Cricket pads. Cricket pads."

"My dear David. After all, it was you who bought them."

Theresa arrived. She only looked at the pads and shook her head. An arm was held up for James to take. A section of the crowd moved aside to let them pass. Dave Parks was left carrying the bag, the pads balancing on top, held between the straps.

After the tight crowd, the narrow hallway and the stairs down, the street was a relief. Streets were quieter now. Emptier. More people back at work to earn the pounds to pay over for the stuff that had just been auctioned and would reappear to be luckily found on the stalls at the weekend. James and Theresa were walking on in front of their bearer.

"I think you've got most of your needs met there, Mr James. What do you think?"

"Almost certainly, my dear Mrs, em, Mrs Kipple."

"Miss Kipple."

"Thank you. There is probably some monies left over to buy groceries."

"What about some cricket balls?" said Dave.

"Now, David. You've more cash than you're lettin on, anyway."

"Oh, Miss Kipple. I refuse to believe it."

"Rubbish. Who's right here, Parks my boy?"

"I'm not listening. I'm too busy lugging this stuff."

"Big man like you can manage it. Is there anything we've missed?"

"Just a pity there were no shoes on offer," said James.

"There's two pair in here."

"Shoes? Don't tell me you're needing a pair of shoes? Those look all right to me."

"A facade, madam, a facade. A shiny exterior only, I'm afraid. Underneath the sole is worn. The wet rains find it all too easy to soak in, I'm afraid."

"They certainly look OK from up here."

"But it is down here, underneath, where the feet get wet. I am, alas, down at heel, and a gentleman should never be down at heel. Like the length of the hair, the shoes are a sign of the breeding. Hair I can use scissors on. I'm afraid I have no skills with a cobbler's last."

"You can talk a bit but. Dave, what time is it?"

"Quarter to."

"The quarter. She might still be there."

Theresa quickened the pace. The holdall was getting heavier. She was heading down someplace by the river. Dave Parks knew. By the route she was taking she was heading for the Lane. The bizarre bazaar. Three hundred yards of reek. Even in high summer the Lane was wet. James was going to be uncomfortable in the Lane. The hole in his shoe would feel twice as holey. Mud was always oozing from between the cobbles, a mutual transfer from shoe to stone and stone to shoe and back again and again. A transfusion of sticky detritus that mixed into and supplemented a stink that was stale, that was fish, that was grease, that was damp, that was the combination that was poverty. This was the Lane.

Hawkers sat or stood by their bundles; fat, oversized women wrapped in heavy coats and woollen hats and scarves; thinner women who blew smoke between the shouting of wares. Old ruddy-faced women, young pale-faced women; men in brown leather jackets with dead-looking fur; men in jerseys that stopped short above shirts that hung out. Men and women watching. Nothing had changed.

Dave Parks had not been here for years. But Dave Parks knew it. Knew the smell. Knew the pain. The pain of standing by, looking away while mother rummaged in a bundle to find a vest without holes, that looked as if it would fit the boy there. Pain as young Davie boy was pulled forward and somebody else's vest was placed against his chest. Pain as huge toothless hawker women held his shoulder to convince every passer-by that it was made for the boy. The pain of a public clout on the jaw if a puzzled face showed the pain: the pain of not being able to understand why not new.

Then fearful pain as the police blocked the ends of the Lane and pulled screaming, angry women away, and kicked at the bundles, scattering the shirts and the socks and the shoes in the mud. And the vests. Ma scrambling for a muddy vest.

"You want some pills, Jimmy?"

"Eh? No. No thanks."

"Here, look, just the fiver."

"No thanks."

"Give us a fag."

"I don't smoke."

"Butter. How about some butter? You want some cheese? Look . . ."

"Ah, fuck off!"

Theresa looked comfortable here. She knew the way. An old woman sitting in a chair beside her two bundles had a hold of Theresa's coat cuff and was talking into her ear. Theresa was

131

smiling. She was comfortable here. James was standing behind, on the edges of his shoes. Theresa straightened up and pulled the woman's black beanie off and pulled it forward over her eyes. The woman leaned forward almost falling off the chair, laughing. She had no teeth. James was struggling to smile, looking round to Dave Parks and all Dave Parks could do was shrug and follow Theresa. Follow her, along, further into the Lane. There was a new smell now to add to the mix. Hamburgers. Onions. Used to be ham ribs and peas.

"You fancy a suit, mister? There ye are. Nice suit that. I know where it's been. Just the style as well."

Theresa was walking on, manoeuvring her way through the searchers and the sellers, past the trestle tables loaded high with money-making junk and past the bundles that sent up their own smell. Smell that touched on feelings still felt. For himself past, or the child standing in the Lane this day. Uncertain. Clothes hung on coathangers along wire fencing. Fur jackets, jackets of faded suede, tweedy jackets and every one a bargain. Women and men with hardened faces shouted to one another up and down the Lane, across the Lane, words coming fast, and laughter coming loud at punchlines unintelligible to the passing buyers. A boy with a bundle on his head found a corner, dumped it, untied the sheet, spilling out the clothes and rags onto the wet cobbles. He sat down behind the pile. Only his head was visible. The shout came: "Everything the five pence. There ye are. Five pence now. Everything the five pence."

Where a building used to be, the gap site was laid out with sheets; lengths of rotting cardboard and curtain lengths, all stuck in inches of rising mud, stinking and sinking under the accumulated weight of other people's rubbish that was worth something to somebody. And was not to be thrown away. Sheets laid out with typewriters, tools and clocks, jewellery, records and tapes and watches that would never go tick again.

On the right, deep railway arches ran under the City's arterial line. Arches long ago made into rows of stalls dim lit, drowning in a flood of dead people's clothes, which were good enough for the Irish, who might even buy their own suits back once they had a wage.

Or good enough for the Lascar seamen who sailed the ships when the river had ships to be sailed. Good enough still for the City poor. Theresa was leading into one of these dim underground clothes stores. James followed on. Dave Parks followed on. A woman rushed out from behind a stall and ran up the aisleway. Theresa was being hugged.

"Tessie. Tessie hen, where've you been? Where've you been? Christ, it's years since I seen you. What's new? What's new? Oh, Christ, you're looking a million dollars. Have you still got some of your punters sticking you up some stuff?"

"Wish I had, Annie. I'd be better dressed than this. How's things with yourself?"

"Ach, not bad. Bad to grumble. Things are not bad. Plenty of poor people goin about right now, so we're gettin the trade. But there's an awful lot o amateurs moving in. Should hear them as well; right plummy voices, you think they'd never be seen alive in here unless they thought they were going to pick up the Venus de Milo for half-a-dollar. But there ye are. Suppose they've got a right to live as well."

"As well as they can, they think. I don't see it myself," said Theresa.

The woman Annie laughed. They had walked back to Annie's stall. It was piled high, higgledy-piggledy, layer upon higgledy-piggledy layer, leaning over, threatening to topple. Annie was now turning her attention to the two men who had brought up the rear.

"Who's this?"

"Just a pair of gentlemen friends. I was thinking of using them as bookends. Unless you'd like to take one of them off my hands."

"Well, this lad here doesn't look too bad. Is this one with the blazer a sailor?"

James pulled a face. Theresa clapped her hands.

"No, no, for goodness sake, no. It's him I'm trying to fix up. D'you have any shoes, Annie? You know what I mean. Shoes."

"Maybe. What size is he?"

"Don't know. What size are you, James?"

"I am a size nine, thank you."

"Christ, listen to him. An accent like that he should be running a stall here."

Annie went behind her stall to search, and disappeared. The sound of boxes being moved could be heard. She reappeared with three shoe-boxes. One lid was removed and the box offered to James. "Here, try them for size."

James crouched and untied his shoelaces as Theresa laced up a new one. The shoe was brown, all leather and workmanship that spoke out quality. Standing on one foot, James tried it on. Annie pulled a jacket from the stall and laid it on the ground.

"That is very kind of you," said James.

"It'll keep the shoe clean," said Annie.

James was making a show of flexing his foot and stamping it upon the jacket. He was smiling. The other was tried.

"They are a rare fit indeed," he said.

"I've got the same in black."

"No, no. Brown's fine."

"Tell you what, I'll give you the two pair for a tenner. How's that?"

Theresa spoke. "Annie, he's not got it."

"Ah, Christ, another sufferer. Right. Seven pound the two pair."

James was looking at Dave and Dave could only nod.

"Just keep them on," said Theresa.

Some more of the Smiths' money was paid over. Soon it would all be gone. And the weekend was coming. As she took the money, Annie moved around the holdall. She looked down. "You into that kind of game?" she asked.

"Me? Game? What game?" She pointed. "Oh that game. No, no, not really."

Clothes were being pushed aside on the stall. Annie was trying to get down into a corner of the stall.

"Here it is. This any use to you?" A cricket ball was being held out on offer.

James took it, turned it in his hand. "The shine's hardly off it."

"Is it worth more to me shiny?" Annie was making a face. Everybody laughed. "You keep it. Here, give me those old shoes of yours up."

James picked up and handed her the old shoes. Annie looked round. The long walkway was empty. One at a time Annie threw the shoes further up the stalls. Each shoe hit the wall and slid down behind a stall further up.

"Moanin' old git him, anyway," she said.

Annie stretched, thrust her hands into her apron pocket and looked at Theresa. "Well, Tessie, is that all you came for? Is that it? And here's me thinking you came to see your old pal. Ah, well. How's Laura by the way? Give her my best, eh?"

Tessie Theresa was ready to cry. A tear sat ready to roll. Annie embraced her.

"Get away, you. There's no need for that. Listen, take a run up some Tuesday. You know we're always quiet on a Tuesday. We can go for a wee drink with the rest of the crowd. They'd love to see you. Maybe get you a toyboy."

"I will, Annie, I will. The same goes for yourself. If you and Bert want to come down some Saturday, just come. That's the night Laura and I get a drink in. Old habits die hard, I suppose."

"OK. If I'm passing. I'll remember, but you know Bert."

"Who doesn't? Don't worry about it. Just if you're passing."

"And you'll come and see us?"

"I will. Honest."

"Don't say 'honest'. You know that's a word we never use around here."

Theresa flattened the teardrop with a finger. "Cheerio."

"Cheerio, Tessie."

Theresa led the way out from the stalls, to the Lane, through the seekers after poor bargains, out to the streets that became drier with distance. She walked alone. Ahead. Behind came James carrying the boxes. Behind came Dave Parks. Dave Parks found that if he stuck the holdall on his head the load was more bearable.

****

This one strip of peel, spiralling round, round and round, hanging on, just, it was going to be a big one, a long one, a peel to be prized but it was off. One potato sliced and one potato put in the pot. Kettle was boiling. Quick rinse, potato pot filled, potato pot put on the cooker. Maybe just in time. Here comes Mary up that path. Peelings still being hauled out of the sink and Mary's in. She was late as well. No smile. A hard day maybe. Bags dumped. A bad hard day sign. Looking in the pot. Looking for bad signs.

—Is that the potatoes just on?

—Fraid so.

—What do you mean, you're afraid so? How long have they been on? Don't tell me, I can see.

—Why ask then?

—Ah, don't be smart. What time did you get home at?

—Round about five.

—Five? Did the kids come home by themselves then?

—Mrs McLeary brought them.

—Oh. Smashing. That's all we need, her telling the world our kids are neglected.

—Ach, don't exaggerate. Did you have a hard day? Sounds like it.

—Don't try and change the subject. Course I had a hard day, and by the looks of things here, I'm not finished yet.

—Oh, give us a break. Look, you go in and get your feet up, and I'll see to this.

—What is THIS?

—I bought some cold meat. We can have that and some beans or something.

—Cordon bloody bleu right enough. Where's the kids?

—Up the stairs.

Away. Peace in the valley. How green was my valley? As green as these peas likely. Plates. The big plates. Knives. Time this

136

drawer was being fixed. Forks. Salt. And the pepper. Salt pepper mustard vinegar salt pepper mustard vinegar hear the word of the Lord. Lord James. James on his own. Except for his Lord. Wonder how he'll be getting on. Clashing his new pans likely. Won't matter whatever James cooks the grace will be the best bit. Steam rising water spitting jiggling bubbles sizzling turn them down. Mark 2 Mark too Mark as well Mark chapter two Who was Mark again? James would know Probably a bosom buddy of his Mark was the one after Matthew and before Luke Dave Parks knows that Matthew Mark Luke Peter John Wrong Dave Parks No Peter Just Matthew Mark Luke and John Why no Peter? Peter He was the one that done in Ananias for holding back on the money How does Dave Parks know that? Plate out Sunday school She told that story And all the time looked at Dave Parks She knew And Ananias snuffed it Oh Christ Peter saw God saw James had enough money A tenner was enough Surely See him through Never for a fortnight Maybe need another visit Theresa Kipple Tessie Theresa Something about her Looks like this is everything ready Mash them up with marge and with milk Here we go here we go here we go

"Tea up."

Mary had changed to her track suit. Keeping track more likely. She had changed Marion and Melanie into their PJs. In their pyjamas. Must be really late or else she's feeling really vindictive. Must have been a real hard day. And now she is sitting with that look on her face. It is going to be one of those nights. New job coming up. Regular wages constant work never any strikes in this game. Never any demand fluctuations. Regular cash coming and yet still there's worry there. And the big sign up: DO NOT DISTURB. Might as well talk to the weans.

"Eat up, kids."

"Don't like it."

"Melanie, these potatoes were specially picked for you. I did it myself, and I peeled them nice and thin so as you would get the best bits."

"Don't like them."

"Melanie. Please."

"Dad, if she doesn't like them she doesn't like them. I don't think I do either."

"That's enough. Do your old Dad a favour, please. Will you eat them? For me?"

"Don't like them."

—Whole thing's like a dog's breakfast.

She had a voice. More than one. This one was the sharp one, that always spoke bluntly.

—Just leave it kids. I'll make you something nice.

—For goodness sake there's nothing wrong with the dinner.

—Dinner? Call that a dinner? Maybe if you paid more attention to what goes on in here you would have a chance of knowing what makes a decent dinner. First it was your studies and now it's your charity case. Y'see these? These wee shoulders are due a break. You kids want a banana sandwich? Maybe some chocolate milk?

They liked.

—You talk rubbish. C'mon, you can't let this go to waste. It's a sin to waste food.

—Who told you that? Your pal James? Holy bloody Joe that keeps you out.

—What do you mean PAL, pal?

—Well, if you hadn't spent so much time with him today maybe you'd've been back here in time to make something decent.

—How do you know how much time I spent with him?

—Well, I presume that's where you were, or were you somewhere else?

—You're cracked.

—Where are you going?

—Through to watch the news.

The news was the same. The same rubbish being talked. Same news in the morning, same news at dinner-time, same news at tea-time, just a little more horrifying at bedtime. Same news probably as all our yesterdays. Some people were going to be shot at midnight because they were handy at the time. Nothing new. Some people were losing their jobs. But somebody was making somebody a new job. Nothing new. Some royalty character was

138

kissing handicapped children who didn't know what their handicap was. Nothing new. Some new fined pop-star was poptificating about death and drugs and a dog had been taught to stand on one leg and bark out the football pools numbers for his master. The newscaster was smiling. Nothing new. The Greeks had always made the last play in the annual binge a comedy. Make em laugh, make em laugh, make em laugh, and fuck the serious stuff.

Scotland's news was on after the main news. Another last-gasp order saved a yard, but another may be closing. But the church was bringing up the evangelist of the inner city.

—Your programme's coming on.

Must be a real maddie tonight. Kids off to bed immediately.

"Goodnight Dad."

"Night night Dad."

"Night. Night. Now be good."

—Will you read them a story?

—Sure.

"C'mon Marion, Melanie, up we go."

It was quieter in the girls' room. Pink room. Pink for girls. Pink reinforcing the blues.

"Brushed your teeth?"

"UH UH."

"Marion?"

"Of course I have."

"Right, what story do you want?"

Melanie looked excited. "Tell us that one about the big strong man on his horse that comes to his sister's house."

"That house, that one Daddy, yeh, and the servants are all away, yeh, that one."

"Eh? Which one's that?"

"Of course you know it. He has a big strong horse and he . . ."

"Oh, that one. I know the one you mean. Right. Tuck in. Settle down."

Two faces. In a clean bed. Two faces on a window in the Social. Two faces. Waiting. Waiting for words that would spin a tale.

"Ready?"

139

> Is there anybody there, said the Traveller,
>   Knocking on the moonlit door;
> And his horse in the silence champ'd the grasses
>   Of the forest's ferny floor;
> And a bird flew up out of the turret
>   Above the Traveller's head;
> And he smote upon the door a second time,
>   Is there anybody there, he said?

And they were caught. Caught outside a big empty house of their own building; caught inside a big empty house; caught by the windows, caught by the stairs; travelling up the stairs, travelling down the stairs, looking for those phantom listeners. They were there somewhere. Little eyes were seeing them, knew they were there, and held their breath with the listening house as the big strong man with the moustache and the shiny brown horse rode away.

> Ay, they heard his foot upon the stirrup,
>   And the sound of iron on stone;
> And how the silence surged softly backward,
>   When the plunging hoofs were gone.

They saw and were silent. They saw. And wondered how they saw.

Marion spoke first. "We were getting about them in school today, Daddy."

"Were you? About who?"

"The Roundheads and the Cavaliers."

"Oh. Do you think Mr De La Mare's poem is about roundheads and cavaliers?"

"I told the teacher. She showed us a picture of a cavalier and I said it was really like the man in the poem Daddy told me."

"That was good. What did she say?"

"She said I had a good imagination."

"And so you have. And that's what the poem is all about, my love, imagination."

"Is it? Is it really?"

"Sure, and if you don't have a good imagination then you'll never be able to see anything clearly. You need imagination to see things for what they really are."

"Have I got a good imagination as well, Daddy?"

"'Course you have, darlin."

"But that poem frightens me a bit."

"Oh, there, there. Don't you worry about it. The man in the poem is a good man. My imagination tells me so. Anyway, I've got one for you.

Matthew, Mark, Luke and John
Bless the bed that you lie on
Four corners to your bed
Four angels round your head
One to watch and one to pray
And two to fly your cares away.

Goodnight."

"Never heard you say that one before, Daddy."

"Must be the company I'm keeping. Now sleep. There you go."

A kiss. A kiss. A wave. Lights out.

A soap on the box. An ethnic stereotype telling another ethnic stereotype the Message for the Month. Unemployment Makes You Depressed. Even Mrs Dale's Diary was more discreet. Now it had not only to be visual it had to be spelled out as well. I say, I'm worried about little Tony. He keeps locking himself in the outside loo. Do you think there's anything wrong? Na, just all that new bran kinda grub he's been eatin. Don't fret my love.

There was space on the settee. No cuddling up. One posted at each corner. Come out fighting and may the best one win. Correction. Come out fighting and may the best person win. Mary would win. In the short of it, or in the long of it. Mary would win.

Coconut bars were fabulous to eat if you could afford to fly to the West Indies to eat them where there was only Cap'n Morgan's treasure and some perverted Ben Gunn who wouldn't come out the bushes but was obviously peering at you through a video camera.

—What time did you get back at?

—I told you.

—What was it you were doing? Did you have to stay with him all day?

—There's no fixed hours on this job. Anyway, I just had a wee talk with the guy and then Theresa and I took him . . .

—Who's Theresa?

—The landlady. I told you.

—You never told me her name was Theresa.

—All right. Her name's Theresa Kipple. Is it important?

—And were you with her as well, all day?

—For goodness sake, the woman was good enough to take us out and get James some stuff cheap.

—Some stuff? What kind of stuff? Could you not have gotten it off that money those people gave you?

—I've hardly any of that left. I gave you some towards the electricity, didn't I?

—Oh, big deal. I'm bloody sure that never finished it. What did you do all day then?

—Well, first we went to an auction rooms and then we went up the Lane.

—Up the Lane? Whose idea was that?

                                               Theresa Kipple

—Nobody's in particular. We just knew we'd get the stuff there.

                                         Theresa Kipple knew

—Thought you hated that place? Funny person goes to shop up the Lane with . . .

                                   Funny Funny Mysterious

—Maybe.

                                   Red hair tied too high

—Funny you to go along with her.

—Aye.

                                   No problems laughs even

Other ethnics were on; yabbering away at one another and Dave Parks, non-ethnic, was definitely feeling élitist. But élitism is sometimes inspired by small things. If Mary was watching this it was because it needed no effort. Perhaps washing the dishes would be humbling and be atonement, penitential. James having an effect upon the vocabulary. Help to sook in.

—What do you want done with this meat?

—Keep it. Put it in the fridge. It'll do for sandwiches in the morning.

Meat put away. Table cleared. Dishes washed. Dishes stacked. Might as well dry them as well. Really sookin in. Put away. News was on. The same. Only longer and worse.

142

                              Theresa Kipple silk and serpent
Everybody dying at midnight. That would be news. That is the
news.

                              Handsome woman in her day
Children were starving in Africa. That's news. Lantern slides
and a penny for the black babies. All starving. And it couldn't be
helped. Give a penny for the black babies. Starvation. The white
man's disease. Somebody else's burden. Run a mile from the black
babies. That dog was on again. Scotland's news came and went.
                              Green eyes Theresa Kipple
Theresa Kipple Theresa Kipple Tessie Theresa Kipple. Still
handsome.
—When are you giving that car back?
—I don't know, end of the week, I suppose. I might as well try
and hold on to it as long as possible in case something happens to
James.
—Is something likely to?
—I don't know. You never know, something might.
—Are you figurin on going back there? To that place?
—I don't know, aye, maybe, how can I tell? Look, what is this?
—You mean, you're going back to see him?
                              see Theresa Kipple Theresa Kipple
—I might. Probably. Aye. Give it a rest, will you?
—Will the landlady not mind you running in and out all the time?
—I don't know. Too bad if she does.
—Don't think she will somehow, do you? Is she good looking?
                              Handsome
—You're talking rubbish, do you know that?
—Think so? You forget I've been married to you for seventeen
years. And right now you're hardly with me. You're hardly in this
room.
—For pete sake. I've got a lot on just now, right at this moment.
This guy James, the car to go back, Bellesmyre on Monday. And
now I've got to listen to this.
—You don't have to listen to it.
—You're bloomin right I don't. I'm away out for a walk.
—To the pub you mean. Down with the rest of the Happy Harrys.

—Where else? Theresa Kipple's maybe?

Theresa Kipple

—Many a true word.

THERESA KIPPLE

—Ah, piss off!

A slamming door; sound that frustrated and satisfied and frightened all at one and the same time. Hardly anybody on the streets. The pub's sign all lit up. Looked kind of welcoming. Not a bad crowd in for mid-week. Pat and Tommy. In their corner. Playing chess. Jimmy sitting on their far side. *Deja vu.* Or routine and habit. Another time, same place, same people, same talk. Social work? Social control you mean. Victorian charity on the rates. Rabble dousers. Dave Parks. Dave Parks was for changing his mind. The pub door didn't slam. It just swung. Walking was better for you anyway. Strong drink is an abomination to the Lord. Is that right James?

Theresa

"What you thinking about, big man?"

"Eh? Oh, it's yourself, Fred. I never saw you there. Aw, I'm afraid I was away in another world there."

"Aye. I noticed. Well, are you coming or going? You for a jug?"

"Thanks, but I was just going up the road, actually. I've left her in herself. I just came out for a breath of air, know what I mean?"

"I know what you're saying. C'mon, have a wee half. That'll sort you out. It's that College stuff, ye know. See when I heard you were off to the College, I thought, aye, aye, there's another good man gone, off to get the napper injection."

"Oh, give us a break. You sound as bad as that lot in there."

"Who? Oh, your mates? Revolutionaries on flat arses now, my son. Factory's away sure. They've no audience whatsoever now, my man. You were the best o the lot o them. If you'd still been in that factory we might have had a fight. That's the way it goes, son. Don't worry about it. C'mon, have a half on Freddie. I had a wee turn at the horses the day."

"Ach, it's OK Fred. Maybe some other time. I'd better get up this road."

"Fair enough son. Please yourself. It's there if you want it."

"I know, Fred, thanks, but I'd better away and keep Mary sweet. See you Freddie."

"See you big man."

The best of the lot o them. Dave Parks. What Dave Parks? That Dave Parks. Him in the memory. Just a memory. Brave days. Good days. Bygone days. Unless . . .

"Hey, Davie boy. Davie."

On the decorative wall outside the pub. Spotlit by the pub sign. Freddie. For your entertainment. Freddie. Shoes flashing, feet and legs kicking, spinning on top of the wall.

"D'ye mind this yin, Davie boy? Follow the Yellow Brick Road, Follow the Yellow Brick Road: follow follow follow follow, follow the Yellow Brick Road, d'ye mind it?"

"Sure; that told them. Now watch you don't fall."

"Same goes for you son. Same goes for you."

****

The dishes were washed up; the sinktops cleared; the table wiped; the draining board stacked, to drip dry; cloth wrung out, rinsed, put in its spot, kids in bed and it was time for the Film on Saturday. FILM on SATURDAY, THE Film on Saturday. As if it was something special. Specially repeated. This one was. Special. This one was being shown in tribute to the lead actor who had just died a week ago. He's dead. Oh dear. What have we got in the stock? Put it on. Save the new stuff for later. Pay the man tribute. Why don't they relaunch the QE II every time one of the welders snuffs it? Too many welders maybe. Could at least put it in the papers.

"Jimmy McCracken, the welder famed for his main runs in the lower bulkheads of the Queens, passed away in his sleep last night. He had been troubled for some time with Welder's lung. The Queen Elizabeth was the most famous of the liners Jimmy worked on, but during a working life spanning some fifty-two years, Jimmy was known to have performed some miraculous runs in cramped, cold conditions, often without the benefit of safety equipment or additional bonuses, on ships of various sizes and shapes. In his later years Jimmy campaigned against the use of uncertificated welders. Of course, this was never held against him by his employers. Due to falling orders there were increasing gaps of time between jobs for Jimmy, but whenever he was needed he answered the call. A memorial service for Jimmy will be held in the bar of The Black Man's on Friday next."

"You watching this?"

"Not really. Thing's ancient."

"Saturday's always rubbish. There's nothing on the other sides either."

"What have we got for drinking?"

"Nothing. The last of the Martini went yesterday."

"Oh."

"For goodness sake cheer up. For the last couple of days you've been like a bear with a sore head. The film is bad enough without you moping about with a face like a Hammer picture."

"Sorry. Fancy the radio? There might be a play on."

"Ach, can we not just leave this? There's a programme on after it I want to see."

"What is it?"

"Can't remember. But I remember looking at the paper and saying I fancy that."

"Oh, come off it."

"Look, you wait till you start work. You'll be glad just to get a chance to sit down and let it wash all over you. I know this stuff's rubbish, but right now it's about all my wee brain is ready for. OK?"

"Aye, right."

—Aye, bloody right. Maybe if you'd do a wee bit more around here during the week I wouldn't be so bloody tired. Lift a Hoover and you want a bloody medal.

"Don't start that again. We'll watch it. Right? We'll watch it."

—Oh, thanks very much. That's very good of you. You'll let us watch it. You sure your superior brain will allow you to watch this stuff?

"For pete's sake, if you don't stop yakking it'll be finished."

—Yakking? Who's yakking? I'm just telling you. For heaven's sake, all I wanted was a quiet night with the television and you start. Is it a crime or something to be able to watch rubbish and accept it for what it is? It's just a simple wee movie.

—Aye, simple's the word.

—Oh and you're that clever, eh? The working-class intellectual speaks. Christ, you're only a Social Worker.

—Mary. Oh, I'm going out.

—Where you going? Thought the pub was losing its attractions?

—I'm going to take that car back.

—On a Saturday night? This is Saturday. They might not be in on a Saturday night.

—We're in.

—Correction buster. I'm in.

—And they just might be. If they're watching this crap they'll be glad of the break.

—Ach, please your bloomin self, you. You always do anyway. Will you bring some milk in if you can get it?

—Can you not get some off the van?

—Very good. OK. Off you go. And see if they'll bloody keep you. The sooner you start work the better. You walk about here bored out of your genius and we have to suffer. Away and take your long face elsewhere. But you better not be late back here.

"I'm away then."

—Cheeri-bloody-o.

***

Saturday night at 24 MacNaughten was obviously a quiet affair. The dog's bark intervened between Dave Parks in the silence outside and whatever whoever was in the house. A spotlight in the roof of the porch shone down. A wooden slat in the door was slid open, closed. Florence opened the door.

"Come in, please."

Piano music rumbling somewhere in the keys of the lower area was being played, but it stopped. The brothers Smith were in the library. Both dressed in black dinner suits. Little Adam had spun his seat and was looking. Robin was looking up from poking the fire. No one was saying anything. Looking at a Dave Parks not too sure where to look. Looking, saying nothing, manufacturing that gap which said: I/We would rather you hadn't come. Silent looking loudly heard. Robin spoke.

"Ah, Mr Parks. Do come in. Just passing, were you?"

"I brought your car back, actually."

"Ah. The car. Yes. The car. Serve you well, did it?"

"Aye, yes, aye, it did. Good car that."

"Never driven it myself. Have to take your word there. Care for a whisky?"

"Don't mind."

"Good."

Little brother marooned in his armchair looked like a snooker player waiting his turn. Tips of a high wing collar fled out from above a velvet, lilac-coloured bow-tie. This one wasn't saying anything as yet, but he had begun to swivel his throne this way and that way and this way and that, watching his brother, watching Dave Parks, watching his brother watching Dave Parks, watching Dave Parks watching the two watching. The whisky was handed over. But no seat was on offer to Dave Parks.

"Cheers, Mr Parks."

"Cheers."

The whisky was most acceptable.

"Here's the keys."

"Thank you. Just place them on the table there. Thank you."

No word of James here. No word from an interested mouth came tripping to enquire. James. Something outside of here now. Something the dog would bark at. The dog had barked at Dave Parks. Dave Parks had put James on the outside. Where people get barked at.

"James is OK."

"Fine. Fine. Excellent."

And now the chair was away.

"Foolish man's fine, foolish man's fine, where's the skinny calf, where's the skinny calf?"

"Might as well give you my bill then."

"Might as well indeed, Mr Parks. Might as well indeed."

"It's a hundred and fifty-five. Expenses as well."

"Then one hundred and fifty-five it is."

A cheque book and pen was brought out from the inside pocket of the jacket. The book was balanced on one knee, flipped open; cheque written, signed, torn off. The cheque was being held out by an arm and hand that was not going to stretch itself. Dave Parks was to go for it. Dave Parks went for it. For this they had to pay.

"Don't you want to know where James is, who he's with, how he is, how he's living?"

"We already know how he is, Mr Parks. You told us."

"He's a fool, that's how he is, a fool."

People could be strangled with lilac velvet ties.

"Forgive us, Mr Parks, we're detaining you. No doubt you want your own car, to be away. Forgive me."

Robin Smith got up. Adam jumped up out of his chair and followed as Robin led, led along the hall to the door out. Florence emerged from a door to the side but stepped back in and closed it. Adam jumped up and pulled a deerstalker from a hook on the coatstand and followed out onto the driveway. Robin led on round to the garage.

"Nice moon, Mr Parks, eh?"

"Yeh, aye, yes, I suppose it is. Night for the werewolves, I suppose, vampires and that sort, I suppose."

"Bloodsuckers do you mean, Mr Parks? I think you'll find that nowadays such species operate on a twenty-four hour basis."

Adam ran to the outer edge of the driveway where it was darker.

"I am the Wolf of Badenoch, I am the Wolf of Badenoch, I am the Wolf of Badenoch."

The garage door was opened and there she was: the faithful old rust bucket. Robin took the keys from a hook by the door.

"*Et voila*, Mr Parks."

It was over. Over for them. Paid their money. James was off. They were free of a nuisance. And maybe Dave Parks had inherited one. No way. One hundred and fifty-five pounds did not buy a transfer of responsibility. Responsibility. Helping somebody even for cash did not mean taking on future responsibility. James would just have to get along like the rest. The rest. Dave Parks speaking of the rest. Dave Parks outside the rest. Two years at a daft College and a promise of the settled future and Dave Parks talks about The Rest. But what could be done for James had been done. He would get his Social. He had a roof; two good new pair of shoes. And a bag of messages. After tonight James was on his own. In the system. After tonight. After tonight.

Theresa Kipple

Robin's sentinel, the wolf, made a howl. Holding his arms up to form paws and now he was galloping over. And stopping. Standing between the car and Dave Parks. Pixie face looking up into the face of Dave Parks. And it howled. Howled. And quit howling. Wolfman Adam cupped a hand behind his ear. Listening. And it was quiet.

Quiet. From inside the house a clock could just be heard chiming. The paws began to claw the air.

"Hear it not, David Parks, hear it not, David Parks, hear it not, David Parks."

"I really must try and keep him inside during the full moon."

"Aye, yes, I think so. Bit of a character your brother, I think."

"He most certainly is, Mr Parks, he most certainly is."

The seat in the car was cold. The whine came. The engine was cold. Whine again. Trying hard. Whine again. Trying hard but getting weaker. A whine. A weak whine. Weaker. A click. Nothing. No power. Flattened. Dead.

"Trouble, Mr Parks?"

"Battery's done."

"I see, mmm."

"Probably start with a shove."

"Ah, mmm."

"Either that or a jump start."

"A what?"

"A jump start. I've got leads in the back here."

"A jump start."

Dave leaned over into the back, rummled about, found the leads.

"See these things. I fix these dragon clips onto the battery of your car and these ones on the other end onto mine. The strength from your battery goes through my weak one and bob's your uncle."

"Sounds complicated."

"It's really quite easy."

"I think we'd prefer to give you a push."

"Please yourself. Suppose that's the quickest way over the problem."

"Adam, come round the back here. We are going to give Mr Parks a shove."

The brothers shoved. The car was moving. Out into the driveway; now into second gear, now moving, down the driveway, slight slope picking up speed, exhaust splutter, exhaust rattle, the engine caught and Dave Parks was away out into the street. In the rearview mirror there was Robin dusting his hands. Adam was waving his deerstalker.

***

Drive. Drive Dave Parks drive on. Where? Upwards? Onwards? Homewards? No. Forever. Drive. Theresa Kipple. Is James all right? Just passing. Must see. Must know. Dave Parks Theresa Kipple. Laura Kipple James. Mary watching the TV. Darkened living-room. Bright TV. Ach. Bright multi-coloured serpentine gowns. A face that laughs. Drive on Dave Parks. Yellow emptying streets. Lollipop commanding lights. Would-be expert drunk driver; swerving. Better get off the road. They'll stop him for sure. Bottom of the hill. Motorway or City? Always the City. Magnet City. Never any question. Newtown blues and the City was never the same. Because not in it Dave Parks. Dave Parks outside observer of the City's wounded. In Bellesmyre near Theresa Kipple. Would she mind? Would she? Theresa Kipple waiting. Waiting. Just passing thought I'd drop by. See how James is. That right? Come in. No one in maybe. Theresa Kipple in a darkened living-room with spray colour TV and Mary's in a darkened living-room with the TV but that's not the same. Not the same room. Not the same woman. Too tired to laugh. Mary's Mary. Theresa Kipple is who? Laura's sister. Crippled Laura in a darkened living-room with a sister that painted her toes but never went anywhere. Laura would be in. She couldn't go anywhere. Obviously been hawkers. Obviously been around. How obviously. Just something. Been around. What does that mean? Knows the score? The street score. The street music. There's a macaroon bar sung to the music of Puccini. Everything the five-pence. Bizarre street cantors selling and singing out. Never too young to know the score. Five nothing. Goals between the lamp-posts. Let me kick it Theresa Kipple. The polis are comin. Pick up your bundle and run. Will they take me away? I just came here because my Mammy said I needed a vest. Dave Parks get a grip. Dave Parks. What is Dave Parks doing. Fleeing maybe. Fleeing from boredom or dirty vests and sharp questions of philosophy and smoke and halfs and pints and talk of football kings and Mary doesn't talk about football somebody does maybe the weans that'll be right so who likes football who likes candy there's a macaroon bar chewing gum's the tenpence Dave Parks used to talk about football but not now football's for the punter. What's a punter? Betting man. A mug punter. Kicked as hard as the balls. Kicked in the balls. The punters are great. The punters get their factories shut and who's to say there's no balls left. Dave Parks maybe. Dave Parks driving towards Theresa Kipple. Fuck factories. Join the white collar brigade. Use the brains. Administrate. Adjudicate at ground level. Take the pay and get on your way. Even football people use administrators and they have it easy. EEEEEEEZy. Fuck that getting your hands dirty. No more Davie Parks. Social Work will do nicely. Save their souls with a smiling face and show them how. Show them how what? How it works? How to stand up? How to walk? Give them a crutch. Give them a wheeelchair. Give them a community bus. But don't give them a rifle. Just show them how to operate their lives within the system come to us for help come to us for advice come to us for money and coupons come to us and grab a gallon of *gemeinschaft* and we'll show you how to cope nicely with the DHSS and the drink and the drugs and the polis and the rentman and the electricity man and the polis and the sheriff's officer and the warrant sale and the gas man and the tickman and the insurance man and the courts but don't ask us to help you help yourself unless you're elderly and want the meals on wheels and maybe we'll get you a run out when it's sunny and this is where you're going Dave Parks. Group meetings on someone's life and we've found the answer. Hallelujah loo yah. Loo. And if your man hits you again we'll get him jailed. We don't really want to and Dave Parks is a part of this and knows the score nothing can save them but themselves. Them but themselves. Us but Usselves. Dave Parks but Dave Parks. Us. All very well Dave Parks. Never Dave Parks. Melanie Parks Marion Parks. Years to go yet. They're awful young and Dave Parks is frightened. Frightened of the future that waits and the revolution that waits and waits and waits. But Dave Parks will be an old man and man and Melanie and Marion cannot live by bread alone needs the Tuna and the Lasagne and can only get it where people sell it people don't give it away. Dave Parks driving. Dave Parks running. Driving. Sitting up straight and driving tired in the City so forget that stuff just doing a job and getting a wage. Salary. Getting a salary. Maybe you can do a bit of educating Dave Parks. Take a group to the theatre Dave Parks. Educate. You know their lives same as your own used to be and Theresa Kipple used to be so you know what's what what's what what is it street credibility street cred. Street credit. Tick. Tick tock never goes off. Never blows up. You can't let people wallow in the muck and starve or whatever. Must help them. Improve them. Victorians taught the women embroidery. *Très gentile*. Immiseration thesis. Let them eat nothing and then they'll revolt. They. They. They. Dave Parks not even started yet and they're a They. Who the fuck is They? Dave Parks is They. I am They. Dave Parks is They. They am I. They is Dave Parks. They is we. But Melanie Parks and Marion Parks not to forget Mary turn around here and turn right into the cul-de-sac. One light on low-down. Leave the car and night City driving that makes for thought.

Walking now and the air is fresh. Even here. Tramp on the bench rising up, settling down, brouhahaing. And spitting.

"Hello, I was just . . ."

"Come in." She was going to her own door. Waving an arm in a flounce of silk. "He's in here."

Inside the room the lights were bright and there was no television on. The room was larger than remembered. In a corner James was kneeling on the floor at the feet of Laura. Her face was overmade up. She was dressed in a white shiny blouse with ruffles at the wrists. On her lap was a book. A Book. THE Book. The Holy Book. Christ. James ceased his deliberations and spoke unto David, saying: David.

And David answered unto him, saying: Hello, James, I was just passing through and thought I'd stop off and see how you were doing, this being your first Saturday night sort of style.

"Most decent of you, sir. Most decent. But Saturday nights are fine nights. Saturday nights are the nights we prepare for the day of the Lord. Is that correct, Laura?"

Laura smiled, nodded, and waved hello.

"Well, as long as you're happy."

Laura giggled. The red on her cheeks was not the make-up. Probably drink. A whisky tumbler sat on the carpet at James's knee. At Laura's feet. A maroon pair of patent shoes with plastic gold leaf creeping over the front. Throw nothing away. James put his head back into the good book.

"Would you like a drink, Dave?" Theresa asking.

"Eh? Oh. No. No thanks."

"Sure? You look a bit tense. You in a hurry?"

"No. Not really."

"Well, sit down. These two are off on a wee tuppenny thing. Suits them but I'm left talking to the walls."

"Hello, walls."

"Pardon?"

"It's a song: Hello, walls, I wanna talk, to you, a while."

"That's right. I think I've heard it before. Sit down."

"OK."

Theresa moved over and selected a decanter from a silver tray set on a dark heavy wood sideboard. Bare feet toes painted. Cherry red. Cherry ripe.

"Sure you don't want something?"

"Well, if I'm stopping, just a wee whisky, thanks. Drown it in water if you don't mind."

"Glad to."

James had found the thought for the evening and Laura looked pleased at the choice. Matthew Chapter Seven. James began to read and Laura leaned forward to listen and Dave Parks was watching Theresa Kipple.

"Judge not that ye be not judged."

"Enough water in it for you?"

"That looks fine, thanks."

Theresa's easy chair was drawn up close. Close. Close enough to smell her.

"Cheers."

"Cheers."

"Or what man there is of you, whom if his son ask bread, will he give him a stone?"

Humans have got to eat, right enough.

"You were just passing then?"

"Or if he ask a fish will he give him a serpent?"

"Well, sort of."

"He seems to be good for my sister. He fair cheers her up when he starts. Likes the whisky but."

"Aye. He's a bit of a boy altogether."

"Enter ye in at the strait gate: for wide is the gate, and broad is the way, that leadeth to destruction, and many there be that go in thereat."

"How did you come to know him again? Was it through your Social Work?"

"Well, I was really doing it for his relations, trying to keep him right."

"Beware of the prophets which come to you in sheep's clothing, but inwardly they are ravening wolves."

"Well, he's OK now, so you can talk to me. I've run out of things to say to the wallpaper."

"I thought I was. Talking to you."

"Well, let's start again. What's the weather like outside?"

"Fine. I think. Fine. Good enough for an old tramp to be sitting out on the bench coughing at the moon. Either that or he was trying to get a moontan."

"Wherefore by their fruits ye shall know them."

"That poor man's been coming here for donkey's. Woe betide anybody that tries to steal his spot. I think he used to live in the building that stood there at one time. Some of those in the newer flats tried to get him shifted, but he keeps coming back."

"Therefore whosoever heareth these sayings of mine, and doeth them, I will liken him unto a wise man that builds his house upon a rock."

Laura clapped her hands. "Don't say it, don't say it."

James jumped up. "I know what you are going to say, my fair pucelle." James knelt down again. "Ready? Ready? Are you ready?"

His hands were out, fingertips touching, thumbs touching, forming a triangle. Laura copied. They began to sing; singing the song, making their hands move as the wise man built his house upon the rock, house upon the rock, and the rains came tumbling down. The rains came down and the house stood still, the house stood still; and the rains came tumbling down. The foolish man had a different estate agent. Or the wise man kept the information to himself. Or maybe the foolish man didn't listen; the rains came down and his house fell down. Laura clattered the sides of her wheelchair as the rains came down, and his house fell down, his house fell down.

"They're enjoying themselves anyway."

Theresa.

"Sounds like it."

"Did you ever get any of that at school?"

"I think so. Maybe. I know whenever I hear these things they ring bells."

"Warning bells?"

"Well, if I was Wimpey, I think I'd pay attention to that one, Theresa."

Theresa was laughing. Dave Parks had made Theresa laugh. James and Laura were laughing and applauding each other and this whisky had not been drowned in water. James was getting to his feet.

"Madame Theresa, may I avail myself of some more of your delicious whisky?"

"Help yourself."

"And you Laura? Shall I make you another of the same?"

Laura giggled and nodded and blew a kiss. Someone was knocking on the living-room door. Theresa rose to answer the knock. James was fixing the drinks and smiling at something in his head. Away somewhere. Two-glass trip to the Holy Land. Someone was being invited in. It was Mr O'Brien, and his hat and his coat; and another man dressed in bluish flannels and a blue blouson-type jacket that was very popular with middle-aged men this year. The smaller man wore spectacles. O'Brien came in; standing just inside the door, looking shy, fingers clasping into the handles of a white plastic carrier bag which he bounced like a ball against his knees. Theresa took him by the elbow and brought him right in. The smaller man followed, waving at Laura and grinning. Laura waved back but turned her attention back to James, looking up him, smiling at him as he handed her down her drink. James took a swig of his drink and picked up the book for another prowl through the pages. He was flicking again.

"You've never met this man, Mr O'Brien. This is James's friend, Dave."

O'Brien stretched his lips. That was it. Theresa continued.

"Have you ever met Mr Manley, Dave? He's one of mine. Number four. Peter Manley, Dave Parks."

"How do you do?"

"Dave."

Chairs were produced from their places at the dining table. The O'Brien man put his bag of booze on the sideboard as if he'd done it before. Theresa was pouring drinks for them without asking them anything. As if she'd done it before. This had the looks of a Saturday night ritual. Manley spoke.

"Thought we'd pop in and see how you and Laura were, Theresa. Just passing the door, so to speak."

"Nothing doing in the pub, is that what you mean?"

"Ah, Theresa, are we like that? Don't be like that."

Theresa passed their drinks to them, sat down, pulling her gown around her. She sipped on her drink. Manley turned his attention on Dave Parks.

"You a pal o the big minister's, eh? Some boy him, is he no?" The man called Peter did not wait for an answer. He swivelled to face James. "What you giving it the night, big man? Hallelujah, I'm a bum. Do you know that one? You soon will, by the way."

James only lifted his glass in acknowledgement. Manley turned back round, but wanted to talk on. "Don't know where you get us from, Theresa. Seems a-bloody-mazin a fine crop like us under the same roof. How ye doin anyway? Listen, did ye hear on the radio this mornin about the man that was . . ."

"Is this another one of your jokes?"

"Aw, ye'll like this joke, Theresa, it's about, it's clean, by the way, clean as Persil, that right O'Brien, clean as Persil?"

"Certainly."

"Well, anyway . . ."

"Peter, I don't think I want to hear it. Your jokes take too long. They go on forever and ever and then a bit and even then you're lucky to get a laugh."

"Ah, you're cruel, Theresa, but please yourself. What's your game, Dave?"

"I'm a Social Worker."

"D'ye hear that, O'Brien? A Social Worker. Works the Social."

"Sure. Certainly. That's a thing to be doin."

"What do you do, Pete?"

"Me? I'm a fitter. Or I used to be a fitter. Just at this minute I go round fixin up the video machines if they go wonky."

"Thought they were all electronics and stuff?"

"Ach. They gave me a wee training course on them. Anyway, they don't break down much, so most of the time I'm only emptying the money out of them."

"Where did you work before?"

"Ach. You name it, I worked in it. Albion, Brown's, Linwood, Singer's, Caterpillar, you name it. If it had a machine in it, I worked in it. Never mind this crack, pass us up a can will ye?"

Theresa passed Manley over a drink via Dave Parks, then one to O'Brien. Manley straightened up, sipped it, and started off again.

"So, how y'doin, Theresa? Never seen much o you this week. Never heard much of the old Madame Butterfly stuff. Wondered where you were when we never seen you flittin about."

"I'm scarcely a butterfly."

"Ah, well, a wee bird then. Ahha, a wee bird, get it, a wee bird."

He slapped his thighs and sipped at his glass and peered with his eyes to see what or who would be next. The look of the fox. This restless man turned his head again. Laura and James were under consideration now, something to keep the mouth going with maybe. But James was reading something in a quiet voice. Quiet voices get respect. Laura's eyes were wide as she looked into the face of her reader.

"This is a fine whisky," O'Brien was saying.

Now someone was was knocking at the outside door. Knocking hard.

"Want me to get it, Theresa?" asked Manley.

"No thanks, I can manage. Don't want you frightening people away."

"Ah, you're cruel, Theresa, you're cruel."

Theresa left the room. Manley winked over at Dave Parks.

"Still no a bad bit o stuff, eh? Still no bad yet. She's been a cracker, I think."

Voices could be heard. A man's. A woman's. Theresa was bringing them in. It was Annie. The woman Annie from the market. She was already taking her coat off. The man behind her was not wearing one. Some sporting logo had begun to peel from his yellow woollen pullover. He held a box of something between his two hands, twiddling with it, turning it. Annie threw her coat on the table, turned and removed the box from the man's hands. The box was going to Laura.

"Here, Laura hen, I've brought you a wee sweetie."

Laura was being kissed and Laura was holding on. Annie straightened up.

"Christ, is it you, goodie two-shoes? Broke my heart charging you that price for them, you know. They fit you OK?"

"A treat, my dear lady, a treat."

"Dear? Bloody cheap you mean." James only nodded. Annie faced into the centre of the room. "Christ, you've enough men here anyway, Tessie. D'you want another one? Bert. For Christ sake, sit on your bum. You're like death on a low peep there. You'd better sit, cos I'm no for leavin for a while."

Pete Manley fetched Bert a chair. Bert sat down, trying to properly place a carrier bag between his feet. The bag collapsed. Cans rolled out. The Bert's face was reddening. O'Brien came over, lifted the bag, the cans, and placed them with the other cargo on the sideboard.

"O'Brien," called Theresa. "A large rum and coke, and Bert takes a wee shandy."

"Certainly."

Two women met in the centre of the room. They hugged. Separated. Hugged again.

"Annie. You don't know how good it is to see you."

Even James had stopped his flicking to watch as the women studied each other.

"Ach, rubbish, rubbish."

They hugged, separated. "Oh, Annie."

"That's enough o that. Christ, Tessie, where's the music? Is this a wake or something?"

"Chance would be a fine thing," said O'Brien.

Annie put an arm round Theresa's waist. Together they moved down the room. Annie was looking at Dave Parks. "You here? Don't tell me you're moving in here as well?"

"No. No. As the man says: chance would be a fine thing. How y'doin?"

"Not bad at all, can't complain. C'mon, Tessie, get some music on here."

Theresa freed herself and crossed over to a stack unit in the corner. From the bottom she pulled out a few long-playing records. O'Brien gave Annie and Bert their drinks.

"Were you anywhere before you came up?" asked Theresa.

"We were at the golf club, but it's the same old faces every week, so, I don't know, I just said to Bert, come on, I know where we're going. So, here we are."

"And I'm really pleased to see you, Annie."

"Cut the cackle. Where's the music?"

Theresa looked up from the records. "Here's one. Peter, could you go and get Bert a chair from the kitchen?"

"Sure thing. Right away. No problem. Here, Bert, you take this one. I'll get one."

Bert sat down and Manley left to fetch another chair. James had moved round to the side of Laura's wheelchair. He was kneeling and reading the words into her ear. Laura was giggling and kept putting her hand up and touching herself upon the ear.

"If you don't like this one, just tell me."

"Oh, just play it. Anything. As long as it makes a noise."

The arm was lowered and the record made scratchy noises before it hit music. It was sixties rock. The group and the song sounded familiar. Dave Parks knew them. A Scottish group. They went to London. Sticky Fingers or something.

"That's better," said Annie, "puts a bit of atmosphere into the proceedings."

"Theresa, I think I'd better get going. I just came up to see James."

Theresa made no answer. But Annie's hand came to grip the shoulder of Dave Parks.

"Sit where you are. For goodness sake relax. You look awful intense. I don't think I've seen you smile since I came in here. Give us your patter."

Dave Parks looked to Theresa. Theresa shrugged her shoulders somewhere inside that gown.

"Well, it's just . . ."

"Whisky you were drinking, wasn't it?" asked O'Brien, handing down a tumbler with whisky in it. Half full. The hand was up and took it and Dave Parks began to laugh.

Pete Manley shoved the door open with the leg of the chair he was carrying. Behind him came Bandy carrying another chair.

"That's it, you can lock up your drink now," said O'Brien.

Bandy smiled all round, but the smile stopped at Dave Parks. Bandy moved to the sideboard immediately after the chair reached the deck. A drink was poured and a can lifted. Bandy settled himself in his chair beside Bert. Bert adjusted his chair to give him more room. Laura was giggling loudly and James was leaning even closer to her ear. The music had slowed. Now the singer was sixteen and running the gamut of all human emotion because his girl had turned out her bedroom light while he was sitting in a tree outside her house playing lovesongs to her on his saxophone.

"That's a good song that," said Annie. Pete Manley was selected. "Right you, c'mon, DANCE."

Pete Manley gulped some drink down, stood up, patted his hair, flicked up his collar and was ready. Annie led him to the floor space between the hemi-cycle of chairs and the table. They danced. They danced close and Annie sung, mimed the song. Annie broke away.

"Right, you two, DANCE."

Theresa Kipple's hand was placed into the hand of Dave Parks. And they were standing up and coming close, fitting together; dancing. Dancing round as the singer sighed; dancing round avoiding the eyes; dancing round and seeing the eyes. Not seeing James; not seeing Laura, not seeing Bert, O'Brien or Bandy. Dancing. Dancing round dancing silent but dancer to dancer loudly speaking. Dave Parks was speaking to Theresa Kipple. Dancing round and the music stopped. Music stopped and dancing round. More music that was too fast but the slow dancing round went on. Dance warmth smell smile: Theresa Kipple.

" Right. Right. That's enough, you pair. The polis'll be in and put you in the jail. Behave yourselves."

Annie moved to the hi-fi. She flicked through the records to make another choice. "Don't have much choice here, Tessie. We'll try this."

Some Latin American music began. Annie held out her arms to O'Brien: "C'mon, you."

"You have to be joking, Mrs. I've not just got two left feet, I've got three. Sure, our family has always been used as the model for the badges for the Isle of Man."

"For Christ sake, what a lot. It'll need to be you Bert. C'mon."

Bert and Annie began to dance a cha cha cha. They did the cha cha, Bert was a dancer, sliding his shiny shoes, skipping his feet in time. Bert could dance some. He was laughing, enjoying himself. Exhibition stuff. The brass music from South America ended. Next up was a waltz. Pete Manley looked as if he was coming for Theresa.

"Shall we try again, Theresa?" Dave asked.

"Don't mind, if you don't."

Manley eased himself down again. Bert and Annie were putting on the style. Theresa came closer. Laura was giggling. At James. James was getting up. James was grasping Laura's wheelchair, pushing it into the dance area, pushing it ahead of himself, spinning himself round, catching it, pulling it back on its wheels until Laura squealed. Spinning with it. Bert and Annie stopped. Theresa stopped. James carried on and Laura carried on with him. Her arms were outstretched as though holding a partner, eyes closed as though enjoying holding a partner. And James did the waltz, waltzing and waltzing, and room was made for the couple on the floor. Annie held up an imaginary microphone.

"Laura's gown is made of the silk from a zillion silkworms doing two nights and a Sunday. Her skirt is made of kumgarra wool bought specially in the Marks and Spencers of the High Street in Tibet. Laura sat up all last night sewing the sixty-thousand sequins on by hand, and now she's just about flaked out."

Laura was keeping her eyes closed, but she was laughing with all of her face. Bert threw her a rose from a vase on the table, but it missed and fell on the floor.

"Laura's partner is, who is he anyway? What's his name again?"

James was pushing and twirling and hauling and spinning and sweating. Beads of sweat caught the light as they formed and ran down leaving trails on a red face. The music stopped. James fell on one knee, swept an imaginary hat off in imaginary cavalier fashion and bowed his head in front of Laura. His voice boomed.

> "How fair and pleasant you are,
>   O love, my love, delectable maiden,
>   You stand like the palm tree
>   Your breasts like grapes a-cluster."

Manley jumped up. "That's enough o that. That's enough. That's no way to talk in front of a woman. She's a cripple, you know. That's dirty talk."

No one spoke and Laura stopped laughing. James rose, turned to face Manley.

"My lady Laura is perhaps crippled in the legs, sir, but that is infinitely preferable to being crippled in the mind."

"What you saying? You saying I'm daft or somethin? You must fancy yourself."

Annie came forward. "Right, that's enough, you two, settle down. Sit on your arse you. All he meant was that he would like to eat her. C'mon, that's it. The pair o ye."

James returned himself and Laura to their corner. Manley sat down in his place. Bandy made some kind of cackle and lifted another can from the sideboard. O'Brien was gathering glasses and giving everybody a refill and Dave Parks was deciding that it would be best to stay on for a bit in case this flared up again and

James needed help. Or Theresa. Annie was speaking.

"Your music's not up to much, Tessie. I think we'll need to have a song. Hey, Paddy, give us over one of those ginger bottles."

'Brien passed over an empty lemonade bottle. Annie leaned forward and spun it. The bottle spun and spun and spun slower and was going to stop spinning and point to Manley, but Annie tapped it with her foot and it pointed to O'Brien.

"Heavens, I'm no singer."

"SING."

O'Brien began to sing. The man was a clear tenor. He sang of living thousands of miles away from the lough where the swans turned red in a summer's evening and danced and slipped and struggled on the ice of the lough as they flew away for the winter. But the swans always got back.

Next on was Annie herself. She sang a country and western song about someone pawning their heart and throwing away the ticket in the wind so the pledge could never be redeemed.

Next spin left the bottle pointing to Theresa.

"Give us one of your opera things," said Manley.

"Let me get a drink first," said Bandy.

"Grand idea," said O'Brien.

Theresa was frowning and shaking her head. "No. Dave, you sing."

An invitation was being extended to Dave Parks, an invitation that was asking for a help out.

"Me? I never sing. Try somebody else. I've a hopeless voice. Don't think I know any songs."

"You must know something," said Theresa. Changing the focus.

"C'mon," said Annie, "sing something, for goodness sake. See trying to get people to sing nowadays. Wastin your time."

"Well, you asked for it. Don't blame me."

"That's a good song," said Annie.

"I meant, don't blame me if your ears curl up."

"Oh."

The song came from nights in the back bar when the revolution was only another tomorrow away.

"Now the final battle rages;
     Tyrants quake with fear.
Rulers of the New Dark Ages,
     Know their end is near.

Scorn the crumbs they drop us,
     All is ours by right;
Onward then: all hell can't stop us,
     Crush the parasite.

With a world-wide revolution,
     Bring them to their feet;
They . . ."

Manley was up on his feet. "Wait a minute, wait a minute, what is that supposed to be for a song? This is a party, mac, just a party. Leave that serious stuff for the politicians. This is a party, know? Singing? Dancin? D'you agree?"

"OK, OK, just leave it. Sorry if it offended you. OK? I've forgotten the words of the song anyway."

"For Christ sake let's dance. Put another record on, somebody."

O'Brien moved to the record player. Bandy followed, but sidestepped to the sideboard. Some kind of music came out. Annie was crooking a finger. "Over here, you. Let's see if you can dance better than you can sing." Annie pulled and Annie held tight. Manley danced with Theresa. Bandy was moving empty cans at his feet, talking, looking up to check Bert was paying attention, and reliving his tale. Bert was nodding. Annie talked as she danced. Non-stop. Non-essential. Hardly allowing time for a nod of the head to agree, disagree. Silent wise looks were the answers and answers. Blethering. This and that and then this and then . . .

"You fancy Tessie? That why you're here?"

"Eh? Who? Me?" A shrug nearly shook the hand off the shoulder. "I just came to see James."

"My arse you did. You've never had your eyes off her the whole night."

166

"Don't think you're right there. I've hardly had a chance to talk to her."

"I never said talk. But please yourself. Not my business anyway."

"It's your business, maybe, if you're her pal."

"What I meant was it's never that important. She's big enough and ugly enough to look after herself."

"Oh, I see."

Manley and Theresa were dancing close. She had her head on his shoulder. James was leaning forward over the arm of the wheelchair. Laura was screened by his back. Bandy was reaching an exciting bit. The eyes were wide. Bert's nods were short, but plenty of them. His eyes were looking round the room for help. James was kissing Laura on the cheek. And groping inside her blouse. After a cluster. Theresa had her head on Manley's shoulder. Her eyes were closed. JCB was definitely groping inside that blouse. Laura's face was red on the cheeks. But she was smiling. Her eyes were closed and she was smiling. James was whispering and pecking her cheek.

"I think I would forget I had seen that, if I were you."

"None of my business."

"Thought he was your pal?"

"Client. Never said he was my pal, or anything like it."

"Anyway, he's big enough and ugly enough as well."

"Big enough for what?"

"Whatever."

"Between you and me I get the feeling that nobody will say too much as long as she looks as if she's smiling."

The music stopped, but moved on to another. A woman was singing The Old Rugged Cross. It was a hard tune to dance to. Annie led the way back to the seats. Theresa lifted her head from Manley's shoulder. She kept her back to James and Laura, moving to the sideboard and pouring two glasses of something. One glass she pushed into Manley's palm. James was carrying on as the singer clung to the old rugged cross. Bandy had reached the high-point of Metra tel Kebir. A quiet knock that was not enough to disturb James sounded several taps on the door.

"Come in," shouted Theresa.

A man wearing black trousers and a heavy grey cardigan over a white shirt came in, but held the door ajar behind him. He stood, scratching at his left thigh with his left hand.

"What is it, Mr Scrimgeour?"

"Oh, I'm awfully sorry to disturb you, you having a party and everything. It's just that my alarm clock has been broken, and I wondered if I could possibly ask you to give me a wee call in the morning?"

"What time?"

"About seven? Or would that be too early? I wouldn't ask, but y'see, it's my old father, he's not well, and I was hoping to catch an early train in the morning to go and see him. Of course, with you having the party and everything, maybe you'll not be going to bed early, and not be wanting to waken early? I know what like it is. I was young myself once. Maybe a bit later then? Could you manage half-past? But only if it's not too much trouble?"

"Half-past would be easier."

"So that's fine then? Sorry I disturbed you, that's fine, I'll away up to my bed then."

"Do you want a drink, Mr Scrimgeour?"

Bandy was on the floor and quietly screaming. Mr Scrimgeour looked at him. "Thank you, but, but I do think I should get to bed and try and get some sleep. I'm not as young as I used to be, and these early starts can be a nuisance."

"No half as much as you," said Manley.

"Oh, if I've disturbed you, I'm awful sorry. It's not that I meant to, you know, it's just, well, I'm afraid, that clock, breaking it was such a nuisance. I'll maybe need to get a new one."

"That'll be the day," said Manley. "There's probably nothing to be fixed in the one you've got. Try winding it up? Usually wakes the whole bloody City up."

"Tell him to fuck off," said Bandy from the floor.

"Mind your tongue, sir," said James, looking round.

Bandy rolled over onto his back and saluted. "Yes, sir."

"You little toad of a man."

Dave Parks was on his feet. "That's enough. Give it a bye, James."

168

James was already repentant, already on his knees. "Come, Laura, we'll pray for the creature."

Laura pulled the edges of her blouse over, clasped her hands, and closed her eyes. James began to pray, asking the Lord to look favourably upon the soul of Bandy. Mr Scrimgeour looked at him, then looked back at Theresa.

"Oh, I am sorry. I hope I've not interrupted you. I didn't really mean to. I . . "

"Mr Scrimgeour, I will give you a call in the morning. If you have an early train to catch, you go to your bed. Goodnight."

"Aye. Fuck off."

"Piss off," added Manley.

Scrimgeour left. James continued his prayer. Laura had one eye open.

"Who the hell is he?" asked Annie.

"Just another lodger. His room is right up above."

"Wouldn't you know it?"

"Bloody creep of a man," said O'Brien. "Pity Jimmy is not here. He's fit for him."

Dave Parks was asking now. "Who's Jimmy?"

O'Brien had his eyes closed and was shaking his head. "Ah, Jimmy. He's a man. He's here, there and everywhere, but when he's here, ah, he's a grand lad."

Annie was stretching her legs out in front of her. Bert had his face turned to her, his nose almost touching her ear. Bandy was trying to attract his attention. Annie let go a sigh. "I don't feel like dancing now. In fact I think that bugger has sobered me up."

"I know what you mean, Annie. I'm sorry. I should've sent him packing, but see when he starts, it's hard. He's barred from the shops around here in case his face curdles the milk. I'm bloody mad. First night you've been here since he died and this character walks in."

"Bugger him. Don't worry about him."

Laura was signalling above the praying head of James. O'Brien went over. She wanted brought down the room into the body of the kirk. O'Brien manipulated the chair around James who never moved and never stopped in his mumbling. Chairs were moved to accommodate the wheelchair and allow O'Brien and Laura through. Laura wanted the small accordion case set against the wall. Dave Parks lifted it over. It wasn't heavy. Felt empty. The case was put down at the side of the wheelchair.

Leaning over, Laura opened it, reached in and came up with a game of Monopoly. "Maybe we should have a game of this now."

Theresa was shaking her head. Bandy lifted Bert's drink from the floor and drunk it. It looked as if the end was coming. James was rising to his feet. Theresa stood up. James turned around. Theresa spoke before he could. "The party's over."

"I was about to say the same thing myself. It is now the Sabbath day. The Lord's day."

O'Brien headed for the door, lifting his hand in a backward wave to indicate his farewells.

James was continuing. "Six days shalt thou labour, and . . ."

Annie leaned on Dave as she laughed. "Would you listen to him? Most people can hardly get six hours, never mind six days."

Theresa's face was angry. "OUT! YOU. OUT! And you, Bandy. Out. The party's over."

Bandy collected up the empty cans of Metra tel Kebir substitute and placed them on the sideboard, lifting two full ones. He left.

James was coming toward Laura. "This is the Sabbath. Later I shall take you in the park and we shall read from the Holy Book and offer up prayer unto the Lord. But for now, kiss me. Kiss me with the kisses of your mouth for love is better than wine."

"Out. And we'll see about the park. The way you carry on it'll have to be a park without bushes."

"Madam."

"Oh, goodnight. On your way."

It was time to call it a day, but Annie was holding on to Dave's arm, and looking up, and winking. Dave Parks was to hold on. Theresa sat down, flopped back in the chair and laughed; laughed loud with her arms hanging down and her legs stretched out and her legs were white and her thighs were smooth-looking. Dave Parks was looking, until Theresa stopped laughing and looked up.

"Would you like a coffee, Annie?"

"No. Not for me, thanks. I'm OK, Bert's driving. He'll be OK. Don't know about this man here, though. Don't let me speak for him."

"Would you like a coffee?"

"Wouldn't say no, as long as it's no trouble."

"It won't be trouble."

Annie was up and gathering her coat from the table. Bert was gathering himself up, stretching. "Well, thanks for a good night, Tessie. Pity about that wee man putting a damper on it."

"Ach, I was getting tired anyway.,"

Laura was kissed. They said goodbye, hoped to meet again and left. Theresa was showing them to the front door and the room was quiet. Recent sights and sounds hung quietly there for recall, but the brain was elsewhere. Laura was holding out the box of tricks nobody wanted to play.

"Could you put this away for me, David?"

"Certainly, Laura."

The box was long, square almost, and there was little to spare for manoeuvring it into the accordion case. Maybe Dave Parks had had too much to drink. It had come out the box easily enough. As maybe, the box was refusing to go in. Turned around, upside down, it still refused to fit. Theresa returned.

"I'll just go and put the kettle on. What's the matter? Here, let me see it."

Theresa tried, but the box kept jamming. Dave Parks had an idea. The case was turned upside down. The lid was on the floor. Dave Parks held up the bottom.

"OK? Now, put the box on the lid there. That's it. Now make sure there's an equal space all round. Let's see, looks OK, right?"

The bottom of the case was lowered down onto the top, passed over it and fitted. Dave shut the latches and placed the case back against the wall, beside the door.

"Do you want to go to bed now, Laura?"

"I think so. It's been a good party. So unexpected."

"Do you want anything?"

"No. No thanks. Goodnight, Mr Parks. I'll see you in the morning, oh, I mean, oh, silly me, dear, for a minute I thought you lived here."

"No such luck for me, Laura. Goodnight. I'll see you again."

"Give me a kiss then."

Laura was kissed. Her cheek tasted of make-up, and she smelt of sweat. Theresa took the wheelchair.

"You need a hand?"

"No thanks, the bedroom is just along the hall. I won't be long and I'll make you some coffee."

"No problem."

Domesticated Dave Parks gathered up the glasses and put them on the table. Empty ones, half-full ones, glasses so full it would have broken Bandy's heart. The furniture in this room was solid stuff. Wood mostly. But all different woods. Light teak table, solid oak sideboard, mahogany shelves done in a Mackintosh style, rosewood chairs with knurled knobs that shone above high brass-buttoned cushions. Pictures on the walls: sepia ships sailing on sepia seas, all hanging haphazardly. Lots hung askew, tilting the waves, tilting the ships, tilting sepia bows to sepia sterns. Abstract watercolours were set beside reproductions of City tramcars. Red bands, green bands, black bands; coloured-coded routes. The decanter was crystal.

"Do you want a coffee?"

Theresa was behind at the door.

"Eh? Oh, sorry, I was just looking at the pictures. No, no coffee, thanks. I'm not too bad. I've been watching it."

"So I noticed. Watching the drink and watching everybody else as well."

"I don't think that's true. if it is I'm sure I never meant it."

"Only joking." She lifted her cigarette packet from the sideboard. "Smoke?"

"Thanks."

"You do smoke? I've never seen you smoke all night."

"Usually I roll them. I, I just couldn't be bothered."

The hand that held the lighter out was steady, and the rings looked bigger close up.

"Dave, can I say something to you?"

"Sure."

"Are you sure I'm what you want?"

"Eh?"

"You know what I'm saying."

"Aye. Look. All I know is that since we went out for that stuff, I've never had a minute's peace with you jumping in and out of my head all the time."

"That's dodgy. The girl in your arms is never the girl in your dreams, as the man says."

"Aye, very good. Don't suppose you dream about me?"

"No chance. You're adult, I'm adult. I have urges, you have urges. No problem. Right now I have a wee urge to see your body. Plain and simple. You're a nice looking man, and right now I need a lift. But you worry me. If what you say is true, I'm wondering if sex will be enough for you. Good uncomplicated sex. No emotional hangovers. All pleasure, no pain."

"Sounds fair enough."

"You're saying that with your mouth, but your eyes tell it different. Something inside is looking for more. Sorry, Dave, I'm not your fantasy woman. But I'm still curious about your body. How you perform, nothing else. I don't want to inherit any hang-ups that don't belong to me. That's the terms."

"Terms? You make it sound like an HP agreement."

"No, Dave, no. Exact opposite in fact. This way nobody pays up anything."

Nobody pays. Everybody wins all ends up. All ends up in anonymity. One body much the same as another. No grasping of the ideal mate. Just what suffices.

"You for staying? For as much of the night as you want, or don't want."

"You make it sound a bit clinical."

"Staying or going?"

"Don't have much option."

"Yes or no is every option on offer."

"I'm staying, I'm staying."

"As long as you know the terms. Bodies I need, egos I don't."

"I'll stay."

Theresa Kipple was kissing Dave Parks. A small kiss and now turning away. A small lamp was put on and the main light extinguished and Theresa Kipple came to dance. And this dance was close. And her head was on Dave Parks' shoulder. Not Manley's, Dave Parks'. Hair irritated at the nose but the desire to sneeze was fought off. A man on a TV programme had once said that a sneeze was as good as an orgasm. Could account for the sale of paper hankies. She was soft. Slowing the dance down; a shuffle; a step from one foot to the other; a bounce; an armful that moved, not dancing, just moving. Moving around and this room of dark light woods and sepia ships and cruising trams and delicate flowers of delicate colours moved round and Dave Parks moved round and closed the eyes. Theresa stopped. The music had stopped. Taking her partner by the hand she led down the room, opened the door on the end wall, and somewhere in here switched a light on. A bedroom done in pale pale orange. Pale orange silk sheets on the bed. From a drawer in a dressing-table Theresa drew out some kind of clothes and threw them over. Dave Parks caught them. Pyjamas. White pyjamas.

"What's this?"

"Silk pyjamas. Wear them, will you? In case you haven't noticed, I like the feel of silk on my skin."

"You want me to wear these? These?"

"Have you ever worn silk pyjamas before? Real silk, I mean."

"Don't think so. Usually don't bother, to tell you the truth."

"You'll like the experience. They'll fit you OK. OK?"

You'll like them. Like them or lump them. They'll fit all right. Theresa Kipple says so. Mammy says so. They fit, there's nothing wrong with them, they fit. PJs from the hawker. Where did she get them? In the Lane? Who died in them? Who died? Her man? Who died in them?

"Theresa, I don't like pyjamas."

"I do. I've got rubbers here as well if you want them."

Them. Plural. Rubbers. Plural. Silky smooth no doubt. Gossamer silk. Extra fine silk. Silk pyjamas and silk rubbers for Dave Parks. What happened to silky skin?

"Theresa, look, I'm not, look, the pyjamas, I mean . . ."

"They're perfectly good pyjamas. They were my man's."

Filling a husband's pyjamas. This is Cary Grant stuff. Filling a husband's boots. Filling a husband's rubbers. Filling somebody else's vest, maybe a wee dead boy.

"Theresa . . ."

"Shh. Listen."

From behind the far wall came the sounds of a giggle. Laura's giggle. And a low, man's voice. James.

"I think your friend has more spunk than you have, Dave. He'll have his work cut out there. And this the Sabbath as well."

"That's as maybe, Theresa. I can't wear these. I don't know, I'm just not into pyjamas."

"Then you're not into me."

"That's, well, what are you saying?

"You know what I'm saying."

"Theresa . . ."

"It's up to you."

She was crossing over, opening the door which led into the hall. "It's up to you."

"For fuck sake, what kind of crazy carry-on is this?"

"They're only pyjamas."

"A dead man's pyjamas. They're a dead man's, aren't they? Fuck me, talk about the spirit moving you."

"Never throw anything out, Dave. And don't get aggressive. You wear them or you don't."

"Ach. No bloody wonder. Theresa, I can't crawl into a dead man's night gear."

"But you'll crawl into his woman."

"Aaaaachhh, Theresa, is it that important to you?"

"It's what turns this woman on. That's all you need to know. It's your entrance fee."

The pyjamas crushed easily in the hands. Smooth. Probably smoother than anything Dave Parks had run across. Smooth. And embroidery had been picked off the breast pocket. The pyjamas were thrown on the bed. Theresa was standing aside to let the man past. The giggling and whispering from next door was getting louder and Theresa was closing the door on Dave Parks.

Mary

***

Mary. Standing there in the padded gown that filled up the door space.

—What you up to?

"Nothing. I'm hungry, that's all. Frying an egg to make a piece."

—Where have you been till this time?

"The Smiths. I told you, I was taking the car back."

—Did it take you till this time? Where else were you?

"I was never anywhere. Honest. I was at the Smiths. You know what like these people are. They just kept givin me these big whiskies. Before you knew it, I was quite drunk. The Smiths made me stay and they gave me coffee, and then I suppose we just blethered."

—Aye. And the band played.

"It's right. Listen, I didn't want to leave because that rear light is broken. They just need any excuse to stop you. Can't afford to take a chance with the old licence."

—Have these people with the whisky to throw away no bloody telephone?

"That was my fault. I never realised it was so late. And I reckoned you'd be in your bed anyway, seeing as how the telly was rotten. Anyway, I'm a big boy now, Mary."

—Think so? Aye. Maybe boy's the word. And I think you're lying. If it wasn't so bloody late I'd give you the bloody Smiths. You're getting worse, do you know that? Bloody worse. Finish that apology for a supper and come to bed. And make sure the door's locked.

"Right. I will, Mary. I'll be as quick as I can."

—Don't hurry yourself on my account, you needn't think whatever I think you're thinking.

"Ah, Mary, just when I was in the mood for you as well. You know you're beautiful when you're angry."

176

—Aye, well, I'm for being beautiful for a long time if that's the case. Mind and make sure the lights are out. And don't waken those kids up. I'll speak to you in the morning. Maybe.

Mary was shutting the door on Dave Parks, but she left it open, just a bit.

****

Dave Parks stood up again from the desk, looked out of the window. At the far end of the street, slap bang across the dead-end, coils of barbed wire ran on angled standards of iron above the top of a wall of red bricks, all crowned by broken glass chunks set cleverly haphazard into a topping of ageing white concrete. That wire and that glass went all around, guarding that scrap-yard, dripping drips of rain from sharp tips, dripping drips of wet rain that ran down, checking and turning here and there, as the pointing between the bricks channelled the runs of water first this way, then another, until the separated waters met on the pavement, fanned out and rushed off the kerbstones to form fast-running shallows that raced to be swallowed by a drain that foamed at the mouth.

Behind the scrap-yard the pylons of the football park held high their ranks of floodlights that would shine down to illuminate that world which spectators and players and the linesmen and the referee had chosen to live in for a while, where everybody knew the rules, the infringements, the punishments.

Dave looked until he was seeing nothing, turned, and sat down again; hands still in pockets, legs stretched, head down, looking, seeing nothing. An automatic hand was drawn from a pocket, an automatic pen picked up, a paper pulled forward automatically, and a signature put on. Automatically. Another assessment signed. One more to go. One more life to sum up and put down for some sheriff to read and contrast with his view of the world. But this next one was a little different.

The previous social worker had compiled and prepared this assessment, but she had got her medal and now she was off. All that could be done would be to explain that fact to whomsoever it should concern. Somebody else had made up this report on this client. Dave Parks therefore, being another somebody else, could not come to any conclusions based upon someone else's objectivity which must be affected by a completely different subjectivity or perspective, or world-view. No way. AND, AND, there was always the danger that the compiler had been totally subjective. She had left to lecture on the subject, so that was a distinct possibility. The report might be really subjective.

So, if the first assessor was not objective, but subjective, or even worse, really emotional, and then along comes Dave Parks with a completely different set of subjective hang-ups, through bad upbringing, bad training or more likely just having a bad day, reads the stuff, comes to some sort of assessment based on the aforesaid, and everything else, signs it and passes it on to the sheriff, who equally well might be subjective, or at the very least have an objectivity arrived at through a completely different set of subjective value-giving experiences, so, so then the person, client, might not appear properly on paper, or at least not filter off the paper through the assessor's prism, as viewed from the perspective of a sheriff, and be seen in his or her true light. This job was fraught with danger.

The pen was thrown down. Dave stood up again. Looked out the window again. Same scene, but the rain had stopped. Sun was shining from somewhere above some roof, reflecting light off the wet slabs of the pavement. A street-sweeper leaned on a close wall. He was looking hopefully up at the sky. He had to move. A little girl was edging her doll's go-chair past him, bumping it matronly down the close steps. Some kind of rag-doll sat inside it, hanging on in there by an arm slung over the side. Further on a reddish coloured dog lay on the steamy pavement. Two other dogs stood almost nose-to-nose, stretching, sniffing each other. The sun was shining like a searchlight onto the graffiti on the red brick wall. This was no graffiti. FUCK THEM ALL. This was pure philosophy, denied a publisher. The defiant cry of the culture, painted on in rough daubs of inarticulate anger.

The dog that had been sunning itself got up, stretched its forepaws forward, yawned the length and breadth of its teeth, straightened up and trotted past the other two. It barked. The other two mongrels followed. They barked. The three barked. The girl pushed her pram. Three dogs ran and barked, stopped and barked. Dodged around the front of the pram and barked. The girl pushed on. The dogs scurried around her and her pram. The girl turned her head from side to side. She was scolding the dogs. They barked. The doll slid down. The girl stopped. The doll was picked up, patted, replaced and a finger wagged at it. The dogs barked. The pram was pushed up a path that separated flat patches of impacted dirt and led to another close. The dogs ran round. They ran round ahead. They ran round behind. They barked. They barked and barked. The girl pushed her pram with her head down, talking to her doll. Now they barked and showed teeth. The pram was stopped. She was manoeuvring the pram around to pull it up the closemouth steps: one and bump and two and bump and three and bump. Her little legs moved backwards up the steps. The pram was pulled up step, step, through the barking dogs. Then another. Then the last into the closemouth. The dogs' barks echoed from the close. Quite clear. They all disappeared up the close. Dave Parks was still looking. The office door opened behind. He turned in away from the window. Just the boss, with another man.

"Hello, Stanley, what can I do you for?"

"Nothing much, old son. You busy?"

A shrug answered the question.

Stanley stood as usual, erect as a policeman, that kind of clean clean: hair neatly trimmed, moustache likewise. The smile was just beginning. Stanley's smiles were always just beginning. The mouth aborted the smile.

"Dave, I'd like you to meet this fellow here. This is John Christie, the new Community Artist. John, this is Dave Parks."

"Glad to meet you, John."

The two hands met across the desk.

"Thanks. Me too. Likewise, I mean."

The man's head was shaking and nodding at the same time. The lips looked out of control. Dave spoke. "Stanley, you've got this poor guy a bag of nerves. What have you been doin to him?"

"Nothing. Honestly. I've had him round everybody else and now I'm just going to leave him to your tender mercies. I've got to be off to a Parents Against Drugs meeting, so I thought you might like to show him the rest of the place. Across the road and so on."

"No problem. I've just finished a couple of assessments, so I could do with the fresh air."

Stanley's head went back, then down toward his watch. "Is there any here? Right, I've got to go. I'll catch up with you later, John. And don't believe anything this man tells you." The door closed. Then opened again. "Listen, Dave, I hear that 'Ragged Trousered Philanthropist' is some show. Do you fancy it for Friday?"

"—ists. It's Philanthropists. There's a whole bunch of them."

"Fine. But are you going?"

"I'll see." The door closed.

Now Dave Parks was looking at John Christie looking at Dave Parks.

"Would you like a coffee?"

"No, thanks. I'm floating on the stuff."

"Well, sit down, for a minute at least."

The man sat, hanging clasped hands between his thighs. His fingers didn't look particularly artistic. Stereotype thinking again.

"So you're the artist, eh? Were you at the College or, I mean, do you make paintings for sale, or what?"

"Well, that's the general idea, but right now this job looks a better proposition."

"Things bad in the painting game then?"

"Just a bit. I'm just back from Paris and I'm totally skint."

"What were you doin over there?"

"Oh, just looking, bumming around sort of. Trying to pick up some pointers, see some paintings I probably will never get the chance to see again, study the techniques, that type of thing."

"Oh. Very good. The old Paris, eh? Some change comin here. What is it you intend to do here anyway?"

The hands became unclasped. The arms were folded. Then a thumb and a finger pulled at a neck. "I'm not really sure yet. I know they've done some good work in some other schemes. I don't really know as yet. But I'm sure there's a lot of good painting talent out there."

"Sure. But how do you get it on to canvas, so to speak?"

The arms were folded again and pulled tight into the chest. "Well, I'm not here to find some underprivileged Leonardos, if that's what you mean. Art covers a wide spectrum, you know."

"Sure, I know, I know. Stained glass and murals and all that stuff as well. I know. There's a few schemes got these murals done."

"Well, that's the sort of thing. Anything that can unlock people's potential, help them express themselves, put down their world as they see it."

At least the bloke was keen.

"You're right. Have you seen the Community flat across the road?"

John Christie shook his head. Outside, on the move, artistic fervour would not be so overpowering.

Dave rose. "No time like the present. I'll take you over and maybe meet some of the girls."

Dave followed the new workmate out the door and locked it behind. A push at the door with the shoulder and a pull at the handle explained it was really locked. He pocketed the key. John Christie was moving along the too-tight-for-two corridor as if he knew the way already.

"Stanley ever tell you these offices once used to be all the houses up this close?"

"Yes. Yes, he did. Good idea, isn't it, having all the staff under one roof?"

"Oh definitely. Definitely."

They passed along the passageway, passing locked doors and passing open doors. A few individuals waved to Dave, Dave waved to a few, a few didn't wave back. He pulled John back at an open door. A broad, blond man moved only his eyes up from the telephone.

"Did you meet this man?" John Christie was just standing. Maybe this was a no. "This is our housing repair man. Does a grand job. One week maximum wait, two weeks for an emergency. Always pleading poverty. 'Give me the dough and I'll give you a show' he always says."

The nod from the man was the least perceptible of nods, and the eyes were cast downwards. He held on to the phone. And said nothing.

Dave Parks was not for pursuing it. He pushed himself off the door jamb. "C'mon, never mind this grumpy old bastard."

The new man followed down the stairs, through the security door, out to the reception area. There was the usual collection of women waiting to be received, leaning their faces into the large glass window, wearing the look that told the woman in front no one was listening to the business underway. Some sat on the bench around the wall, nodding to each other, and underlining important bits by blowing billows of smoke above nodding heads. A baby being bounced on a wide lap was sucking a thumb and shooting a million questions from wide eyes. There was the usual pause while they watched to see who had come out from within, then the frieze came nearly alive again.

"Excuse me a minute," said Dave. He crossed the space between.

A woman sitting in the centre of the bench looked up, waited.

"Sally, I'll be going up to the Panel with you and your boy after all, OK?" There was no response. "Right. Now, for Christ sake, will you tell him to wear a tie if he's got one. Will you?" The woman's eyes slipped from Dave to John and back again. She nodded and that was all.

Dave turned to go, but a woman with a coil of dyed grey steel-wiry hair tapped the shoulder. "I've been lookin for you the day."

"For me? Chrissie, I've been here since morning."

"Well, I was told you were busy."

"What you after? Hold it. Don't tell me. Don't tell me here. Look, can I just get this guy a coffee and we can go to the office?"

Nothing showed in her face either. Just the same sideways slippage of the eyes. Dave waved John over and they passed through to the café. Two women stood at the counter of the food co-operative feeling at a loaf and exchanging views. At the café counter a man sipping at a paper cup moved away as they approached. A tall but bent man in a flat cap came out of the kitchen. Tony.

"A coffee for our artist friend here, Tony, if you don't mind. I'll need to pay you after. I've got somebody else to see."

John went rummaging in a pocket. "I can pay. It's OK. I'll pay it myself."

"Good lad. I won't be long. I'm really sorry about this."

"That's OK."

A pool cue tapped Dave Parks on the shoulder. "When's this game comin off, big man? Have you got the pitch booked yet?"

"Ah, Joe, for Christ sake, give us a break. It's no done, but I'll get round to it. Right? And listen, while you're here, what's this about that brother of yours changing his plea?"

The young pool player's head went down and he fumbled in a well-worn waistcoat for some chalk. Dave put a finger under the boy's chin. "Fuck sake, Joe, I made up that assessment for him on the basis he was for pleading guilty. I mean, what's the score? Never mind, the best of luck to him. I'll see you about the match later." John had been served the coffee. "You be OK here? I'll be as quick as I can."

Dave went back through the reception area and buzzed some buzzes at the security door. The young receptionist behind the panel of glass pressed a button after she had keeked out to see who was wanting in. When something at the door clicked Dave pushed it open. The door was held open for Chrissie who went through, yanking a child with her on the length of his arm.

Dave walked round the desk to sit at the other side of it. He glanced out the window. The street was empty. Not even a dog in sight. He sat down. And listened. And it was as expected. A Section Twelve. The man had got off with the book yesterday, and he still wasn't back yet. There was no cash. It wasn't for herself, it was for the weans. Seven quid. Seven. That would do it.

Dave Parks lifted his forehead from the upward press of a forefinger. "Jesus, Chrissie, you're making it hard. I gave you seven yesterday. There is absolutely no way I can lob you seven the day. No way."

The child was heaved onto the lap. The cigarette was stubbed hard and harder into the ashtray. But the smell coming over was not nicotine alone, but a mixture of damp unclean clothes and the expensive perfume of the cheap bevy.

"Chrissie, look, if I go to the boss for another seven for you he'll chase me. He'll never countersign it."

The child's hair was getting the palm treatment now. She spoke as she brushed. "But I'll need seven, Dave. I need that even just for some bread and milk and something for the weans's tea. Dave, I'm no at it. Honest."

"Nobody said you were at it. But what do you think this is, a bank? Chrissie, we're only allowed so much for Section Twelve emergencies and you are definitely not the only one that's hard up in this scheme." The hand brushed on. "Right, I'll see him, but don't hold out too much hope. Weans or no weans."

Stanley looked up, took the paper, began a smile, made the seven into a five, shook Dave away with a shake of the pen and returned his head to his work.

The woman took the fiver. Dave swung the boy three steps at a time down the stairs. The boy was far from being heavy. The café area was arrived at. Chrissie smiled a goodbye with a smile that beat the Mona Lisa for enigma. John stood, legs crossed, pretending to be watching the pool. A laughing boy made an approach.

"Sam. Later. Please. Later. My wee napper is nippin right now."

The boy shoved up two fingers. It was best to laugh.

Outside the sun was still shining. The broad street was totally dry. Some boys were moving off the pavement, crossing the street. It was the young team. Dave shouted. "Hope you lot never touched my motor."

The group let them catch up. The bald-headed one inclined his head towards them. "fuck all on that thing worth nickin. Time you were gettin somethin decent."

Some laughed, all agreed, some kicked the tyres. One pointed at the licence plate. "Aye, that's right, brings the place right down, man."

"Dave pointed at the last speaker. "Well, well, I forgot you were due a turn out. You back for a week?"

"Aye."

"Keep off that glue mind."

"Ah, fuck off."

"Fuck off fuck all. You're the only mug that's still sniffin. The next time you get a balmy buzz and perform something stupid they'll keep you in weekends as well. Tell you soldier, if I'm here and you feel like you're dying to get on it, give us a shout. Promise?"

"Aye."

"Well, see you mean it."

After the rain the street was clean. Dandelions were giving a brave show on the central reservation. Up ahead the sniffer broke from the group, ran on a bit, kicked an empty can and shouted: "Promise fuck all, you. Promise nothing. Promise fuck all."

Dave shook a clenched fist into the air. On the far pavement John tramped on some dog shit. He lifted one leg in a fair impersonation of a stork. Two girls were looking out a window in the tenement they had arrived at. They were laughing. John scraped the muck on the edge of the pavement, and followed on down into the close. Dave opened a dark door in a dark corner and motioned him through. The place smelled damper than usual. Scuffed red and black checked linoleum peeled up in supplication. Along the lobby Dave held a finger to his lips and pointed to a door. He tiptoed up to the door. He knocked and pushed it open, all in more or less one movement.,

"Open up, it's the polis here. Where's Andy Scott?"

A man pulled the door wide open from the inside. "Come in, Dave, we know it's you."

Dave laughed and entered. John hung back a little. In the centre of the room a small single-bar electric fire gave out some heat. In a large semi-circle around it, in seats of various designs, shapes and sizes, sat the four women and two men, of various ages, shapes and sizes. A fat woman leaned forward.

"Who's your pal, Dave? How's about giving Maisie a wee knockdown?"

"This is John Christie, your new Community Artist. John's been sent here to help you create. I told him the only thing you lot create is merry hell."

"Aye. Especially if you're miserable at the Section Twelves. Where is this man, then? C'mon in then you. Give us a looksee."

John stepped forward a shuffling step. Another woman called out, "Come in here, arty-crafty, let us see; what size is your drop?" They all laughed. Even John Christie could not hold a laugh back. He was in. The teaser continued: "Are you arty-crafty people no supposed to have a good imagination? I think you'll need it for this lot."

"You speak for yourself you."

This time they only smiled. But they were looking at John just the same. Watched and smiled. Evaluating the reaction. Weighing the man up. Street psychologists, carrying an encyclopaedia of social psychological interfacing and body language around in the head, and referring to it constantly. Only the best conmen or the better organised had ever got the better of them and their ilk. Got the better of them, but never really fooled them. And Dave Parks was standing right in front of them. And so was the Community Artist. The artist lad was smiling. A wink was the best Dave Parks could do to reassure him.

Maisie spoke. "If you're a painter, I know where there's a ceilin needin done. A white emulsion'll do me fine thanks. But I hope you don't take cash.,"

"Ah, cut it out Maisie." An arm was thrown round the new boy's shoulders. "You're embarrassing the boy. John is here to unlock your creative potential."

There were hoots and laughter and more shouts and John grew red in the face. He moved a little under Dave's arm and there were more laughs. Andy Scott pulled at the zip on his fly, up and down several times. "Mine is never locked away at any time, son. Don't believe in it."

A woman at the far side joined in. "Don't need to for the wee potential you've got. You could show what you're worth to the whole world and they'd never arrest you, they'd only feel sorry for you."

Everybody laughed and Andy stuck his tongue out at the woman. He sat down and they waited. Waited for another laugh. Something to make the day go. Half-formulated cracks and giggles settled down into relative quiet. Old Tam Winters leaned forward in his chair and aimed, flicked, and missed the ashtray that sat in the middle of the floor. It was quiet now, for Tam was ready to speak. Quite a clever guy Tam. He was given the floor.

"No a bad wee number, Community Artist, eh?"

John Christie just smiled.

"What are you for doin for us then? You for organising the community bus an taking us in about the galleries? Or are you for taking us up a big hill and telling us to make a landscape of the City?" He flicked more ash. "That would be good. Give us a chance to look at the place from away up there instead of permanently down here."

Dave Parks let his arm drop.

John Christie flushed again, but he took him on. "I hadn't really thought much about the job yet, but I would've thought there's plenty material around here."

"Oh there is, there is. Are you for making us all like the Glasgow Boys then? Do you want to be a New City School yourself? Is that what you're here for? Surely it's already been done, son? Are we no a bit played out?"

"I know what you mean, but I'm just a painter."

"Just a painter. You'll need to be mair than that here, son."

Tam Winters stubbed out his cigarette. It was finished. The room was in silence. John Christie was looking confused. He was young. His face was reddening again. But he came back.

"Well, I hope I'll have you to keep me right."

"Oh, I'll keep you right all right."

The door burst open.

"Maisie, Maisie, for fuck sake Maisie, come quick, come quick."

Maisie leapt up and grabbed the woman by the shoulders. "What's up? What is it? What is it?"

The woman kept her head down, eyes tight shut, twisting her neck one way then another, making sounds, struggling to speak.

"It's the wee lassie Paterson. Oh Maisie, no no, oh no, the dogs got her, they och, the dogs have got her. She's killed, Maisie, she's killed."

Maisie pulled the woman to her and held her head into her breasts. Tam lifted a quarter bottle of whisky from behind the fire regulations. It was passed over and the woman didn't want to know. She sobbed. "The boys got them, but they were too late. They chased them, but the wee lassie was deid, she was deid, Maisie, deid. The polis are there, but, och, she's deid."

Maisie passed back the whisky which was replaced. She led the woman out. The others filed past John Christie and Dave Parks and they were left alone.

John sat down heavy on a seat. An artist was looking at Dave Parks with an open mouth that was trying to put words to the questions that were in his face. Dave Parks could only fold the arms and hands behind his head. Bright Paisley patterns on a dark base filled the seeing spaces. Questions. Explanations?

"Fuck fuck fuck fuck fuck fuck fuck fuck fuck fuck FUCK!" he said.

The head was up, but the only thing up there was the ceiling. He let the head slump onto his chest. The community artist was there sitting, waiting on words. There were none to give him that could be right. John was saying something.

"Are you all right?"

"Me? Me? I'm all right. Fuck me, I'm all right."

John wanted to speak.

"I don't know what to say. I feel, I really feel pretty sick and pretty useless as well. Maybe what they need here is a dogcatcher."

Dave rubbed at his face, straightened up, spoke.

"It's different things, John, different things. You have to do what you can in your own way. You're a painter. Show them what it's all about. In your way."

John nodded. Dave had more to say.

"But do me a favour will you? When I go through this scheme I do not want to see the local vigilantes guarding a fancy painted brick wall. Don't give us any of that art as *gemeinschaft* crap. Make them see, and make them paint politics. Politics."

"But I . . ."

"Never mind the buts. You're not here to have them paint walls. You're here to make them look at this place with some kind of eye that'll make them see it. No just look at it, see it, and put it into a painting that'll make other people see it and feel it. That's what you're here for." A chair got a kick and flew over. "Y'see the

189

people here, John? They've been fucked up by the system and its language for so long they're dumbstruck. You go ahead and show them how to use their eyes and then the paint and tell them that every time they mix a blue or a green, it's their blue and their green, no other fucker's. Just tell them to paint what they see, will you son, so that at least maybe some people will see what they're saying."

What Dave Parks didn't see. Head-butting the edge of the door wouldn't do any good. But it felt like something. Like deserved. But not enough.

The boy could only sit. His eyes were wide. All the better to see. Dave turned to the door.

"C'mon, John. Just make sure before you start teaching them anything, you do plenty of looking and seeing yourself."

Dave turned back. He reached behind the fire regulations. The whisky was brought out. There was enough for a decent slug. Dave Parks finished the whisky. He could always buy them some more.

***

It was just as well Mary had wanted to get here early. A queue had formed already. Some cars had been parked on the spare ground opposite but there was still room for one or two more in the theatre car park. "Just go in the car park, Mary." That was a mistake.

"Who's driving, me or you?"

"Sorry."

The car swung in, and there the headlights picked out John Christie's lemon and blue Citroen Diane with its large orange stars. The car was parked and the shrubbery cut through to get to the queue. A girl in a red sweater and yellow jeans was immediately in front, knees bent, back curved, head bobbing up and down with the inflections of her voice. Silent Dave Parks felt an anger. Rain began. Multi-coloured and black and white sponsored golf umbrellas went up. Mary put hers up, a bent spoke catching in the hair of a man in front. He took it in good humour. The chatter level was going up under the umbrellas. A hand tapped Dave's shoulder.

"Right, Parks, how did you get here before us? Were you away early?"

"Hi Stanley. I take it you're only joking, by the way?"

"Ah, Christ, that was a silly thing to say. Ach. How was the funeral? Was there a big turnout? At least there was not even the beginnings of a smile.

"Aye, the whole scheme turned out. I told a few of them you couldn't manage."

"Good. Thanks."

The queue was moving in. Near the entrance a man held his poodle on the lead while it shat in the gutter. The dog finished and was taken away and put into a car. The man rejoined the queue, near the front. The dog barked.

"Mary, can we give this a bye? I'm not really in the mood for theatre."

"It's up to yourself. I'm easy."

Dave Parks was not in the mood to speak, to apologise, to say cheerio to Stanley and his wife. Monday would come too soon. A nod was enough.

****

A woman. This woman opposite must've been young at sometime. Younger. Younger at sometime. Must've laughed at sometime. Played at skipping ropes. Cawed; skipped in, skipped out: Polly in the kitchen, doin a little stitchin, in comes the bogey man and out pops she. Laughed probably. Played chase, catch, kiss. Giggled probably. Screamed hysterically for somebody. Elvis, Cliff, Beatles maybe. Went dancing likely. Eyeing the talent; being eyed by the talent. Standing round the edge, ready with the answers, waiting; watching for the dream boy. Winched a few dream boys. Or maybe just smiled at the one. And smiled at a wedding photographer somewhere, with face all lit up, and now she was sitting opposite Dave Parks, with black pouched red-rimmed eyes that were disappearing into a skull that provided the frame for a clay-coloured skin that stretched and sunk its way into the crevices and hollows encased by the bones. A skull that was close to screaming. Dragging succour from a cigarette, gusting the smoke back out in a burst, turning her head again for another draw, turning her head to blow the smoke away, turning her head on the cigarette to keep her eyes on the move, away from Dave Parks. Keep the eyes distracted. In case she ever saw herself in the eyes of whoever was opposite this time. And today she was talking to Dave Parks.

"I want you to help me, Dave. That's what you people get paid for, is it no?"

"Have you seen Tam Winters?"

"Tam? Tam? Tam's just a punter like me. That Parents Against the Drugs thing is not what I need right now. Counselling. I'm flooded, drowning in the fuckin stuff. I want my boy and I want that bastard that's shovin the stuff. I want my boy, Dave."

"Where was he the last time you heard?"

"He's still in the area. He has to be near that bastard."

"Who is it that's shovin the stuff, Chrissie?"

"Fuck off Dave. You know and I know who it is, so don't tell me any lies. You know and the polis know, every cunt knows. Just get me my boy."

There was wet in the eyes. Not tears. A wet film that covered the eyeballs. Maybe the tears were held back by the white stuff stapped at the corners of the eyes; put there by the pills from the GP. And every cunt did know Collier. From behind the cigarette Chrissie was ready to say something.

"His pal Batsy says Billy is kipping in a motor in the scrap-yard at night. I've been watching it the last couple o nights, but I've never seen him. Can you find him, Dave? He likes you, Dave. He talks to you."

"Any idea where he is during the day?"

"Where do you think? In the city. Tea-leafin for the cash for, aah, fuck, Dave, you know the score."

Dave Parks knew the score. Heard it that often now he could write the score. But never be a singer. In it, but not of it. And the line between Dave Parks and these people was a payline. Only a payline. A silver thread. Dave Parks, a couple of million Dave Parks, hanging by a silver thread.

"Dave, the kids on the street'll talk to you, can you no find out for me where Billy is? Please. Please."

"I'll do my best, Chrissie. I will. But will you do me a favour? Go and see Tam Winters. He'll help you get through this, till we find Billy. Will I contact him?"

"Just you find Billy. I'll see Tam, honest, I know where he is. But you get Billy, get him before something terrible happens."

"Can the polis help?"

"Fuck the polis. If I'd wanted the polis I'd have went to the bastards. I came to you. You're supposed to be good, just like one o us. Fuck you and your polis."

Chrissie rose. The cigarette was stubbed out, ground down into the base of the ashtray, stubbed hard until she was only banging and screwing her fingers into black ash. The telephone rang, and was lifted.

"There's a Mr Black to see you, Dave."

"Aaaafff. What is he after?"

"I'm sure I don't know."

"I'll be down."

Telephone was replaced. Telephones could be a nuisance.

"Sorry about that, Chrissie. I'll do what I can. Chrissie, I'd like to be able to say I'll get to Billy before anybody else, but I doubt it. I'll do my best." More smoke was blown in the air. Chrissie rose to follow it. "Wait and I'll get you down the stair." The keys were hunted, lifted, door opened, door closed. Door locked.

"You make sure you have a cup of coffee before you go up the road. Try and calm down a bit."

"I'll calm down when somebody gets that bastard out o this scheme."

Downstairs James was waiting in the reception area. He got up, but had the sense to sit down again. Chrissie refused coffee. She walked straight through the café area and out through the door. One of the young team got up from the pool table and came over.

"You got that pitch booked, big man?"

"Eh? Oh. Sorry, Bernie, I was away there. Right. The pitch. No. The buggers say it's fully booked for the next month."

"My arse."

"That's what they said. Only thing left is the cricket pitch."

"Can we no get a game on that? Stick a couple o poles in for goal or something?"

"No chance."

"Hey, big man. You're quite new here. I don't think you appreciate the needle that's in this game."

"Sure I do. Nobody wants this game played more than me. I'd sooner see you lot kick lumps out each other as have you chip bricks up and down the street. I'm definitely not into that kind of rockery."

"Well, get us a game then. Man, we've hardly had a decent game in about two months. Now that's deprivation, so will you do something about it? Throw those snobby cunts off the pitches and get us deprived people a game."

" I don't run the pitches, Bernie. I have to go. I'll see what I can manage."

"Manage fuck all you."

"Give us a break, Bernie. By the way, if you see Billy Roy, give us a shout. Any time."

Bernie nodded. No need for a story. The street knew.

A voice shouted. Bernie's pool partner was being impatient.

"Talking about breaks, it's your go. C'mon."

Bernie flicked up his cue through his hand and held it up high and out like a spear. "Tell you, big man, there's a loada bad energy buildin up. Could be trouble." The spear was shaken.

"Just make sure you put chalk on the cue first. Now piss off you. Bampot."

"Ok, big man, do your best."

James was sitting with his legs spread out in front of him and his hands clasped in front of him on his lap. His neck was stretching as he tried to see what was going on in the reception area.

"How y'doin, James? To what do we owe the pleasure?"

"Ah, David. It's a fine day, isn't it? I was simply taking the air, a little walk, a little exploration, and lo and behold, I am here."

No doubt asking the natives the whereabouts of the Dave bwana as he walked.

"Very good. Well, c'mon up and I'll give you a decent coffee."

Buzz given, received, door freed. James followed on up the steps, looking around, looking in all the offices as he passed. Inside the sanctum sanctorum of Dave Parks he settled himself and waited for the coffee from the pot. He settled back with the coffee. For Dave Parks it was time for a roll-up. A roll-up was made and lit as James watched.

"Hope I'm not disturbing you."

"Not a bit, but you'll have to excuse me for a tick. I've got a phone call to make."

The number was on the corner of the desk blotter, but it came to the memory without trouble.

"Sergeant Naismith, please. I won't be a minute, James. Gerry? Listen, I think our pal is back in action again. One of our women was up here this mornin. It'll be him OK."

James was up; going over to the window, blocking out what light there was. Gerry Naismith was wanting to know too many definite articles.

"That's as much as I can say, Gerry. Can I get back to you? There's somebody here." The conversation was over and the telephone settled back in its cradle. James turned around and took his seat again.

"So, how's things, James?"

"Admirable, Mr Parks, admirable. Well, nearly good." He pulled at his collar. "I'm afraid the lady I give my shirts to is a little overzealous with the starch."

"What do you mean? Are you saying you get your shirts laundered? James, you can't afford that."

"So I am quickly coming to appreciate, my dear David."

"You'll need to think that right away."

Theresa

"How you and Bandy gettin along?"

"Ah. A lovable rascal, I'm afraid. I have to admit that your character assessment of him was correct. I submit to your superior knowledge. The man is, what you called, a ponce. But I'm afraid it's not so much drink he gets from me as heat from my fire. Every time I light one the man is at my door in a flash. James paused for a sip of the coffee. "Giving the heat I do not mind, but being coached for the position of curator of the military museum at Stirling Castle I do find a trifle tiresome."

"Can well imagine it."

And Theresa. How is Theresa with
the body wrapped in silk?

"How's Laura?"

"Ah. Laura. Proving a most equable companion, my boy. Most equable. I have found that she too has a fondness for the Books of the Old Testament. It is a joy to read with her."

"Imagine it must be. Any more parties?"

"None that I am aware of since that particular one you attended."

Attended and left. Unpicked monogram.

"Ah well. Pity that, it was a good night."

"An excellent evening."

James Cameron Black had walked in here. Large as life. And he was not part of this Scheme. But he was going to keep popping up. Why here? Why didn't he go and impose himself on the Smiths?

He had known them longer. They were the ones that had really benefited from his old man's knowledge. Why come here for the chat? A knock at the door was followed by Stanley sticking his head in the door.

"Sorry, Dave. Will I come back?"

"It's OK, come in." Stanley came in, carrying a rolled-up poster in his hand.

"James, this is Stanley Hutchings, the chief ganger around here. Stanley, this is James Cameron Black, a former client of mine."

James stood up and proffered a hand. "How do you do, Mr Hutchings?"

Stanley shook it, "And you, James. Listen, will I come back? I only came in to give you this poster, the one you always said you fancied."

"No, don't go away." Dave stood up and took the poster, unrolled it a little, turned to the wall, and let it roll down and open. An unsmiling face of Karl Marx looked out on the office. Dark eyes above a dark beard, eyes that seemed to look everywhere. The smaller head of a man with a sharp nose was tucked into the shoulder of Marx. Dave signalled to James with his head. The sellotape was wanted. James passed the tape to Stanley. Between the two of them Dave and Stanley taped the poster to the wall, behind the desk. They stood back and admired the poster.

"Do you want the Che Guevara as well? I'm fed up looking at it. Thought I might put up some from the miners' strike."

"Well, if you don't want it, I'll take it. James was sipping at his coffee. His eyes were on his cup. "You'll know this man, James, eh?"

James shrugged. "Yes, yes, of course I do."

"Religion is the opiate of the masses. Don't think that's your cup of coffee."

"I'm not quite sure if he actually said that, David. Personally I find his theories on religion as the manifestation of the human's fear of being left alone, in a world dominated by the struggle of the individual to survive in a cash society, a much more intellectually challenging way of putting it."

"Eh? I thought I just said that. Up the workers, anyway."

Stanley was scratching his head and making faces. James had said a mouthful.

"Well," said Dave, "it'll fill up a space." He sat down. "Stanley, while you're here, I'm having trouble getting a pitch booked for the two teams. Any suggestions?"

"Sorry, Dave, not my line at all. Did you try Community Education?"

"Ach, those people haven't a clue. Problem is, this is my spare time. I can't use the Bellesmyre clout on them."

Stanley shrugged his shoulders, and his lips could offer no suggestions. His forehead was purling, lips were pouting, but there was nothing coming.

"Sorry, old son. Can the Sports Centre people not squeeze you in somewhere?"

"Kiddin? They're trying to squeeze us out. Only thing they've offered is a cricket pitch, and they think that's a great joke."

James slid his coffee cup onto the desk and straightened up.

"Cricket? A joke? Who said that?"

Dave Parks should have known not to mention the word. "Relax, James. Nobody here knows one end of a cricket bat from another."

"Then I shall teach them."

"James, the kind of blokes that I'm talking about are waiting to commit legalised criminal assault on one another. If a man goes down, they're queueing up to strike him with the booted foot."

"Then they have been taught the wrong sport."

"James. That's as maybe."

Stanley was weighing up the situation. Smile just beginning. Getting ready to stir it. "We could always get some gear. Community Resources, that sort of thing."

"Stanley. Are you having me on? You wouldn't get that lot within a mile of a cricket pitch."

"Don't know. Before we came here the Mormons used to have them up there playing baseball, until somebody spilled the beans they could be the CIA."

James was on his feet. "I am not CIA, neither am I the Secret Service. What I do, I do for the Lord."

Stanley's eyes had widened. James's fervour was real. James was stamping a finger on the desk. "If you can get the place and the players, I shall do the rest. I shall coach them, explain the rules, show them how to play, with no criminal assaults."

"James, I don't know if we could allow a civilian out with them. Stanley, tell me you're only joking."

"Worth a shot."

"Stanley."

"Let's go and see Bernie."

All down the stairs Dave Parks made his protest, but Stanley made a joke of it all. James had made his face into something awfully serious. Cricket was being talked about.

Bernie listened and called over Popeye, who was taking a turn at the table. Popeye leaned on his cue like a shepherd on his crook. Meditation. He spoke.

"Don't know, man, that's fuckin weird."

"What's weird in it?" asked Bernie. If Popeye said it was weird, then to Bernie there was fuck all wrong with it.

"Fuckin cricket, man. Get a grip."

"Looks no bad on the telly. Might get a chance to skelp you bastards with that ball. It's solid, man."

"Skelp me fuck all, you. Try it and you'll get a stump up your arse until it knocks your teeth out the way. Who's showing us how to play?"

"James here, and I'll give a hand. Just so we can get a game."

Stanley added his encouragement, for what it was worth.

"Be a laugh, if nothing else."

"Cricket is a serious business," said James.

"What do you say, Popeye? Are your boys game? Mine'll be there."

"Mine are always game. For anything."

The leaders of the young teams had agreed. The game was on. Just like that. And Dave Parks was getting involved with James again.

"James, looks like we've got ourselves a game. Two o'clock Friday."

"What about transport?" asked Bernie.

199

"We'll get the Community bus," answered Stanley.

No bother. We'll get the bus. But Stanley was not going to be there. James stepped forward and took Bernie's hand and shook it, turned to Popeye and shook his till the dragon on his bicep wobbled.

"May the best team win."

"Aye, we will," said Popeye

"Win fuck all you. C'mon, we've got a game waitin."

Looking back, Dave Parks saw Popeye look up from his preparation for a pot and tap his head. Dave Parks had the arm around James's shoulder and was guiding him to the door.

"James, I don't want to be rude, but I've got quite a busy day ahead. Can you maybe give me a ring towards the end of the week and I'll tell you what the arrangements are?"

James agreed.

The outside door led onto steps which ran down to street level. Dave Parks was going out for a breath of fresh air and to make sure James was safely away. Up the street a crowd was gathering. An ambulance siren was getting louder. A boy had broken from the crowd and was rushing the news down to the centre. Up the steps he came, pushing past James, trying to push past Dave Parks.

"Hey. What's happening? What is it?"

"Somebody got Collier. Stuck him. A breadknife man. Right in the street."

"Is he dead?"

"Don't think so, don't know, but he'll be off the scene for a while, that's for sure."

"Who was it?"

"Fuck me, I don't know. Fuckin would never tell you anyhow."

Dave Parks stood aside, let him in. James was waiting at the bottom of the steps, looking up the road. The ambulance had arrived and the crowd was making space.

"Anybody you, know, David?"

"Ach, just some minor crook around here. On the drugs scene."

"Oh. Somebody attack him for his drugs then?"

"Could be."

"It's a bad business."

"Aye. It's bad. That's us in the papers again."

James looked up the street. The crowds were ringing the ambulance.

"If you give me your phone number, David, I'll be away."

"Did I not give you it? Sorry. Have you got a pen there?"

James held out a battered green notebook. "Put it inside the back cover."

"There you go." The number was scribbled on the back page. "Sorry I'm in such a hurry, James."

"Not at all. I understand. You have your work to do."

The news from the messenger was bringing out the rest. Bernie pushed by. Popeye followed him still carrying his cue. Women were bringing their children out from the café, unemployed males and females brought to life by a near-death.

"James, I'll need to go. I'll see you."

James waved a hand in answer and went striding down the street.

"Hey, James. James. You're going the wrong way. You go up that way."

"Thank you, David, but I thought I'd try and find a way back down that way."

"Please yourself, but I don't think there is one."

James waved again.

Inside, Stanley was talking to the receptionist, through the tinted glass. He straightened up. "Dave. Wee bit excitement, eh? Collier, was it? Couldn't have happened to a better man. Suppose that means we'll have our pal Naismith running about."

"Could be. Aye. As long as he keeps out the café. Don't want him scaring away our custom. Took us long enough to get them in."

"Lot o thanks to you for that, Dave boy."

"Sure. Where you off to?"

"Dinner-time son. Man cannot live by deprivation alone. I'm off to the Poacher's Friend for a wee pub lunch. You for coming?"

"Not for me, thanks. I'm a bit busy just now."

"C'mon now. Get a grip. Give you a break."

"What about them out there? Who gives them a break? Can they stop for a wee pub lunch? They pay for it, we eat it."

"Ah, come off it, Dave. That's crap. We work amongst it, OK, right, this is where we work. We do our best, man, that's as much as we can do. Start bringing them in food parcels and they'll throw it in your face. They know the score. This is our work. We try to help them get as much out the system as possible. That's all they want. They don't want us to be their bosom buddies. No way. C'mon. Get a grip. I don't think anybody out there will grudge us a pie and a pint, as long as we do the business for them."

"I know, I know, I know I know know I know. I'm sorry Stanley, it's just . . ."

"I know as well. Don't let it get through to you, Dave. You'll crack up, you'll be a goner, man. Seen blokes like that. No use to anybody at the finish up."

"Aye, I hear you. You're right, but ach, sometimes. But you're right, you're right. It's no our fault. OK. Just to show you how laid back I am, I'll come with you. Wait till I get my jacket."

"Good man. Good man. You won't regret it."

The receptionist freed the door. Stanley stuck his head round and shouted after Dave Parks. "You will not regret this, my man. They do the best lasagne in the City. Ah, man."

****

The cricket pitch was all the grassy parts left over on the edge of the sports enclave made from the reclaimed sites of the fallen factories that the people of Bellesmyre used to work in. Ground now impacted, grassed, astro-turfed, set out and surrounded by staked-up saplings and high overlooking banks of floodlights. A pavilioned oasis set in the sandstone city, of bowling rink, tennis court, football pitch for all weathers, a rugby pitch that doubled for American football, hockey pitch and, at the far end, a cricket pitch whose far unmarked boundaries touched the lines of the pitches for rugby, and ran along a screen of young dark green trees, imported specially from Western Germany because they grew quicker.

The car park was full. Mary turned the car and was off. No wave. The lads were here: two bunches of them milling around in front of the sports centre building, kicking at bits of paper, sitting on their haunches. There was no sign of James. Unlike a gentleman not to be punctual.

Bernie was coming forward to be the first to moan.

"Hey, big man, they'll no give us the keys for the cricket pavilion. What's the score with these people?"

Dave Parks gave the Dave Parks shrug.

The woman behind the till at the reception put her mouth to the hole in the glass and asked: Yes? which asked everything. After explanation and showing the Social Work ID the keys of the cricket pavilion were passed over.

"Have you got equipment?" she asked.

"We were hoping you would have some."

"Cost extra. And we've only got one bat and one ball and one pad thing here."

"Pardon?"

"One bat, one ball, one pad. The club has the rest."

"The club?"

203

"The cricket club. They play at weekends, and it's hired out sometimes during the week if anybody wants it."

"So where can we get the equipment?"

"Oh, I'm afraid we let the club take their equipment home. Saves us having to take care of it. But the secretary told me there should be wickets in the pavilion."

"Ah, give us what you've got."

The single ball, battered shapeless, and the single bat, with peeling rubber grip on the handle, and the single, dusty pad were brought out from an adjoining room by a silent instructor in a blue tracksuit. Dave Parks did not offer any thanks. Passing the reception he stuck his mouth into the hole in the glass.

"You won't mind if we come back and use the showers, will you?" The morning was off to a bright start. At least the sun was shining.

Bernie wanted the bat. So did Popeye, but he settled for the ball when he found how hard it was. He began to throw it at members of his team who ran and dodged. Bernie waved the bat in the air. A smaller boy who had settled in by the side of Dave Parks got the pad which he carried bearer-style, settling the radius of his head into the inside curve of the pad. The two teams were here. Two workmen were here over in the far boundary by the trees. Need to be some six to hit them out there.

The pavilion was empty; except for a small tall-legged table and three empty bottles of Robinson's barley water. which sat in a neat group in a corner. Benches along two opposing walls. The other two walls held the ranks of lockers. All locked. But probably empty anyway. A canvas bag stuck out from under one of the benches. Dave pulled it out. Inside were the wickets and bails. Dave stood up.

"Just as well you lot have nothing to change into any-way."

"Bloody cold in here mister," said the boy with the pad.

"Benches would make a good fire," said somebody.

"Give us a break lads."

Popeye had found a door and found the lavatory.

"Might've left a bit of soap," he said.

Another door went somewhere, but it was locked. None of the keys fitted the lock. Dave Parks was for saying nothing, but Popeye had been watching. He wanted to know.

"What's in there?"

"Something that's either too good for you lot, or maybe it's gear that belongs to somebody."

"I thought this was a public pavilion?"

"Aye, well, it is, and then again . . ."

"Then again it's no for us. Is that what you're sayin?"

"I don't think so."

"Will I kick it in?"

"It's a good job I know you're kidding."

"Think so?"

James was on the verandah, at the door. In his white flannels and white shoes; wearing the whites. James Cameron Black in his whites and with his cricket bag had come for a real game of cricket by the looks of it.

"Good morning, David."

"Mornin JCB. How's things?"

"Very well, thank you. And you? Raring to go?"

"Aye. Raring to go. What do you think?"

"Looks fine. A trifle Spartan, but that was never a fault. The pitch looks well."

"Never knew it was sick."

"What's the matter, David? You don't sound too enthusiastic."

"Ach, don't bother about me. It's just the mood I'm in. I've a wee bit on my mind just now James. Carry on. You're the expert."

James looked around. Some of the boys were sitting on the benches. An empty bottle rumbled as it was rolled from one bench to the other. Some of the boys were sitting on the edge of the verandah, swinging their legs, passing the smokes, shouting across to one another in friendly cricketing rivalry, in a language that an Australian umpire would have frowned upon.

"Well, David, if you just tell these young men to get changed, we'll make a start."

"Changed? Changed? James. This is it. This is them. Ready to go."

"Oh, I see."

Dave Parks hung up his jacket and called on those with jackets or parkas to hang them up. JCB's pullover had a green chevron at the neck and green rings around the cuffs. Popeye hung his pullover up and turned from the wall. He was wearing his white T-shirt with MOTORHEAD and lightning jags printed on it and all ripped over his breast. A blue and gold striped tie hung around his neck, neatly tied in a schoolboy knot. He was putting on a green cap.

"I can see you're taking this seriously, Popeye," said Dave.

The players were mustered outside, and almost naturally formed up into two teams, except for the pad-bearer who now had the pad strapped to his right leg and limped first to one side, then the other, and finally settled at the side of Dave Parks. There was nine on one side and eight on the other. Dave Parks became Solomon.

"You take the wee man, Popeye."

"Aye. Very good. Can we no get you? Sammy's a bit on the wee side."

"We'll see. You can toss for me or James."

"We'll take the old boy," said Bernie.

"Can you play this, Dave?" asked Popeye.

"Well, wee bit maybe."

"Suppose we'll take you then." Bernie did not protest.

Dave asked James to take over.

James nodded an agreement as he knelt down and unpacked, untied his gear from his bag. As well as his two pairs of pads, his beloved bat and his ball, James produced one pair of batsman's gloves and a pair for a wicket-keeper.

The players had mustered outside, standing around, kicking at the turf, wrestling, abusing the wrestlers, impatient to be doing something. James came out carrying the equipment which he placed on the verandah. He asked, in a voice that ordered, that the table and a bench be brought out from inside. Bernie pointed to two of his team, flicked a finger and they moved to oblige. Popeye did likewise and two moved, one giving him the two fingers. The table and bench were brought out. James took up a position as near the centre of the muster as was possible.

"Boys, we are here to play cricket. The object of cricket is not to win, but to play. To play, play up and play the game. THAT is the object. To play. While playing, each team must, of course, try and score more runs than the other, whilst the other, fielding side, tries to stop this happening by bowling them out or otherwise dismissing them. But always this is to be carried on in a spirit of fair play."

James was a preacher, and there was an element of the sermon in here. James was using his administrator/preacher voice. The capers had ceased, the cynical interjections had ceased. The natives were listening. James continued.

"Has anyone ever played this before?"

Two or three said a couple of times at school. Some had seen it on the telly, some had fallen asleep to it on the telly.

"Fine," said James. "Now, what I want you to do is listen closely to what I am about to teach you, then I want you to forget all about it when the game starts. First, line up in your two teams, in lines, each man face a man."

The trainees shuffled into two lines, each man facing a man. Popeye faced Bernie. Dave Parks took up a blank file. James paraded between the two ranks, then stopped in the centre. His arms and bat were held aloft for silence. When sound had settled to silence, he spoke.

"I want you all to, now, listen. Listen." James stopped speaking. He adopted a batting posture. "Listen. Sssh. Listen."

Everyone looked at one another. Some giggled a bit, but one by one listened. A bird sang somewhere. A lorry of some sort passed outside the ground. Two pigeons made gurgling noises on the pavilion roof, their feet tapping on the tiles. It was quiet. James was a frieze. It was quiet. Sammy's eyes were wide and his mouth had fallen open. He was listening with all his might. But somebody could listen no longer.

"Hey mister . . ."

"Sssh. Listen. I want you to hear it."

They listened. And Dave Parks was listening. But the impatient one couldn't listen.

"Hey mac, what are we listening for? What are we supposed to hear?"

"Listen for the sound of this stroke I am making. Listen for the sound of the stroke."

"Oh, aye."

James came out of the batting position; straightened up.

"A stroke is made when the ball strikes the bat, would you agree?" Some nodded, some looked doubtful, some spat. "Well, when I make the stroke here, if you listen you will hear the sound of the stroke made by the batsman and the bat."

"But you're no hittin anything, you're only hittin mid-air."

"And if you listen you will hear the sound of the stroke. Shoosh. Listen."

James stepped, leaned into the stroke, brought the bat down square, held it at the stroke.

"LISTEN!"

"Fuck this mister, hit it a wallop, and we might hear it."

James eased himself straight. He ignored the doubting Thomas.

"That was for your ears. Now we will try your eyes."

James went to Bernie, Popeye, gave each of them a bat. Both were natural right-handers. James adjusted their grip, aligning their hands, talking to them, swinging their arm through the stroke, showing them the grip. Now he spoke to the teams in general.

"In batting it is normal to present a square bat. Push it out, bringing your body with it, lean into it, and listen, and hear the sound of the stroke. Hear your square bat push the air around its face, hear the sound of the willow on the leather."

He demonstrated and made Popeye and Bernie imitate. They tried and were congratulated. Now James made the two lines face each other directly, man to man, face to face, each in the batting posture.

"NOOOW, bat."

The two lines made batting movements to one another, and held the bat in the square position. James passed up and down the lines, tucking their heads in, squaring the bats up where necessary.

"Right. Again. Ready? NOOW, bat." They batted, held the stroke. "Who heard the sound?"

"Me, oh me," said Sammy.

One or two others grunted ayes, some grunted, most were looking at James with question marks stamped on their faces.

"I heard fuck all," said the hard listener. "There's fuck all to hear."

James called on the lines to go through the motions again, this time demanding they expel air from the lungs as they made the play, and to gasp out, haaah-HOH, as the knock was executed. James passed among them as they moved, panted out, gasped out, shouted out, and made their play. He kept calling: again, together, again. Dave Parks looked up. Both lines were executing their shots together. Both lines were moving as one.

"Head down, Mr Parks."

"Haaaah-HOH!"

James called on the teams to stop. He switched to the basics for hitting the runs: keeping the bat close, watching the wrists, but always listening for the stroke. The coach turned to bowling: demonstrating the difference between a throw and a good ball. The two lines were put back, released to run up towards one another, to stop a yard short and bowl straight-armed, arm brushing the ear. Some were carried by their momentum to be met and pushed to the ground by their counterpart and have playful kicks administered to the ribs. James yelled for quiet and waved his bat for order. When quiet came he addressed the ranks.

"That is all I can teach you in this short space of time. This is your last instruction. Always remember: the last instruction is the one you obey. Now. Forget everything I have said to you. Everything. Forget it all."

"Ah, thanks very much," said Popeye.

"That's easy done," said somebody behind James.

James held up his bat. "You must forget about method. Do not think of how you are going to do it. Batsmen, think only of the sound of the stroke. Keep your eye on the ball and do not think of the stroke, hear it. But remember, whatever ball game you are involved in, you must always keep your eye on the ball. As you listen and watch, your body will respond. Do not think, play it."

"What about us bowlers?" asked Bernie, making part of his team selection known.

"Bowlers also must not think about how to bowl. There is only the wicket. See the wicket. See the wicket until it becomes the only real thing on the pitch. The eye must see and the mind must be full with the wicket. The body will respond."

"Can we no just get a fuckin game goin?"

"I think we should, James, eh?"

"Certainly, certainly, but remember, forget the method. Look with your eyes, hear with your ears and let your body respond."

Dave Parks stepped in. "Popeye, Bernie, c'mon. Toss to see who's in."

A coin was spun. Popeye called heads and it was tails. Bernie chose to bat first.

James went back to his bag, delved, and came up with some pieces of paper. He brought them over to Bernie. "Mister Bernie, here are some score cards."

Bernie studied the card. He turned to Dave: "How d'you keep this filled in, Dave?"

Dave took it for a look. At the top it was marked Cliftonpar School. "Don't ask me. Too many wee boxes and funny names there for me. Use the back. It's blank. Just put in who's batting and how many they've scored; then we'll add them up. Never mind about the bowlers."

Bernie turned to one of his team. "Davie, you deliver the milk, you be the scorer."

Davie took the card and looked at it, pulled a face. "You got a pen?"

Dave Parks gave him one.

Popeye kept a hold of the ball. He wanted to be the first bowler. Dave Parks set the field, with Popeye waving his arms in endorsement. Sammy was made wicket-keeper because somebody said he was a good goalie and he had not parted with the single pad. Two near enough slips were set, one near enough mid-off, and the rest put around with an equal distance between them, alternately nearer and further from the wicket. A classic field. Popeye waved his agreement.

Bernie came in with a team-mate called Harry. They came forward like some form of alien life, experiencing difficulty in walking with the pads on. Bernie positioned the bat, asking for centre. Harry held his over his shoulder like a hod.

Bernie shouted: "Hey. You. Is this centre?"

Harry shrugged his shoulders.

Popeye was walking away from the wicket, stepping out his run-up. He turned. Bernie footered at the crease, until, "Right," he shouted.

Popeye ran; ran up, swung his arm up and over and the ball was pitched up. It pitched well clear of the wicket. Bernie hung his bat out to dry, waggling it away. Dave Parks turned to face the pavilion, arms extended.

"What you doin?" asked Bernie.

"The ball was wide. I'm signalling a wide. Your team gets a run for that."

"You the umpire as well then?"

"Well, I . . ."

"I don't remember anybody askin you. How can you be a player and be umpire at the same time?"

"Bernie, I was just trying to keep the scorers right."

"But you're playin me. I mean, obvious this time, but you're really playin for them. Know what I mean?"

"It was just a wide." Dave signalled James to come and umpire from square leg.

Popeye was shouting. He was waiting to bowl. Bernie tapped the ground with the bat and nodded hard. Popeye ran. Bernie hit, and somebody was off on a gallop through near enough the covers. Bernie and Harry ran three. Popeye was swearing at the fielder. Next ball up, Harry knocked his own bails off and threw the bat to the ground. Popeye danced like a high-trotting horse.

Next man in strapped the pads on, picked up the bat and Popeye nearly took his head off before he was ready. Number three wanted some more time. He called Popeye a mad bastard and took up his guard. Popeye was walking back and put the two fingers up.

Next ball up was short and bounced high over the batsman's head and over Sammy's head. Sammy ran, limped after it. Dave

Parks took the ball to bowl from the tree plantation end. On the run-up a decision was made to bowl it easy to Bernie. Bernie stuck the bat in front and another run was made. The team on the bench shouted and yelled and the scorer slapped the table. Anybody listening must have heard the word wanker. Dave Parks bowled three wides. Third bat was out caught behind by Sammy, after a ball from Popeye struck the fingers of the batsman, who hopped around, waving his fingers and cursing at Popeye.

"You should've been listenin," shouted Popeye.

Most of the players managed to get some kind of strike at the ball, and the umpires were turning a blind set of eyes to any foot infringements by the bowlers. The balls came in from all angles. In its own fashion the game went on. The street repartee between the curses was making James smile. When the batsmen were changing over and taking up the pads there was a chance to speak.

"Is this the cricket you know and love, James?"

"Excellent. Could not be bettered. 'The green sward level, the sun on high, my chums around me, athletes all, brandishing bat and bowling ball, speaks of an England that will never fall'."

"Is that a poem or are you just time-warpin again?"

"An Old Boy said it about the School."

"Oh. Never said that about mine. Only thing people said was, thank Christ I'm finished in there."

"David."

"Sorry. Thank whoever, I'm finished in there."

Play continued. Bernie was proving to have some talent for the game. Probably because he was the leader and never listened to anything anybody ever said about anything, if it disagreed with his own thinking. His team had made a creditable forty-two for six when it became a not quite so creditable forty-two for seven. James was the last man in. He buckled up the straps, took up his bat, and tapped it around in front of the wicket until Dave Parks acknowledged the centre. He was ready. It was Popeye to bowl. Popeye came in fast and the ball was a throw. James dodged it by moving his head only. A movement from above the shoulders and a fast dangerous throw was made to look simply wayward. Popeye came again. Fast in, and James put his head down and lifted the bat.

The sound was clean and the ball flew; players scampered, and the pigeons at the pavilion scattered as it cracked upon the tiled roof and rolled down to drop on the ground. James was causing a stir. Dave Parks signalled a six.

"Many's that they are?" shouted Sammy.

"Forty-eight," shouted Davie the scorer from between two lengths of long wiggly hair that surrounded his face.

James eased back on Popeye. Now he was contenting himself to placing the ball where he and his partner could run the twos that would let him keep strike, playing the ball where the fielders always had to run; run hard in hope but never quite get there in time. On one ball, James's partner got greedy and tried for three, came too far, and Sammy got the ball from extra cover and Sammy the wicket-keeper got him out with a long throw. All out for sixty-two. Sammy was delighted as James patted him on the back. Popeye was trying hard to be the sportsman.

"Think he fancies his chances at the cricket, old boy, eh?"

"Could be, Popeye. But can he play pool? Who's going in first?"

"Thought me and you."

"Can I go in first?" asked Sammy.

"You? You can go in last, that's where you're goin. Best men first. Me and Dave here."

"Best don't always go in first, you. Shows how much you know."

"They go in first in this team, right?"

"He can go in my place, I don't mind."

"Nothin to do about mindin. I'm skipper, right?"

"Right."

"So what I say goes. It's me an you Dave. Right, you?"

It was right for Sammy. Dave Parks and Popeye Hunter opened. Bernie was bowling. James took up the wicket-keeper's position. Bernie bowled and Popeye waved his bat at it.

"Wide," shouted Popeye.

"No wide," said James.

"What d'you mean, no wide. It was wide a mile."

"That ball wasn't wide."

"Think you need specs mister."

Bernie delivered another, and Popeye managed to get his bat in front of it. The ball bounced to mid-off and Popeye ran when he saw Dave Parks was running. Dave Parks settled and waited for Bernie. It came in straight, only bounced up a little, but Dave Parks stepped to it and slashed it to gully or near enough, but it flew between the two slips. James signalled a four.

"Well done, son," shouted Popeye.

The bat was lifted in acknowledgement of the congratulations for this cracking shot. The next proved an easy single.

Bernie brought on as bowler the tallest man in his team, who was the tallest person in Bellesmyre; a thin lad of about six-foot four in height with long skinny arms that dangled. By Bernie's actions he looked as if he was miming out the precise way he wanted to ball to be bowled and from what height. The lad was nodding on down.

Popeye had the strike. The young giant stamped in. An arm came up like a solitary bladed windmill. The ball hit short and bounced close-too, but past Popeye's head.

"You tryin to kill me? Hey, ref, what about that? Did you see it?"

"A perfectly good bouncer, Mister Popeye. But he's not allowed to do it too often."

"Better not be. And don't call me Mister Popeye, you. I'm just Popeye."

The human maypole stomped in again. This time Popeye managed to duck.

"Fuck sake, you. What you on? Did you see that one, you?"

"Yes. But I don't think he means it. If it happens again maybe I'll warn him."

"Warn him? I'll cut his fuckin fingers off."

"No need to speak like that. It's a game we're playing. This is a game"

"Some game when some cunt's tryin to kill ye."

James went down the wicket and spoke to the bowler who looked down from his height and shook his head and nodded away and shook his head. James returned to his position.

"You tell him?"

"I told him."

The bowler came in. His arm came round. A ball bounced and Popeye lifted his bat to protect his face. The sound of willow on leather was heard and James was jumping high and shouting: owzat? as his hand held the ball.

"What you shoutin about? You don't think I'm going out to that? He's fouling. That was too high or short or somethin. You're not on."

"It was a good delivery. You're out."

"Hey, Dave, d'you hear this man? He's tryin to tell us that's out. You tell him."

"He's the man, Popeye. If he says out, I'll go along with that."

Popeye was staring. "Whose side are you on anyway?"

"Not a question of sides, Popeye. There's got to be an umpire somewhere."

"Aye, but him? He's on the other side. The other side, man. And you're takin his word. Fuck me. I mean to say; I'm daft an I can see that's flamin stupid."

Dave Parks was shrugging again.

Popeye threw the bat down. "Fuck you an your cricket!" Popeye walked to the pavilion and gave up the pads.

Next man in began in the classic ducked-down position and more or less stayed there until the young giant's spell was over. Bernie bowled on and was not very good. James had to dive to save the wides. Each time he dived shouts would come from Popeye and his cronies at the bench. The score crept up. Dave Parks hit two fours and a single off the tiring giant before number three was caught out at what passed for second slip. Next two were out for ducks and joined Popeye on the bench, adding their shouts to his. One of the batsmen skied one and it travelled, nearly hitting one of the workmen who were working their way nearer.

The score scraped along to forty-five for five. Bernie asked James to bowl. Bernie took wicket. James was using a short run. So James was a spinner.

First ball up and Dave Parks stepped down the wicket and whacked it far away over James's head for six. There was no recollection of seeing it, the body had responded. Lucky strike. James was standing, waiting on the ball. His face was giving the game away. Dave Parks had upset the man. And Dave Parks did not know how it had been accomplished. It was just a step, a swing, and a hit. There it was. Away. And James was none too happy. James was thrown the ball by an out-of-breath runner. He rubbed it between his palms. He rubbed it on his trousers. He stepped up and Dave Parks watched, had the eye on the ball, saw it come through the air, saw it land, saw it bounce, tightened the grip, lifted the bat and the ball was dancing around the ankles somewhere as the bat became a shovel.

Dave Parks lifted his head. "LBW?"

James gave a nod. Dave Parks was out.

The boy who came in at number seven was a round lad whose stomach almost protruded downwards onto the pads once he had manoeuvred them on. This man had a plan. He survived by leaving all balls alone, playing the percentage game: if no play, no error. If lucky they might miss both himself and the stumps. The other batsman in was a swinger, and Bernie from the other end had four taken off the first two balls of an over to some solid swiping. On the third ball the batsman stepped back and touched his bail. The bail slipped, but jammed between the wickets. He stood and looked at it. Fieldsmen came for a look at it. People from the bench came for a look at it. Popeye led them out from the pavilion for a look at it. Around the wicket one or two tried to blow it down. Others stamped the ground. The bail stayed in place.

"I'm afraid that's out," said James.

"How is it out?" asked Popeye.

"It's the rules. It's out."

"How can it be out when the wicket's still up?"

"The bail is off, that's why."

"Ah, but the bail's no on the deck."

"It's off."

"It's off but it's still no hit the deck."

"As long as the bail is off the wicket it's out."

"But supposin a gust o wind came and blew it right up in the air and left it back in its place, would that be out?"

"I suppose in such cases it would depend upon the length of time one waited for a wind. It's silly. The game must go on."

"Are you sayin it might no be out?"

"Mister Popeye. The rule is quite clear. Law twenty-eight. A disturbance of a bail, whether temporary or not, shall not constitute a complete removal, but the wicket is down if a bail in falling lodges between two of the stumps."

"I don't think you can argue with that, Popeye."

"This you stickin up for him again?"

"The man's right, Popeye. That's all there is to it."

Popeye was staring, scratching his chest. "You think he's right in everything, that's your trouble. Just because he knows the rules."

"Popeye, we're talking about cricket here. The man knows his cricket. It's as simple as that."

"Aye, so it fuckin is."

Sammy was nudging the batsman put out. He wanted the pads. JCB helped him strap up and showed him again how to grip as Popeye led the rest of the team away, still muttering and cursing his luck and the rules, and the umpires.

"Many do we need?" asked Sammy.

"Ten," said Dave.

"Ten hundred with that old bastard," shouted back Popeye.

"Ten to make and a match to win," said James.

"What's that mister?"

"It's a poem:
    'There's a breathless hush in the close tonight,
    Ten to make and a match to win —
    A bumping pitch and a blinding light,
    An hour to play and the last man in.
    And it's not for the sake of the ribboned coat,
    Or the selfish hope of a season's fame,
    But his Captain's hand on his shoulder smote —
    "Play up! play up! and play the game"'."

"Don't know it," said Sammy.

Sammy took up position at the crease.

"Go to it young Sammy!" yelled Dave Parks.

JCB was bowling from the sports-centre end. Sammy staved off the first ball. Second ball Sammy never saw, but it skimmed past the off-stump. Third ball Sammy straightened up before it left

JCB's hand. Down it came, and off it went, and up and over the ropes being put across by the workmen. It was a six. Sammy had scored a six off JCB. JCB applauded, and gave a shake of his head to Sammy as he got the ball back. James came in again, bowled. Sammy was swinging the bat tight to his body, square elbows up, connected, and followed through. The ball went to mid-off but the fielder muffed it and Sammy was off down the wicket, lugging his legs inside the pads, turning, screaming at his mate to come for another and running, running, stretching back and got in. Bernie came over to James.

"You takin it easy on him or something? Another wee four and they've won it."

James opened his mouth to say something, but closed it. JCB made his run up, delivered. This ball was a slow one, up in the air, curving, coming down and Sammy swung and Sammy missed and the ball hit a rent in the turf and spun away, miles away, from the stumps. Sammy was saved. Bernie returned the ball.

"You're definitely at it, old man."

JCB caught the ball but said nothing. JCB changed his approach. He was standing more side-on. The approach was hardly two long steps. He was bending hard and his arm was up, slower, holding the ball, releasing, and the ball came and came and Sammy was watching and Sammy was waiting, preparing, and the ball bounced and it spun and Sammy's bails had fallen as he held his bat in the air and stood still and looked back to see them fall. Sammy was out.

Bernie's boys were jubilant. The game was finished. And they had won. James came up and shook hands with Sammy and clapped him on the back.

"You're as good a natural cricketer as I've seen."

"Aye. Says who?"

JCB drew the stumps. Dave Parks tried to console Sammy. "Hard lines wee man. Thought you might do it there for a minute."

"That'll be right. No chance. He was only kiddin me on."

"You think so? Ach, I don't think so. Not his style. Plays the game right, y'know. Plays it right up. No favours."

"Reckon?"

"Positive."

Bernie was holding out a hand to Popeye. "Good game, man, eh?"

"Fuck off. That old cunt gave you the game."

"Did he hell."

"He did. Every time he opened his mouth, we had another man out. Him and his fuckin rules. Knows the rules OK, but that's nothing. Maybe that means he can cheat easier."

James was passing and shook Bernie's hand. Popeye turned away and went into the pavilion. James went round and shook as many hands as he could find, then sat on the verandah. Sammy threw him the ball. JCB threw it back. "You keep it, young Bradman." James went into the pavilion. Players came in and slumped on a bench, passed out the smokes. The other bench was brought in. Popeye was scratching something on the wall.

"Can I see the score-card?" asked James.

"We done it in our nappers," said Popeye. "Don't need a rubber there."

"Doesn't matter. It's simply that if one puts the scores on paper, it helps to recall who did what."

"Never needed to score anything as long as you were referee." Popeye kicked at the door that was locked. It opened. Lots of equipment filled a small room, as though stashed away in a hurry. "Hey, have a swatch at this."

"Don't go playing about in there," said Dave Parks. "Leave it be."

"OK Dave. Just looking."

Dave Parks went outside for the table. Sammy was parrying and thrusting with a bat.

"Still practising, wee man?"

"Aye."

"Still mad at James for getting you out?"

"Getting me out, that was nothing, I told you."

"But if you think he was making it easy for you, you forget one thing."

"What's that?"

"You might have been playing well."

"Ah, but . . ."

From inside the pavilion there was shouting. Scuffling. Probably wrestling. A scream. The day had been too easy for Dave Parks.

Dave ran to the pavilion. The giant and two others barred the door. Dave Parks tried to get through. They were too strong. Dave Parks was turned and held against an outside wall.

As James screamed he struggled. Somebody was holding his ankles. The net came first. Netting, and somebody inside it: James. Popeye and a team were pushing at the bundle and JCB was down. They rolled him, bumped him off the verandah. James was wrapped in the practice nets and being rolled around the outfield. Popeye took the bat from Sammy and began striking at the bundle on the ground.

—POPEYE, YOU BAMMY BASTARD.

A head butted Dave Parks. Blood came from the nose.

—I'll remember you son.

—Touch me and you'll get your books.

James had gone quiet. Dave Parks tried to talk reason. Popeye continued to swing and strike at the bundle as his team rolled it around like a carpet.

—Referee fuck all you. How's this for ungentlemanly conduct? What's the rules say about this? Will I get a yellow card?"

—FUCKIN LEAVE HIM!

A head connected again. Dave Parks struggled, trying to knee a groin, balls, anywhere, bite anything. Another one piled on. Dave Parks bent at the knee. The whole pile dipped. Now they were on the verandah.

—HIS HEART, MIND HIS HEART!

There was some hesitation The two workmen were running over. They carried mallets. Popeye was hesitating. He stood back, two hands around the grip. The bat was drawn back above his head, and let fly into the heap. The net was not moving.

—C'mon to fuck. Leave the bastards.

Popeye ran. His team ran.

Bernie's voice came from above Dave Parks. A hand was slapping the face. "Sorry about that, big man. But there's no way we can go to war for you or Freddie Truman there. See ya."

Bernie ran. His team ran. The workmen shouted and waved their mallets, but the young team were off. Sammy ran, came back, dropped the bat, ran again.

"You OK Jimmy?"

"Sure, sure, get James, get that man there."

The net was unravelled and there was James Cameron Black. His head was cut along and through a bruise on his forehead. Blood stained and was sticky on his hair. James moved. A shaky left hand went to his temple. James Cameron Black was not dead.

"How you feeling?" asked one of the workmen.

James groaned. Dave Parks put his head down closer.

"James. Are you OK? James. James."

James was trying to lift his head up. His head was either trembling or nodding quickly. James rolled over on his back and looked at the sky. His arms came up, straight up: a plea for assistance. Tears were in his eyes, and his hands shook.

"I don't think we should move him," said a workman.

James was trying to sit up. With a workman at each arm and Dave Parks pushing from the back, James was lifted to a sitting position. James put his head between his knees and held it there, slumped.

"You OK Jimmy?"

James croaked: "I think so." James rubbed his legs, brought his head up. "My knees. He hammered my knees. Help me up, please."

"Are you sure James? I was considering getting an ambulance."

"No. Not necessary. Please." From the sitting position was harder. JCB's legs were reluctant to hold him up. He was staggering on the spot. "David. Your face. Do I look as bad as you?"

"Well, I had a bad start."

James coughed and spat. Dust and blood came off his lip.

"C'mon, we'll get you blokes to the sports centre. There's a café there. We'll get you a cup of tea or something."

"Thanks. Can you make it, James?"

James lifted an arm up, palm out. The workmen made to grab James as he went on his knees, but they stepped back as they saw the hands come up, clasped together. James was praying. James was praying for the forgiveness of the young people. James was praying for the misguided. The workmen drew back.

"Is he always like this Jimmy?"

"Yes. Always."

"Christ, he'll be all right when this man comes." The workman was pointing with his mallet to the area they had just roped off.

"What man?"

"The American guy. Jason McNeely. One o they evangelists. Christ, where have you been? It's been on the wireless every other day."

"Oh, right. Now that you mention it I think I did see a poster somewhere."

"You mean a million?"

"When's he coming?"

"Middle of the week. Not too bad. We'll get this Saturday and Sunday out it anyway."

"Doing what?"

"Putting up the marquee." The man held his mallet up, pointing to the ropes they had been slinging round to mark off an enclosure. "What do you think this is all in aid of?"

"Mmm. Right."

James had stopped praying. He was moving again. Trying to rise. The workmen moved to him.

"C'mon, Lazarus, up on your feet. Lift up your whatever and walk."

"I'm afraid for the next while I shall be wanting into my bed, not out of it."

"That's the spirit, mister. Feeling a bit better, are you?"

James did not answer.

Dave Parks gathered in the nets. One workman came to help. Together they gathered it in, folding it up, rolling it up, rolling it round as best they could until it formed a cigar-shaped loose mass. Dave took it up, dragged it, jerked it and threw it into the storeroom it had come from. The door was well and truly burst. The door to the WC was open. The WC had water. A dry grey covering of plaster chips and dust showed there was no water in the hand-basin, but the taps were tried anyway. One tap handle flew off and skited around the inside of the sink, but no water.

"James, c'mon in here a minute, we might manage something here."

222

The two workmen helped James; one at either side, one hand out under each of the man's elbows. James came into the WC.

Dave held out a hand. "You got a hankie?"

"I have, yes." James was fumbling in his pockets.

One of the workmen said: I've got one I think, but James had found his.

Dave Parks took it, flushed the cistern, bent and soaked the handkerchief in the rushing water. The hankie was squeezed and Dave wiped at JCB's sore face. After the wipe, the handkerchief was squeezed out over the bowl. The handle on the cistern was pulled again, but the cistern was still filling up.

"What you thinking about?" asked one of the workmen. He pressed into the WC, reached and pulled at the lid of the cistern. It came off. "There you go." He put it to the side. Water was splurging in through the feedpipe. The ballcock looked battered and lumpy.

The green square of cloth was dipped in the tank, wet, excess water squeezed out, made into a pad and dabbed at JCB's face. The process was repeated until the face had at least been wiped of dirt and most of the drying blood.

"Here, do you want this back?"

"Mustn't go without it, David."

"Aye, I suppose so, if you say so." The wet cloth was pocketed by James.

The workmen backed off, James backed out, and Dave Parks followed on out. The workmen were being concerned again. Dave Parks went back, replaced the lid. For no particular reason the handle on the cistern was pulled. The water flushed.

The pavilion door was locked and Dave Parks pocketed the key, giving the padlock a final rattle before stepping off the verandah as James and the workmen moved away to the Centre. The sun had moved round in the sky. It must have been near teatime.

Outside the Centre the men were thanked for their help. James called them Good Samaritans. The men offered to buy James a cup of tea. The offer was refused. The workmen left. Dave turned to James.

"James, I'm going in here to phone for a taxi. I don't know how to put this, but if this thing in here sees you, she'll use it as another excuse to bar the people from Bellesmyre. Know what I mean? No, unless you want to go in and get cleaned up — c'mon, maybe you'd better."

"It's all right, David. I'm fine here. I understand. I do. I'll wait here."

There was no one at reception. The keys were shoved under the glass. A taxi firm's card was pinned above the phone. From somewhere amongst a pop song somebody said the taxi would be five minutes.

"Taxi will be five minutes, James."

"I hope so. I do feel, I'm afraid I, I'm afraid I'm starting to feel it now. All over."

"Do you want to go in and sit?"

"It's all right. Here's fine." James lowered himself onto a brick box that was holding in a fading forsythia. The man was looking his age. Old. The man was feeling the pain. Mental unseen pain, bruising physical pain that was turning features black and blue, and feeling pain because he knew they did not know what they had done and he was probably wishing he could make them see. And Dave Parks hadn't been much help. Maybe you can only be a Samaritan if you get a clear run across the road. Samaritans. He gave tuppence. After he took him in.

"You know about this evangelist that's coming here, James?"

"Yes. I've got tickets."

"Tickets?"

"Well, more properly, Laura got them from her church. Theresa and I are taking her."

"Oh. When is it? Wednesday night?"

"I think so. Oh." JCB was in pain.

"What is it? Where is it?"

"A trifle. Don't worry."

The taxi turned into the car park. Dave waved, but there was no one else there anyway. The taxi drew up. The taxi-driver didn't look too sure. Dave helped James in.

"Are you coming?"

"Well, can you manage yourself? The taxi will take you to the door."

"I just thought, perhaps, Theresa would be pleased to see you."

"Just tell her to see to you, James. I'm sorry about this, James, I really am."

"Not your fault. Oh."

Dave stepped out and closed the door. The taxi-driver was given the instructions and a fiver and tipped his finger to his forehead. Dave waved, but James was facing the front. James was off in the taxi.

****

The woman that was the voice of Scotland on the radio made a pun and a man tittered and that was the news. Next titbit. Today was the day the evangelist had come to town, sponsored by the Ecumenical Trail Blazers for the Bible, and the native Churches. In the five-minute interview the man spoke of his mission to bring the Word to bonnie Scotland at a time when so many were feeling the pain and despair of unemployment and deprivation. The Ecumenical Trail Blazers for the Bible had called him and he had been only too ready to come over — honoured to be asked — he had to come, come to try and win Scottish souls for the Word and set those burning crosses alight, aflame, not only in the wonderful glens, but in the deep canyons of the inner city. He thanked the Organisation for the chance to blaze this particular trail, and hoped the old Scottish clans would rally to the burning cross and come to the meetings; come and be saved, and given new life. Today he was real glad to be in this City, a fair City, a no mean City, a City that reeked of tradition.

Today. Tonight. Dave Parks would be there. Dave Parks was going and not sure why. All reasoning ended up drifting. Going to watch out for James. He was sure to be there. Going to watch for Theresa. Theresa might be there. Let that thought drift away. Don't think about it.

Theresa Kipple

Just get up and go to work as usual. Throw the legs into the trousers; just get ready. Mary was turning over.

"You making the toast?"

"Sure. No problem."

"No problem? Makes a change."

The kitchen was cold. Other side of the venetian blind looked cold. A mist hanging over above the garden. Wet drips dangling from the washing line. On the kitchen radio the voices of Scotland were introducing the same news, the same features; setting today's loop of taped news off on another turn around. On the Clyde station the evangelist was repeating his message. The cat was trying to catch a drip from the tap. Better watch in case the washer bursts. The first roses were about ready to burst out from bud, coloured slips of petal ready to come out and reach for the sun, signal the bees to come suck, and then to die. But come again. Two hostages had been shot somewhere. Those roses should have been pruned back further. Where had the time gone? Where had the interest gone? Mary was up. Slippers padding above; doors opening, doors closing. Mary Parks meeting the day. Meeting Dave Parks for the day. Mr and Mrs Dave Parks. Mrs Mary Parks. What did that mean? Mary Parks had married young Davie Parks, unskilled masher of metal, daft as a brush. Now Mary Parks was the wife of Dave, or David, Parks, ex-factory floor hero, Social Worker, ex-mature student educated into loneliness. Lonely? Lonely. Maybe that was it. Maybe made the break too late. Stuck midway somewhere. In the class, not of the class. Maybe should give the Flosfy Klub another go. But something was different. A silver-threaded payline different. Part of the system different. Maybe. Maybe Dave Parks had changed his stance on Social Work. Maybe butter was better than gunpowder. Maybe Dave Parks had changed his politics. Maybe Dave Parks had changed. Period. Maybe the napper injection had taken effect. Maybe education was the solution Dr Jekyll played around with. Poor people, inarticulate people, alienated people, fucked people, looking to educated Dave Parks. And Dave Parks had emerged from the crowd and taken up his post as a gateman. Only a gateman. A gateman that holds the gate and lets some through to a deeper part of the maze. A gateman that chews lasagne sandwiches and reads the *New Statesman* while the pass is sold all around. Maybe that is Dave Parks. Maybe. Just part of the maze. People presenting problems then passing on, sometimes coming back to check the instructions given, but never far out of sight. People presenting their problems and passing through. Friendly enough. But wary. Wary of Dave Parks. But Dave Parks knew the poverty. I've been there, man. I can relate, man. Sure. Dave Parks wary of the poverty. Avoid it at all costs. Might be contagious. Keeping it

227

at arm's length and so people knew: Dave Parks, gateman. Pallier than most, maybe, but a gateman nonetheless. Lonely gateman in his box. Goggling.

"You got the toast on?"

"Ooops, sorry, I was away there."

"You've been away for a while now."

The toaster accepted the bread. The kettle was filled and last night's teabags cleaned out from the pot. Toaster pinged and crusts appeared over the rim. Bit more in. Teabags to the pot, boiling water to the pot, butter, marmalade to the table, more bloody news and a new day is beginning.

"You want some of this bran on your muesli?"

"Just a spoonful." The Loving Spoonful. What was that record of theirs again?

"I'll need the car today, remember."

"What?"

"I'll need the car. Do you never listen? Wish you'd take your nose out your own backside some time. I'm going out to that chemical place, you know, out thingmy way, what-d'ye-call it? Where they're still waiting on their first covered waggon."

"Oh that place."

"Y'know where I mean. Anyway, I'll need the car."

The toast was nice. Whatever nice is. Nice is nice. Nice is not Theresa Kipple.

"That OK?"

"Sure. It's just that I'm going to be a bit late tonight as it is."

"Why's that?"

The crunch that was coming was going to match the toast.

"I thought I might pop over and see how James is. Sort of see how he is after that doing he took."

"Why do you need to go there? Can you no just phone? Or go during your dinner hour? Apart from that, he's not really your client, is he?"

"You forget I was there."

"So? You were there. Doesn't make you responsible, does it? He's a grown man."

228

"I just think I should go and see him. Right? It's through me he came to be there."

"Don't get carried away with this now. You were there and he was there. That's about all there is to it as far as I can see. Anyway, Marion thinks you're going to see her in her wee school play."

The mist was rising from the garden. And Theresa Kipple was standing looking in the garden window.

"What school play?"

"She told you."

"Oh, aye. What time is it at?"

"Seven o'clock."

"I'll do my best."

—What do you mean, you'll do your best? She's expecting you to be there. You be there.

—I'll do my best.

—Well, I don't think it's very nice to let Marion down to go and see an old man you can see anytime.

—I never said I would let her down.

—Don't give us it. I can read you like a book. You've no intention of going. Dave, what is that man to you?

—Nothing. He's nothing. I just worry about him.

—I wish you'd do some worrying about what goes on around here. Why don't you just let his landlady worry about him?

The bitten toast was put down on the plate and snapped in two. The chair scraping back. She was going to waken the kids. Nothing surer.

"MELANIE. MARION. TIME TO GET READY FOR SCHOO-OO-OOL."

Time to get ready for school. Time to come down and put the pressure on. Not nice.

—Well, if you're taking the car I'd better get ready and go for the bus.

No answer. Only the standing aside to let a man pass up the stairs. The bathroom was reached before Marion and Melanie. Dave Parks' face was in the mirror. Theresa Kipple's face was in the mind. Why that after-shave? That was usually for weekends

229

and weddings. Or funerals. Somebody's little fist was banging on the door.

"I'm coming. Nearly ready."

Marion and Melanie were waiting. Clean, tired faces. Clean, crumpled cotton pyjamas.

"OK, on you go."

"I'm before you."

"I was first. Sure I was, Daddy?"

"Well, I was inside. I didn't really see."

"I need a wee."

"Well, you better go first."

"But I was first."

"But you're a big girl."

The big girl hesitated, and that was enough. She would have to wait.

Marion was following on into the bedroom, watching as the socks were pulled on.

"That sock's got a hole in it."

"Matches the hole in my head."

"You haven't got a hole in your head."

"Yes I have. My mouth."

Marion's smile was like Mary's smile. Like Mary's smile used to be. Who changed the smile? The man with the hole in his head. Dave Parks.

"Have you got a tie for me, Daddy?"

"A tie darlin? A tie?"

"Yes; for my play. I'm a boy, remember."

"Oh. Right. The play. Sure, we'll find you a tie. What colour?"

"Any colour; as long as it's old-fashioned."

"All my ties are old-fashioned darlin. How about this one?"

"Don't like it."

"Neither do I. Well, let's see what else we've got here."

"What about that one? I like that one."

"Oh, that's a College tie; your mother bought me that. Tell you the truth, I've never worn it. But anything for you, sweetheart. Here."

That tie was the tie. Marion liked that one. Liked the pretty colours.

"Can I keep it for always?"

"Sure. Course you can. There, that's Melanie finished. The bathroom's free. Off you go."

Mary was waiting at the foot of the stairs. "That you off then?"

—That's me away.

—What time will you be back at?

—Told you: I don't know.

—Did you tell Marion?

—No point if I might be back, is there?

—Please yourself.

Marion was in the bathroom. Daddy would have to shout.

"Marion. I'm going now. Best of luck with the play. I'll try and be back to see you."

The bathroom door was opening, Dave Parks was waving and out the front door and off to his work.

****

The marquee had been pitched just beyond the cricket pavilion. In length it had to be two hundred feet or more, for it took up the wicket, the far outfield and the spare grass beyond. A pole stuck up from each end of the marquee, each flying a white pennant; on each pennant some logo: a silhouetted globe of the world, and above each globe the letters ETBB. Between the poles a line of smaller pennants was slung: all carrying the same logo. In front of the large marquee a smaller marquee formed an entrance. Across the two poles arising from the ends of the roof of this marquee similar pennants flew, with the same logo. A cable dipped, hung, running down from one of the banks of floodlights. Pennants were strung on the cable. With the same logo.

Loudspeakers were attached to the top corners of the smaller tent. Letters had been painted on the individual ruches above the entrance to the marquee. These flapped in the breeze, now and again settling down to spell out WELCOME. Little pennants fluttered from the guy-ropes and showed the logo. Coconut matting ran out from the floor inside to form a large square, in the centre of which was the white globe of the world below the letters ETBB.

People were arriving. People were getting in. Dave Parks was waiting. Dave Parks was loitering. Waiting. Watching to see if Theresa Kipple would turn up. After that Dave Parks did not know. People passed. Passed by in their ones and twos and family groups. And Dave Parks waited for Theresa Kipple. The car park was full. Cars were being parked out in the road. No one from Bellesmyre had passed yet. A person with that logo stuck to the lapel of a grey suit jacket passed. She was giving out pamphlets. Dave Parks took one, and got one of the smiles and a thank you.

Jason McNeely smiled out from the first page: finger under his chin, eyes up as if in thought, and perfect teeth. Inside told the tale. Jason McNeely had been a car thief, a gang leader, a drug pusher. Hush my mouth, Dave Parks, he might have come from Bellesmyre. And he had come to this end of this city to show that there was a way out, a way forward, a way to live. The Lord was waiting. And Dave Parks was waiting on Theresa Kipple.

Organ music sounded through the speakers. At this distance the tune could not be made out, only the emphasising chords. The music was mixing with the sounds of the increasing crowds heading towards the marquee. People were all around. In front, behind, all around. There was Maisie from the crèche.

"Hiya Maisie. Never thought this was your scene."

"Hah. Nor yours either. For goodness sake. What are you doing here? You picking them up on their way out?"

"Ach, I'm trying to catch a pal. I think he's coming here."

"You'll need eyes in the back of your skull. It's pretty crowded already, an time's gettin on."

"Aye, you're absolutely right. Look, don't let me hold you back."

"I think you're wantin rid o me." Maisie walked away, then turned. "I'll away in here and see if this guy can make a better offer than you lot and your Section Twelves."

"No chance."

The sound of singing voices was coming from the loudspeakers. Tambourines were being rattled in there somewhere. The gospel singing. All the way from the US of A. And no sign of Theresa Kipple of the markets. No sign of James even. No Laura either. She would miss it. The singing had gone a little up-tempo. Hands were clapping. Quite clearly clapping. Hands clapping and clapping and clap clap clapping for the Lord to carry them home. Carry them home to Old Virginny. And there was a taxi-driver helping to set up a wheelchair and it was Theresa he was helping; between them they were supporting Laura who leaned on them, watching her feet, until she made it into the wheelchair. Theresa was tucking a blanket round Laura. She paid the taxi-driver and now she was heading along the shingle paths that separated the various pitches. Heading this way.

And Theresa was here.

"Hello, Theresa. Hello, Laura."

"Well, well. Look what the cat dragged out. Going religious, are you?"

"No, but, eh, you going in here? I'll give you a hand."

"Don't see as I need one, thank you. You need a hand, Laura?"

"Don't be so cruel, Theresa." Laura looked up, smiling, tapping her fingers on the Bible which lay in her lap. "Dave. You come along if you want to. I'll be glad of your company." She turned her head to Theresa. "Can we go now? I don't want to miss any of it. Can we go?"

"Do you mind if I join you, Theresa?"

"Suit yourself."

Laura was visibly excited. The heels of her feet bounced on the step of her wheelchair, her fingers tapped, and her head kept turning round, and looking up, her face sought confirmation that the journey was really exciting. At the entrance to the marquee two young men in dark suits approached, smiled, offered up pamphlets, and checked their tickets.

"I don't have one."

"I'm terribly sorry, sir. Could we ask you to wait? I am sorry, but we are restricted for safety reasons to those who have tickets. The service is being broadcast on tannoy of course. If we ascertain later that the people with tickets have not attended, we can let you in. But until then, may I ask you to listen here with us?"

"Thanks."

Laura was fishing in her handbag. She pulled out a ticket. "Here. Take this one. It was meant to be for James."

"Where is he?"

The young man took the ticket, smiling. Theresa was pushing on inside.

Tiers of plastic seating ran up high on three sides, each bank of seating separated by a gangway. These coconut matting paths led all the way down through the seating to a platform situated on the far fourth side. Several other wheelchairs sat in front of the platform. On the platform sat a tanned, dark-haired man in a blue suit, white shirt, blue tie with white logo. Two ministers of the collar sat, one on either side of him. To the right a black man sat playing an electric organ in front of a choir of purple-robed women and men.

Theresa was pushing on down to the front, to ensure Laura was there, at the front. As the Theresa and Laura arrived at the front the choir were holding on a long vowel sound and making their tambourines tremble. Theresa manoeuvred Laura's wheelchair between another wheelchair and a handicapped girl sitting on a white plastic seat, whose head kept falling onto her chest, jerking up, and falling down again. The song or whatever ended. The people applauded the choir. One of the minsters was standing up, turning toward the choir, clapping them his appreciation. Now he had turned and was holding his arms up for quiet. He leaned on the lectern.

"How come James never came?"

"My friends, before I introduce you to our friend from across the sea, I would like to lead you all in a little prayer of thanks to the Lord for Mr McNeely's safe journey to us; for our safe journey here tonight; and for the wonderful work Mr McNeely has done in his journeyings in the other cities of our land. Let us pray."

And there was the usual coughing, stamping and scraping of feet as people closed their eyes, and some clasped their hands, and some bowed their heads.

"Lord, we thank you for bringing safe to our City, Mr McNeely, who has come amongst us to do your work. We thank you for making your presence felt among the people of the Ecumenical Trail Blazers of the Bible, and inspiring them to sponsor Mr McNeely on this trip. We thank you. We thank you for this fair evening you have seen fit to grant us, and hope that this heavenly mixture: your servants, searching souls, music and good weather, will combine to produce here tonight a realisation that the only way to the good life is the Lord's way. Lord hear us as we humble servants come here this night to nurse any seeking soul back to your path. Amen."

The organist played a chord. The choir sang Amen. Amen. A-aah-ah-aah-men, on a shivering of tambourines. Coughs that were missed and held on to were coughed; and the eyes, feet, heads, put back in their usual places. Theresa was leaning forward.

"This suiting you, Laura?"

235

"Fine. Oh Theresa, it's fine, fine. I've seen that one on the Epilogue, you know."

"That's right. That's him that cracks all the jokes, isn't it?"

"He looks just the same. Well, I think he does."

"He certainly does."

"Theresa, can I ask where James is?"

"I don't know and I don't particularly care. The man is no longer one of my lodgers."

"You're joking. What do you mean?"

Theresa was looking up to the platform party. The minister had introduced a tall, black man. He was going to sing a spiritual. The organist rambled over his keys, hit and held a chord, and the man started. His voice was low. Deep and low. As deep as any singer Dave Parks had ever heard. He was singing the only spiritual Dave Parks knew, *Swing Low Sweet Chariot*. Theresa altered Laura's chair so that Laura sat facing directly onto the singer.

"Where is James, then? What's happened?"

Theresa Kipple was looking over the head of Dave Parks. The look was quizzical; she was biting her lip. She was weighing something up, and answering herself. The face cleared. Now she answered Dave Parks.

James had come home on Friday night with Bandy. Two in the morning they were shouting, arguing. Three in the morning they were singing. Tops of their voices. James was singing *Rule Britannia* and Bandy was singing *A Scottish Soldier*. At three-fifteen they were fighting. Three-thirty they were on the street where James had stood on the pavement and insulted Theresa Kipple with his Bible talk.

"What did he say?"

"Nothing. Something about strange women having lips like honey and backsides full of worms and razor blades." She was searching for a reaction.

"That sounds like James."

"Think that's funny, do you?"

"Och, I don't suppose so, but that's just his way."

"Well, his way can be elsewhere now."

"Any idea where he might be?"

"Bandy knows his way around. They'll probably be at the Imperial. It's the only place that would take them in at short notice."

"The Imperial? For Christ sake. Will you consider taking them back?"

"I generally only give my people one chance, Mr Parks."

Mr Parks

"Did you know James was mugged on Friday?"

"Nope. I suppose that would explain his face. Too bad. He's out."

The spiritual was finished. The man with the voice bowed to the applause. The other minister was rising to his feet. He crossed his hands in front of him and waited for the audience to settle down. When it was near enough quiet, he spoke.

"Brethren. First of all, on behalf of all who have worked so hard for this night, may I thank you for attending. It is your attendance here which makes it all worthwhile. Before I introduce you to the man whom you have all come to hear, may I say a few words about our friends who have made it all possible, the Ecumenical Trail Blazers of the Bible. In 1979, in America, groups covering many of the Christian churches in that land were aggrieved to hear of the deprivation in our streets, the aimlessness of our youth, and, we do have to say it, the decline of the power of the established churches over the preceding years. They looked at the land that had sent forth their own Pilgrim Fathers; they looked at the uncertain times ahead in the land which had given so much of their own Christianity a beginning; and they were sore aggrieved. But always positive people, they resolved that as well as sending forth to us more missionaries of their own particular churches, they would sponsor people like our guest this evening, the fine evangelist, Mr Jason McNeely."

There was the applause. Claps and whistles. Mr Jason McNeely was hiding his blushes behind a dismissing hand. The minister continued.

"So the Ecumenical Trail Blazers of the Bible organisation was born. These Trail Blazers of the Bible are blazing out not only new paths, but they are blazing a way out over our old paths, making them new again, and setting new feet on the paths to glory. These fresh Trail Blazers are bringing new roadmaking ways, but

237

their route plan is still the Bible. But without people to travel their roads, their time has been wasted, empty. You will be asked here tonight to set your feet upon a path for the Lord. No matter your church, we have counsellors here to help you, to guide you, guide you back on the way, and help you blaze a trail for others. Before I introduce Mr McNeely to speak, another gospel song from the men and women of the Westonho High Congregational who have come all the way from Surrey. This one is called: *Bringing My Light to the Lord*."

The fingers of the organist moved off at one hundred miles an hour. Tambourines were having all hell clapped out of them. The song swung between the sections of the choir in question and answer fashion. People were joining in: a few singing, some clapping, some stamping out in time with their feet. The faces of the congregation were sweating. Summer heat in a marquee with hot gospel bringing the sweat onto their foreheads. James and Bandy were coming down the aisle.

"Theresa. Do you see who I see?" Dave pointed back.

"Hope it does something for them."

James and Bandy came right down. Bandy had more than a few days' stubble. JCB's face was worse. Swellings had grown up underneath and around cuts, with dried blood still stuck there; blue bruises had formed; and little clumps of hair jutted out where it had been too tender to shave close. His hair was matted. JCB was dirty. Unkempt. James was smiling about something. He came right forward, clapping as he came. Bandy was waving to the crowd as if he was a hero being welcomed. James bent over and kissed Laura. James was smelly. Laura held his head down on hers until she had to let go. She was pleased to see the man. James patted her hair.

JCB whispered: "Hello, David." His breath reeked of some kind of drink.

"Hello."

Bandy was just looking around, winking and waving here and there to people in the crowd.

The singing stopped. Applause was long and loud. Jason McNeely did not wait to be introduced. He jumped up, leaned forward and drawled into the microphone.

"Do you want some more?"

"YES."

And more they got. Even slightly louder this time. Slightly faster. Jackets were coming off now. Sweat was running in streaks now. Eyes were wide and smiles were fixed and choruses were being shouted. People were punching the air on two beats at the end of the line, Bringing my light to the Lord. Hoh Hoh.

"Theresa, can I speak to you?"

"What about?"

"We. You and me."

"There is no you and me. There is only you."

"You know what I mean. Please."

"I'm here to watch Laura." Her face was giving nothing away.

"James'll watch Laura. Look, I just want to talk to you."

The foot stamping, and singing, and shouting, was getting louder. She nodded. James agreed and saluted. Bandy was squeezing himself into one of the rows. People were moving up. Theresa patted Laura on the shoulder. "I won't be long, Laura."

Laura never moved. Laura was keeping her eyes on the singers and the organist and was clapping away.

Outside it was cooler and not so loud. The speakers were sending out the joyous sounds over the empty sports field. There was no one listening. Over in the car park a policeman was leaning out a car window speaking to a man sitting on the running board of an ambulance. The police car turned and drove away. The sun was going down, leaving its sunset traces to remind that it had been there.

Theresa pulled a cigarette from her handbag. "Do you want one?"

"No, thanks."

Dave Parks was glad to wait until the cigarette routine had been gone through. There was a lot in this mind to say, but a blank was forming between the head and the mouth. Theresa Kipple was here. Dave Parks was here. The waiting, the anxiety, the wondering, over. And just beginning again. She was here. And Dave Parks didn't know what to say. Had an idea what to say. Knew in some unformulated way what was to be said, but there didn't appear to be the vocabulary for it.

"Well?" A cold hard question.

"Can you take James back?"

"Is that what we came out here for? To ask me about him? Is that what we came out here for?"

A cheer came from the marquee. Probably Mr Jason McNeely rising. Dave Parks' feet were kicking the ground. Theresa Kipple was walking with him, shaking her head. Walking aimlessly, in no particular direction, just moving. Away from the marquee. Away from the light. Jason McNeely's voice was booming out into the air. There was no one else here to listen. McNeely was confessing to his past. He had the crowd laughing.

"Sounds as if he's been a bit of a boy."

"Dave, what's the score here?"

"What d'you mean?"

"Don't mess me about, Dave. This is Theresa Kipple you're talking to. You asked me out here as if you had some state secret to tell me. So what's your problem?"

"I don't know. I know but I don't know. It's you and me and, ach, I don't know how to put it, I was never any good at this . . ."

"Why don't you just say I'd still like to try my luck with you, Theresa?"

There was another cheer from the marquee.

"I think there's more to it than that, Theresa."

"Think so? That's your worry."

A worry. What was the worry? That unformulated bit. The bit that stuck there in the top of the head, because some other bit of the head refused to put words to it.

"Listen, Dave, don't look so down in the mouth. If it's any help to you, I still fancy your body." Theresa threw the cigarette on the ground and stamped on it. "In fact, if you fancy it right now, if that's what you're trying to say, that's OK by me. Same condition. No emotional hang-ups."

"What about the pyjamas? Don't tell me you carry them around in your handbag?"

"That's ideal conditions. If and when available, to be preferred. But as I say, I only fancy your body. You can romanticise all you like."

That was the offer. Stark. Now the unformulated blank spot was slipping away. Nature was taking over. Nature was making the eyes look round to see nobody there. The car park was far enough way. But there was no cover in the sports field. Only the cricket pavilion. Theresa Kipple preferred straight talk.

"What about the cricket pavilion?"

"Suits me if it suits you."

They walked to the pavilion. Excitement in the stomach was childlike: churning, bit frightened, nurses and doctors for adults and Dave Parks and Theresa Kipple. Dave Parks stepped up on the verandah, took another look around, hesitated, stepped up and kicked at the padlock on the door. The clasp gave way and tore from the wood and Dave Parks felt pride there somewhere. Theresa came forward, smoothed her skirt and followed in.

The door was jammed shut, jammed shut with the small table. Some light was getting in through the windows. Dave Parks went to the storeroom and pulled at the practice nets. The nets came out easily and spread easily, just sufficient to form a makeshift mattress that would do for the moment. Just enough to take two bodies. The spread was ready.

Theresa had her jacket off, her blouse open and she was freeing her bra. Dave Parks lay his jacket along the nets. Theresa laid her bra down, knelt and signalled. Dave Parks knelt in front of her.

Theresa began by unbuttoning the shirt, holding the waist, and kissing at the nipples. Theresa Kipple was kissing at the side of the neck, under the jaw and moving round and her tongue was in Dave Parks' mouth and Dave Parks was falling onto the nets with Theresa Kipple.

Lying there in the gloom touching; touching more; fumbling; kissing; fumbling more; groping; catching fingers in the netting, dust, letting a sneeze out, bit by bit, quietly, over her shoulder, sweating and groaning and feeling no touches now only the touches at the points of contact, but feeling strong, feeling superior: this Dave Parks, this Dave Parks is Dave Parks. Theresa Kipple and this blank unformulated mind is going dark at the groin. Theresa relaxed backward, pushing the body off.

"Have you a hankie?"

"Christ, no, it's a thing . . . no, I meant to . . ."

"Give us my bag over. I've got some Kleenex in it."

Dave Parks stretched, got a hold of the bag, passed it over. Tissues were pulled from the bag.

"Do you want one?"

"Thanks."

The tissue was taken and Dave Parks wiped clean. Theresa was standing up, clear of the nets, fixing her clothes. Dave Parks zipped up, sorted himself; picked up, rolled up the nets and piled them back in the storeroom. Picking up the tissues he took them and flushed them away in the WC.

Theresa was moving to the door: "Ready?"

The table was removed and the door swung open on its own weight. Dave Parks pulled it shut, but it opened again. And again. From the jacket pocket a pamphlet was taken and folded and jammed under the door. It stayed shut.

The sun had disappeared. The night was clear, starry. Light cut a bright rectangle at the entrance to the marquee. Nearer the tent church organ music could be heard. The choir was singing. The singing was faint. They were singing *Amazing Grace*. McNeely's voice boomed through the speakers above the singing and the organ playing. The accent was straight from the Grand Ole Opry. The lost souls here this night were being asked to come forward to be found. Somebody was moving round the edge of the tent. One looked like Popeye.

"Theresa, can you go in yourself just now? I think I've just seen somebody I know. I'll come in. I will come in."

"It's up to you. If you come in, I'll see you. If you don't, too bad." She shrugged her shoulders.

Dave Parks looked, then moved around the side of the marquee. Popeye and two others of the team were huddled at the side of the marquee. Dave Parks moved towards them, came near, whispered: Popeye Popeye.

Popeye looked up. "Well, fuck me, look what we've got here. This is about as much as we need. Another Holy Joe and matches that don't work. It's no our night, boys."

"What you up to Popeye?"

"If it was your business I might tell ye."

In his hand Popeye was holding twists of newspaper. The matches were being stuffed into the pockets.

"Popeye, for fuck sake man, get a grip of yourself. There's people in there, man. You fuckin cracked? Popeye, Popeye, look, you're wastin your time. You're wastin your time."

Dave Parks arrived beside them, knelt, fiddled and tugged for a piece of canvas. "See this stuff here, this, it's specially treated. It's fireproof, man. You'd need a fuckin flamethrower to start it. They treat it before they let it go from wherever they make it. And then the hire people treat it every time they hire it out. Just to be sure. Popeye."

"Rubbish ya bastard. You're just sayin that."

"Popeye, it's the truth. Think about it, for fuck sake. D'ye think the people that made the tent never thought there were folk like you goin around? Get a grip. It's flame retardant, man."

The other two were looking to Popeye. There was doubt in their faces. But Popeye was losing.

"Ah, fuck off, you. You're just saying that. Anyway, suppose we better no light it or you'll be shoppin us."

Popeye had shifted the ground. Fireproofing story hadn't stopped him. It was Dave Parks. A shopper. Voices came from the back of the tent. Relief.

"Sure. That's why I came round here mob-handed."

"Aye, but if we had lit it would ye have shopped us?"

"Popeye, there's people in there."

"Supposin it was empty?"

"Popeye, this is a bit fatuous."

The voices were getting louder.

"Oh, 'bit fatuous', fatuous, why don't you fuck off?"

Dave Parks was pushed in the chest. Popeye was leading his two mates away. His face had been saved. He was mocking: a bit fatuous, a bit fatuous, this is a bit fatuous, Popeye. The tent had not been set alight but he had made a silly cunt out of Dave Parks. Dave Parks let some breath go, turned and went inside. Inside the flap the two young men in the suits stirred themselves from their master's voice and came forward to offer up the smiles and the pamphlets. They stopped smiling and turned back to listen to Jason McNeely. There were gaps in the seating. There was a crush of people down at the platform. People were moving down the centre aisle; others were rising, following them out and down. Jason McNeely was standing at the microphone, hunched over, slapping a hand on the pulpit, calling the people to come forward, come forward, come forward and seek out the Lord. He was urging those menfolk at the back to bring the little women on down and not to take no snash. The choir was still singing *Amazing Grace* and the organist had his arms extended and his eyes closed, keeping up the accompaniment.

Dave Parks moved on down the aisle, moving close behind people; dodging in close behind people; bumping people; edging people aside, hurrying, saying excuse me and not saying excuse me. Bandy was still there, sitting in his row. His head was on his chest. He was sleeping. James and Theresa were there, standing by Laura. Dave Parks was slowed by the weight of numbers; slowed down, almost stopped; waiting; waiting until this file of converts, old and new and old and young, made their way forward to the counsellors waiting at the front to take note of their names and addresses and religion, waiting to smile at them, be happy with them and shout hallelujah with them, before sending them out into the night, through two big open flaps at the back.

Jason McNeely was going to go home this night and praise the Lord. He was sure the Lord was moving here, right here, right here in this City, in this tent, here, moving among all the people here this night who were crying out for Him. McNeely could feel it, and he was asking everybody else to open up and feel it; feel it and come forward here, come forward for the Lord. Laura's voice shouted: I feel it, I feel it. Dave Parks made it forward as far as Theresa Kipple and James, who was looking sober and hanging on every word McNeely was preaching.

†

James Cameron Black was standing in this tent, under this canopy that the man said was a canvas home for the Lord this night. He heard this man from America call for people to come forward and meet the Lord, come forward to make friends again with the Lord. James made no move but watched this man, listened to this man, but did not feel or hear the Lord; for James Cameron Black heard the accent of an American mercenary soldier, the vanguard of the missionaries come to protect the mission with his gun. James did not see the Lord moving here; he saw only the same white teeth, the same wide eyes. James Cameron Black put his hand on Laura Kipple's shoulder, but she did not stop crying out, nor stop kicking her feet, but only shouted louder to tell Jason McNeely she wanted to come. And James could see that this Jason McNeely was feeling the power; feeling the power that had helped him blaze a trail through the troubled cities of this land. And now he was come here; and Laura was crying louder and kicking her feet in answer to his call. Laura's calls were insistent. This made Theresa push the hand of James Cameron Black aside and grip the handles of the wheelchair; grip it so hard the knuckles on her hands turned white. And Laura's cries made Jason McNeely look over and down toward her, and he was stretching out his arms, beseeching, saying, Come forward, don't be afraid, come forward, come.

"Come along, bring this child of the Lord; you, sir, come too, blaze a trail for the Lord this night. Blaze a trail for the Lord, forget that hell fire. Why, if any of them devils get in your way, then just you remember your ammunition is in the Bible, so just you shoot from the hip and blast away at them spooky devils and let them feel them bullets. Why, those bullets are made from the Word of the Lord and don't you know it every one of them bullets is a killer-diller for the people of the Bible, so you come along here, make those bullets count for the Lord. Don't you wait none for no badman devil to blast you, blast away, and blaze your trail right here and now for the Lord."

James was hearing this and knew this; and he moved forward to Jason McNeely. An outreaching young counsellor was pushed aside as he tried to hold on, talk to James, but James moved on, forward, until he stood under the open arms and welcoming smile of Jason McNeely, the preacher of the Word. And James spoke to him.

"Do you know what you are saying? Do you realise what you are saying?"

"Pardon, sir?"

"Do you know what you are saying? Guns and bullets are articles of war. They kill people. Kill people. Have you seen people die? Have you seen the faces of the dead?"

"Why, sir, I was speaking metaphorically, metaphorically."

James pushed on right up to the podium, until his face was under McNeely's face. "People don't die metaphorically. People die. They just die. Die. They die." James lifted up his fists and beat upon the podium with the sides of his hands, crying:

> "Dost thou work wonders for the dead?
> Do the shades rise up to praise thee?
> Is thy steadfast love declared in the grave?"

James McNeely's mouth was opening and closing. "Why, sir, I say to you, why should it be thought a thing incredible with you, that God should raise the dead?"

James looked, and James knew why.

James lowered his head between his arms, looking now at the floor, but seeing James Cameron Black peeling back the black waterproof that made unnoticed puddles run on and over his shoes; seeing James Cameron Black standing erect, holding up the tarpaulin like a trophy hunter, for the photographers and scribblers; seeing James Cameron Black holding it high as a backdrop, up and above the woman who clutched her baby, that child who had suffered and come unto mother and died. That child who screamed to be buried but James Cameron Black had made her wait for the photo-call for the Ministry until her face bloated.

Dave Parks put his arms around James, pulling him in, away from the arms of two other counsellors who were reaching.

"James, c'mon away, c'mon."

The two men in suits were standing by.

"It's all right. I'll get him. He's OK. I'll get him."

Dave Parks held the shoulders, bringing James away as McNeely lifted his head and spoke again to the rest of the congregation. Two counsellors fell in behind. Dave was leading James back to where Theresa had been, but Theresa was pushing Laura in her wheelchair out to the front. James saw this, pulled free, pushed through and lunged for the chair, grabbing Theresa's hand and the handlebar in his grip.

"Don't take her out there. You cannot. Theresa, you cannot take her out there, to a man that speaks of bullets, no. Theresa. No."

The two men who had followed were pushing their way to James. James was pleading for Laura.

"Theresa, not here, let her come with me, I'll take care of her, I'll help her, I need her to help me, Theresa."

"You? You can't even take care of yourself. You'd be the last man I'd let take my sister anywhere, even if I could watch you every inch of the way." Theresa pushed with her free hand. "Out my way."

Laura looked up at James and slapped her hands on the sides of her chair. "I want to go, I want to go."

Theresa was trying to push the wheelchair. "Right, I'm taking you, right, right."

One of McNeely's counsellors reached past James and held Theresa's arm. The other leaned unobtrusively on James, but enough to force him to the side. Theresa pushed free, pushed on, and James slapped his hand over hers again.

Theresa Kipple put her face to his: "I told you, bugger off. Go away. Permanently. It's you and your Bible nonsense that caused me to be here." She ripped her hand free from under James Cameron Black's grip. "But if this makes her happy for a night, that'll do me. Now out my way."

James let go, and Theresa paused: "Tell you something: don't let me see you near our place again. Ever."

A counsellor edged around and placed himself between Theresa and Laura and James. David Parks managed through, but Theresa was off.

James looked after her. "Theresa," he said.

247

The pressure eased a little as the two counsellors checked Theresa had made good progress.

Dave looked into James's face, hesitated, spoke: "C'mon, James, ease up now. C'mon, old son, I don't think we're wanted in here."

But James Cameron Black only stood, his head turned, watching Theresa Kipple manipulate Laura forward. Laura looked back and waved. James lifted a hand but it would not wave. One McNeely man was standing looking up the aisle at James, his hands crossed over in front, smiling.

James watched. Theresa was pushing the wheelchair into the clear area, over to the section of the floor near Jason McNeely, who was leaning over his podium, talking to a man. And when he saw Theresa, McNeely's head was lifted, he leaned up and smiled toward the oncoming Theresa and Laura. McNeely had one arm extended, palm out, indicating where counsellors were moving amongst other disabled people. Theresa did not look back, and Laura was too excited. James and David Parks stood and watched together.

"James, I think the air is cooler outside."

"No doubt," said James, but he stood still where he was, watching Theresa push Laura forward until they became absorbed within the mass of people who had come to be converted or repledge themselves.

Dave Parks touched him at the elbow. "C'mon, James."

James nodded, speaking as he did so: "Yes. Yes. I have dwelt too long in the tent of Kedar."

"Eh?"

"My soul has long dwelt with him that hateth peace. I am for peace: but when I speak they are for war."

"Look, James. C'mon. That's your trouble. You know too much stuff like that."

James turned to walk up the gangway. "Correct as usual, my dear David."

The two men turned and moved against the flow of descending converts. As they passed the line of benches where Bandy sat hunched and sleeping, James leaned over and wakened him from his slumbering.

Bandy's arms moved from his chest to his side. "Sir."

"Time to go, my man."

"I'm with you, sir."

"Good man."

Bandy staggered to his feet and joined them in the push to the park outside, people standing aside for them as Bandy grimaced and showed his only two teeth out over his bottom lip. Outside people were scattered over the sports pitches as if unsure as to where to go next: uncertain people who had been reunited with their faith and now looked around for someone to tell the tale to; eager-faced people waiting on tardy friends who had hesitated just that little bit longer, and people who had been unable to commit themselves but who now waited to hear from companions who had. Chatter was loud, smiles were wide. They moved slowly; disorganised; some tried to walk in groups gathered in half-circles, individuals chattering across the individual chatter of others attempting to explain the different way the experience had come upon them. In the darker light their faces shone, as they told how the power had moved them. The people moved at various paces down the single path to the car park, some moving through the cars, to the main road, going home, each keeping private counsel. There was a large group making a lot of noise over at the cricket pavilion. A crowd was gathering round it, congregating in a half-circle. James looked and saw that it was on fire. Flames were coming out of the windows, the blaze had well and truly caught. James ran to it, saying excuse me after excuse me and moving people to the side to clear his way, but once through there was nothing for him to do but stand and watch. The cricket pavilion could not be saved.

When Bandy and Dave Parks had caught up through the thickening crowd, James was on his knees. The light from the burning pavilion lit up his face. Tears were running down his cheeks, reflecting the light intermittently. James Cameron Black was praying. James Cameron Black was trying to be a Christian. James Cameron Black was ex-Cliftonpar Public School, and there was nothing he loved more than a decent game of cricket, but James Cameron Black was still praying for whomsoever had set alight to this cricket pavilion.

Bandy was scratching his head as he looked at the fire, looked at James, and looked at the fire. Bandy looked at Dave Parks, but he only shrugged his shoulders. Bandy waited until James had stopped praying, but as soon as James had finished Bandy leaned down to him and pulled at him; pulling him, pulling him to his feet.

"Hey, partner, that's enough." Bandy wiped his partner's eyes. "Hey. That's enough, you'll have grat enough for two fire brigades, give over. It's only an old fuckin pavilion." Bandy pointed to the burning building, nodding at the same time as if to confirm that it was only an old burning pavilion. "It's no as if it'll affect anything. They'll probably get a better brick thing now. I mean, it'll no stop your bloody cricket, will it? An you can see it in the TV basement at the Imperial, and if somebody is for switching on the other channel I'll stick it on them. C'mon, up ye get." Bandy gave a big effort and James came kind of sideways to his feet. "C'mon. I'll even sing you a chorus of your stupid *Rule Britannia*."

James walked backwards on Bandy's pull; people made room for him to pass through, standing aside, quiet now. James staggered a few steps, gained a stride, and walked away, Bandy's arm around his shoulder.

Before they had reached the car park Bandy's voice could be heard half-singing, half-shouting Rule Britannia. The voice of James Cameron Black could not be heard. Dave Parks stood where he was, at the edge of the crowd, watching the pavilion burn. Watching it burn and seeing himself and Theresa Kipple when there had been a pavilion there. He watched until men from the fire brigade came and asked the crowd to disperse, for they had decided that since there was no danger, the fire could burn itself out, but people had to stay back from it.

Dave Parks looked around the crowd, but could not see Theresa or Laura. He moved back up towards the marquee, but there was no music coming from there now, and the coloured lights were out. People and counsellors were coming from the back in dribs and drabs. Dave turned, looking, and saw her, in the distance, at the car park. Two young men in suits were assisting Laura into a taxi. Theresa got in with her. The taxi went away.

****

Outside, down on the streets, men were weeding the dying dandelions from the central reservation; shaking the fine soil free from any tangled roots, flinging the remainder into wheelbarrows, to be carted away. Somebody must have sent them. In front of the Community flat they hoed, picked up, shook, discarded, dug over, tried to break the lumps into less coarse tilth, and brushed away any dirt that spilled over out onto the street.

Tam Winters sat at the pavement edge in front of his house, watching them, puffing at his pipe, leaning forward, hands crossed, his arms resting upon his knees. Tam Winters, the quiet man, just watching, but probably thinking plenty. The telephone rang.

"Hello, David Parks here."

"Hello, David? This is Robin Smith here. How are you?"

"I'm fine. Yourself?"

"Oh, fine, fine. I'll tell you why I'm calling, David. I'm looking for you to help me; if you can."

"What is it you're after?"

"Well, I don't know how to put this to you really, but, eh, tell you what: I'll give you the broad outline, see how we go."

"Fair enough."

"Our father, dear old man that he is, is just a touch past it. We were wondering if, in your line of work, you knew of a good sort of old people's home that you could recommend, or, failing that, if you could find us one for him. You know the type of thing."

"That's not really my line, Robin. I . . ."

"We wouldn't expect you to give your advice for nothing, you know. We would expect to pay a fee and meet your, how shall we say, incidentals. Mm?"

"Well, it's . . ."

"Don't answer in a hurry, David, what say we meet for lunch? Lunch all right?"

"Em, aye, I suppose, but . . ."

"Shall we say Holiday Inn? I'm seeing someone here at the moment anyway. Two o'clock? Good man. I do hope you can make it, but business calls, must dash. Until two then. Bye, David."

David Parks did not answer. He held the phone, hesitating, then replaced it. Robin Smith was looking for David Parks to do another wee moonlight. Ach. David Parks looked out the window again. Tam was still sitting in the sun, on the pavement. It had been a while since he'd had a blether to Tam. No time like the present.

Downstairs he passed through the café area. Popeye and Bernie were playing pool. Bernie turned his eyes to studying the top of his cue as if putting the chalk on was a skill in itself. Popeye had his eyes and his nose buried in the green baize as he set up a pot.

Outside, David crossed over the street, kicking a stray clump of weed back towards the workmen. He sat down beside Tam. The kerb felt warm through the arse of the trousers. Tam only nodded a hello. David leaned forward in the same posture as Tam.

"Nice day for it Tam."

"Aye. Depends upon what IT is right enough."

"Aye. You're right there."

They watched the workmen. David broke the silence. "Those guys must be roasted in those boilersuits on a day like this."

"Aye."

That Aye was reeking with all sorts of signals. Might as well take the bull by the horns.

"Somethin the matter, Tam? Between you and me like?"

"Nothing I can think of, but the day's young yet I suppose."

"Ah, give us a break."

Tam took the pipe from his mouth, studied the bowl, looking down into it, jabbing a curled finger down inside it. "If you really want to know, Dave, this place is in a wee bit uproar about the way that mate o yours Stanley lifted Chrissie's weans the way he did."

"Oh, that's what's the matter."

"Aye, that's whit's the matter, an like it or lump it, you work out o the same office as him. People here thought we were due better than that. Know what I mean? Thought we were promised all sorts of communication by you people."

"Aye, but it's weans Tam, it's weans." David looked down, lifted a foot and repeatedly hit his heel into the kerbstone, and kept his head down while he spoke. "There's times when you've got to move fast, Tam. You know that. Especially where weans are concerned."

Tam spat. "People are as concerned here about their weans as anywhere. You should know that. Whether it's their family, or somebody else up the close, or even the street. Bringin up a wean is the only job they're allowed to perform. Bringin up weans is somethin everybody here sees everybody else doin. That wean when it's grown up is the only thing that represents us in the world, for good or for bad. We brought it up made it into a man or a woman, helped it survive. Tell us we're bad at that and we've got absolutely fuck all."

"I know what you're sayin, Tam, I know, but . . ."

The shoulders were shrugging to signal there was a mental confusion somewhere. Tam was looking round, looking right into the eyes and maybe right past the eyes. Tam jerked his head upwards.

"Ach well, as long as you know. Never mind the now, we'll see how Chrissie gets on, eh?" Tam gave three sucks on his pipe. It was out. "Did you know Isah had a wee turn last night?"

Tam had decided to swing the conversation round. Three hunded and fifty-nine degrees. David was eager to take up the new point for discussion.

"Did she? Is she all right?"

"Eh? Naw, the bingo man, the bingo. A wee turn at the bingo."

"She win much?"

Tam laughed, turning around and shouting towards his open window. "Hey, Isah. Isah, ISAH."

Isah came to the window, filling the frame with her bulk, which was exaggerated by a shapeless grey thermal cardigan.

"Who you shoutin at?" she asked.

"Ach, Isah, it was just so you'd hear me, that's all. See us those lamps you won last night till I show Dave."

"They things? Oh. Wait till you see these." Isah went inside.

Tam started to fill his pipe from his pouch: "Aye, wait till you see these, m'son. Seen some in my time, but these things are definitely on their own."

Isah came out the close carrying two brass lamps with shades on. She brought them over, handing down one to Dave and one to Tam. She rubbed a hand on her cardigan.

"Actually they're no that bad. I think you could get used to them after a while." Isah spoke, but sounded doubtful.

Tam looked at her. "Aye, ye could maybe get used to them if you lived in a chapel."

David studied a lamp. The lamp was made of a cheap rough brass, painted black in places. From four ornamented curling brass feet at the base, a broad statue of St Mungo in heavy surplice and mitre rose up, two women in attendance at his knees. One woman carried a shovel, holding it high, and the other held a rake. St Mungo had two fingers raised to bless them. At the top of his head, where the mitre began, the frame for the shade was attached and flat wire ran up to hold the shade. The shade was a yellowing map of old Glasgow, with the Clyde running around it, underneath the Molendinar. The districts of Glasgow were picked out in olde worlde lettering and language. The lamp was big and high and thick.

"Ye ever see anything like that in your life?" asked Tam.

"Can't say as I have Tam."

"Beauties, eh? See, there, the bulb screws down right into his hat. And the Lord said let there be light right enough, eh?"

"No half."

Isah reached down for the lamps. "Give us them, you. You'll be glad o them when the lamps we've got are done."

"Aye, ye think so? There's no way I'm having them. No way. Somebody can get them for Christmas."

"Oh, that'll be right. You could never affront yourself givin them to anybody. Especially somebody you knew."

David laughed. "Don't blame you, Isah. They're a bit OTT."

"Well, they're certainly never for the likes o us. You'd need to have money to spare to buy things like that. We might be daft, but we're no that daft." Isah took the lamps and headed back to the house. "I feel like I've lost a fiver and found fifty-p."

"Know the feelin," shouted Dave.

The door closing echoed down the close. Tam was puffing away again, watching the workmen. The workmen had stopped for a break. One was moving off towards the Community flat carrying a kettle.

"No signs o work for you, Tam?"

"Signs? Signs? At my age it's no signs ye're lookin for, it's miracles. Maybe I should've rubbed those lamps."

A blue van, travelling fast, drove in to park beside them, making them draw their feet in. A man in a black pullover, not as black as his curly hair, got out. The man's face was tanned, lean. He approached David.

"I've got a carpet here."

"Sorry, I don't live here, I'm just a neighbour."

The man turned his attention to Tam and began again.

"I've got a carpet here."

"Much?"

"Twenty."

"Size is it?"

"No sure. Six by four, seven by four, might even be eight by six."

"Well, I don't, wait a minute, I think she was lookin or talkin about a carpet recently. Wait a minute."

Tam got up, walked across the impacted dirt that had once been his garden, and shouted in the window for Isah to come out. While they waited the man looked around. He took out a cigarette, lit it, blew the first draw of smoke away. When Isah appeared he moved to back of the van and slid the tailgate up only enough to put the carpet on view. It was nylon; pink and brown whorls on a backing of thin black rubber. Isah felt a corner of it.

"What you lookin for?"

"Twenty Mrs."

"That's no' bad. Twenty. That's a bugger. Day before the Giro comes as well."

The man closed the tailgate hard.

"Oh, wait your hurry, wait your hurry," said Isah. "Fancy a swap?"

"What've you got?"

"Lamps. A pair o them. Brand new. Never been out the box. Just won them last night at the bingo. They're no stole or anything."

The man bit his lip. "Let's see them."

Isah turned, but Tam was already at the closemouth, going in.

Tam brought the lamps out. The man took one, turned it around and said: "Fuck me!"

"Must be worth twenty the pair anyway," said Isah.

The man half-scratched, half-pulled at his hair with his free hand. Still scratching, he decided. "Aye, OK, right, let's get this thing off." The man pulled open the tailgate, accepted the lamps and put them into a corner. He began to drag the carpet towards him. He turned to David. "Give us a hand here Jock?"

David stepped forward, and stopped. He clasped his hands together in front and shook his head. The man looked at him. Tam came forward.

"He's no allowed."

"No allowed? What's up? He got a fuckin bad heart or somethin?"

"Na, it's just, he's, I'll get it, c'mon."

Tam took the front of the roll of carpet and led the man straight across the garden to the window. "Just stick it through here," he said. "I've got the feelin you're in a hurry."

Isah had gone in the house. She pulled and the two men pushed until the carpet slid in and fell with a thump on the floor.

"OK, see you," shouted the man. He ran to his van, jumped in and was away in a crashing of gears.

Tam turned to Dave: "Too hot for this kind of thing. I think a cup of tea is in order."

David nodded. Tam pulled at his chin and mouth. "Eh, Dave, I would ask you in but, eh, you know what it's like, just, I mean, wi Chrissie's weans an that."

David took a half-step backwards, shrugging. "Ah, it's OK Tam. I need to be away anyway. Must be lunchtime."

"Lunch is it? Mind it used to be dinner-time."

David nodded. "Aye, me as well. But I'll need to away. I've got a man to meet in the Holiday Inn at two."

"Not bad, eh, not bad. Don't do too badly, eh?"

Tam moved to his close as David moved across the street, passing the workmen who were sitting down munching sandwiches and sipping at their tea.

"Hey, Dave!" shouted Tam, "make surte you have one on me."